PIGEONS OF THE DOMES

PIGEONS OF THE DOMES

STORIES ON COMMUNALISM

EDITED WITH AN INTRODUCTION BY
RAKHSHANDA JALIL

NIYOGI BOOKS

Published by
NIYOGI BOOKS
Block D, Building No. 77,
Okhla Industrial Area, Phase-I,
New Delhi-110 020, INDIA
Tel: 91-11-26816301, 26818960
Email: niyogibooks@gmail.com
Website: www.niyogibooksindia.com

Editor: Gita Rajan
Design: Shashi Bhushan Prasad/Cover: Dsgn Unplugged

ISBN: 978-93-85285-09-7
Publication: 2015
Reprint: 2019

Printed at: Niyogi Offset Pvt. Ltd., New Delhi, India

To Rajen Prasad

CONTENTS

Introduction 9

Fear
Gulzar 33

The Ones with the Signs
Abdus Samad 39

The Line
Tariq Chhatari 57

The Wolves are Secular
Zakia Mashhadi 65

Rogue
Syed Muhammad Ashraf 83

The Wail of the Black Breeze
Ajeet Cour 101

I am a Hindu
Asghar Wajahat 119

At the Zebra Crossing
Deepak Budki 129

Flowers of Mustard
M.K. Mahtab 137

Soil
Tarannum Riyaz 147

The Last Lesson
Joginder Paul 161

The Culprit
Jeelani Bano 175

Another Great War
Ratan Singh 183

Pigeons of the Dome
Shaukat Hayat 189

Hysteria
Khalid Jawed 203

A Life in Transit
Noor Zaheer 221

Blank Call
Khurshid Akram 233

Bars
Keki N Daruwalla 253

The Vultures of Doongerwadi
Ali Imam Naqvi 263

Glossary 271

Notes on Contributors 276

INTRODUCTION

Aao ke aaj gaur karein iss sawaal par
Dekhe thhe humne jo, voh hasin khwab kya huwe

Come, let us ponder over this question
Those beautiful dreams of ours, what became of them
Sahir Ludhianvi, 'Chhabees Janwary' ('26 January')

My concern in putting together this volume is primarily in tracing the secular thread in the fabric of modern India, a thread that goes back to many centuries. When I set myself the task of putting together an anthology of short stories that deal with the issue of secularism, it seemed a good idea to first go looking for those stories that seem to be about its dark twin, communalism. For, I do believe, secularism cannot be understood without understanding communalism, and vice versa, especially in India where secularism does not mean the absence of religion; rather, it means accepting the 'other' and according it acknowledgement and space in most cases, if not respect and tolerance.

For a long time now I have been keen to see to what extent the secular impulse finds reflection in the modern Indian fiction from Upper India. My sense is that a belief in pluralism and composite culture is intrinsic to the Indian ethos. It is being challenged day by day, yes, but is not fully eroded yet. The horrific communal violence of the Partition, the continuing communal clashes in the decades thereafter, the sense of besiegement and alienation that came in the wake of Partition-related violence have been sufficiently and exhaustively studied by scholars and literary historians. My interest, in this volume, is to explore how the modern writers who started their career immediately after the Partition generation, that is, those who came after Manto and Krishan Chander, Fikr Taunsvi and Tajdar Samri, Ibrahim Jalees and Upendranath Ashk, and the stalwarts of the 'Partition generation' deal with communal violence.

The secularists and liberals among us have long cherished the notion of the durability and sturdiness of the Indian 'brand' of secularism, one that is distinct from the western version, for it has been woven from the warp of religious-cultural pluralism and the woof of respect for all faiths. In the process of editing this volume, I wanted to study whether, and to what extent, continuing instances of communal violence in the new republic born after a long and bloody parturition, the rise of a militant right-wing nationalism during its years of infancy, and then the eruption of militancy in Punjab, separatist movements in Kashmir, and events triggered by Ayodhya and Gujarat, as well as the emergence of communally-divisive political parties have challenged or weakened the idea of secularism in the past six decades. I wanted to pluck the picture that emerges from a study of modern Indian literature – and I must confess I had to limit this study to the languages I know and understand, namely Urdu, Hindi and Punjabi – and place it for a larger viewership through the medium of translation. I must also confess that for the purpose of this study, I have limited my trawling to the genre of the short story; at some point in the future I propose to take up poetry and other forms of prose writings such as journalistic writings, novels and memoirs.

A word about the abundance of Urdu stories in this collection; I have chosen more Urdu stories than all others put together for two reasons. The first and most obvious one: the majority of victims of communal violence have been Muslims and the subject of communal violence has crept up repeatedly in Urdu literature. At the same time, it must be clarified that while Urdu is most often used by Muslim writers, and Muslims have indeed featured in more though not all instances of communal unrest in this country, it is also used by writers from Punjab and Kashmir, and by writers who live in other parts of the country but are not Muslim, such as Gulzar for instance. The other three notable examples of non-Muslim writers writing in Urdu in this collection include M. K. (Mahindar Kapoor) Mahtab who has written about militancy in Punjab, Deepak Budki who has expressed his anguish regarding the exile of the Kashmiri Pandits from the Valley and Ratan Singh who has written an allegorical story about the futility of fighting with each other when, regardless of who wins or loses, the consequences only make the poor still poorer and the weak weaker.

The second reason why the majority of stories here are from Urdu is a more personal one; the bulk of my own work in recent years has been about translating or contextualising Urdu sources. Urdu is the language I know and understand. While I read Hindi with equal ease, I am well placed to pick up the cultural nuances, the sub-text and the complexities of Urdu *zubaan* and *tehzeeb*, the inter-play of literary and cultural sensibility. I am convinced a study of modern Urdu literature can reveal what culture means, how Muslims interpret it and the importance it has in their daily, lived lives. It can also reveal whether and how far tradition continues to remain important, how Muslims in particular and Urdu writers in general, deal with issues of culture and identity. I am interested in seeing how modern Urdu literature reflects the concerns of the present generation of Urdu writers, and to what extent this modern Urdu is capable of walking the tightrope between tradition and modernity. I must clarify that this selection is part of a 'work in progress'; my interest in secularism continues and will find expression in a more detailed literary history of modern Urdu writings at some point in the future.

Needless to say, I had read dozens upon dozens of stories before selecting the eighteen that are included here. A word that crops up repeatedly in the stories included here as well as others of this 'genre' is *fasaad* in Urdu and *danga* in Hindi; translated as 'riot' in English it has an entirely and peculiarly Indian connotation. When used in India, a riot is more often than not a clash between two communities and is a word loaded with communal intent unlike the original English usage whereby the word, free of any sociological baggage, merely refers to unruly or disorderly conduct by a group of people.

Scholars such as Muhammad Umar Memon have argued whether communal violence in itself can be the subject of good writing, for a merely compulsive dwelling on blood and gore and a cataloguing of the violence inflicted by one community upon another surely cannot yield literature that has any lasting value, for such literature falls under the category of *waqti adab* (topical literature). Surely, a story must rise above its time and circumstance and speak of universal concerns, if it is to free itself of the label of topicality. Memon notes the 'knee-jerk quality' in much of the Partition-related literature and the occasional lack of 'depth and conviction' leading to a formulaic quality in the burst of writing that emerged from what was, nonetheless, a great human tragedy of unsurpassed proportions. Many writers resorted to, as Memon rightly rues, a rough and ready way of dealing with the consequences of communal violence rather than looking objectively at the causes. This has been a worrying trend for much of the literature of this genre; even now, as I found to my dismay, an attempt to be even-handed and politically correct overrides the impulse to understand and analyse. The Urdu writer has, regrettably, neither fully comprehended the consequences of the human tragedy that was the Partition nor learnt to analyse the reasons for the continuing communal clashes and the fault lines that mar the surface of day to day life.

Two previous anthologies have dwelt on stories that deal exclusively with *fasadat* (plural for riots). There is the excellent selection entitled *Kaali Raat: Fasadat ke Afsane* ('Dark Night: Stories of Riots'), edited by Zubair Rizvi and published by the National Book Trust in Urdu; it was subsequently published in Devnagri by Rajkamal Prakashan. It has neat sections entitled 'On the Riots of 1947,' 'On the Riots after Independence,' and 'On Recent Riots.' Rizvi points out that, with the passage of time, one community emerged as the victim of communal riots and those writers who wrote of their trauma ended up gathering the readers' sympathy. These riots of the 1970s and 1980s culminating in the Ayodhya-related riots of the 1990s created a state of 'constant terror,' so much so that fear became a constant in the psyche of a particular community (namely the Muslims) and the stories of this period dwell rather excessively on fear and trauma. Again, there is little attempt at analysis or even comment.

The other collection, selected and edited by Asad Zaidi and Vishnu Naagar, is entitled *Aaj ka Paath* ('Today's Lesson'); published by SAHMAT in Hindi, its title page bears the following legend: *Hamare samay ki loktantric aur dharmnirpeksh parampara ko samarpit* ('Dedicated to the democratic and secular tradition of our times'). It takes the diametrically opposite view from Rizvi's, instead of resignation it highlights voices of protest, instead of victims it searches for unlikely heroes and heroines, and instead of instances of barbarism it goes looking for reflections of pluralism and multiculturalism. Taken together, the two collections are a classic instance of the glass being half empty and/or half full.

I am not interested in a binary of either/or. I am as interested in communalism as I am in secularism, for I think they are conjoined twins; to study one you have to study the other. I am also interested in the anatomy of a communal riot. How does it start? What keeps it going? How does it end? What happens to the two communities that had been living together either peacefully or at the very least without overt hostility before the riot? And what about situations that appear seemingly calm, but simmering beneath the placid waters of community life lie sheathed hostilities and mistrusts?

I have chosen stories from the dozens upon dozens that I read that attempted, at the very least, to answer some of my questions. In 'Fear' Gulzar writes, '... when the mob is in a frenzy, they do not stop to ask names. Their thirst is quenched with blood or fire alone. Burn them, kill them. Finish them off. Their anger is subsided only when nothing is left.' Barbaric though it sounds, at least this seemed to be an answer of sorts.

In 'I am a Hindu' Asghar Wajahat writes, with his tongue firmly in his cheek, how riots have changed over the years:

> 'Those days, the riots were not like they are now. There has been a sea change in the politics, pace, perspective and policy of riots. Till about twenty-five to thirty years ago, people were not burnt alive during riots, neither were entire neighbourhoods laid to waste. Nor did rioters have the blessings of the powers that be. Riots were usually orchestrated by small-time, local leaders with short-term, immediate greeds and concerns. Business rivalries,

> land grabbing, garnering the Hindu or Muslim vote in the municipality elections – these were the usual compulsions behind most riots.'

And then, most damning of all, comes this summing up of the riots of the good old days – which seem infinitely 'better' compared to recent ones – again from Asghar Wajahat's pen:

> 'The riot had started in our city as it usually does in most small cities, that is, a parcel of meat had been found inside a mosque and without so much as inspecting the meat, it had been decided that just because the parcel was flung inside the mosque it must necessarily contain pork. In direct retaliation, a cow was slaughtered in Mughal Tola and a full-fledged riot was stoked. A few shops were burnt; most were simply looted. Seven, maybe eight, people were knifed to death in scattered incidents but a sensitive administration had immediately clamped a curfew. It wasn't like today when even after thousands of people have died politicians go about smirking and saying whatever happened was just and right.'

While riots may start for any number of reasons, they usually end due to sheer pragmatism, as enumerated in this story by Khurshid Akram:

> 'Rioting began to abate. For how long could one exchange blows, after all, without a square meal! When people become desperate for food and water, who could worry about reports about numbers of

> people being killed by those on one side or the other? And then the children's education was being interrupted. Somebody had to take his father to the hospital for an eye-operation; another person's pregnancy had come to term. Somebody had to arrange his daughter's marriage; a girl wanted to make a call to a boy in the neighbourhood. There were so many tasks to be attended to, for sure!'

And so, by all accounts, while riots may start with a bang, they usually end with a whimper. Incidents of communal violence may start with inflamed passions, they usually taper off as passion dies down and pragmatism takes over, or as the business of daily life and living begins to make its insistence felt. But even when they end, they leave a high toll: not merely of casualties but more importantly of greater mistrust and fear. The boundaries between 'us' and 'them' become more sharply defined, the communities more clearly demarcated by invisible but strong *cordon sanitaires*, and while the wounds may heal with time the scars seldom go away altogether.

Coming to the stories included in this volume, let us start with the first: 'Fear' (*Khauf*) by Gulzar. In riot-hit, curfew-bound Mumbai, Yaseen, a Muslim, has been hiding for several days. A Hindu has helped him, given him safe haven and even fed him meat even though he himself is not a regular meat eater. Finally, one day when the curfew is relaxed, Yaseen gathers the courage to board a local suburban train to make his way home. He gets into an empty compartment but is alarmed to see another man there. 'There was no trace of fear on his face. He was definitely a Hindu; this was Yaseen's first reaction.' Taking the situation to be one of 'Kill or be killed', Yaseen pushes the man off the running train into the bay below – the very bay from which many dead bodies were said to have been retrieved during the recent riots. Inexplicably, however, the man screams 'Allah' as he falls off the train to his certain death below. Yaseen's reaction is one of mild surprise: 'Was he also a Muslim?' That night, when Yaseen returns safely home, he confides in his wife, 'If I had not done what I did, what proof did I have of being a Muslim? I wouldn't have got naked!' In his complete absence of remorse, or even the slightest twinge of conscience, Yaseen is reminiscent of Manto's nameless rioter in 'Black Margins' (*Siyah Hashiye*) who kills a fellow Muslim and upon making the vital discovery of the dead man being circumcised, merely tut-tuts: 'Mishtake!' Evidently, the more things change, the more they remain the same. Gulzar's Mumbai is in many ways no different from Manto's Partition-ravaged Bombay. The same fear that stalked its blood-stained streets in 1947 has come back to haunt this bustling metropolis years later. But had the fear ever really left the city? Was it merely biding its time, waiting to strike? Does that fear go away for some time, only to return? Will it always be so?

In Abdus Samad's 'The Ones with the Signs' (*Nishaanwale*), we travel from Mumbai to a nameless town where nothing is said openly, where there are no overt signs of communal tension let alone rioting or curfew. Yet, 'the machinery of fear' is present all around. A family moves into a new flat and discovers, to their utter consternation, that their neighbours are 'the ones with the signs.' What those signs are we are left to infer from the narrator's haunting memories of his childhood fears replete with oblique references to 'their unique uniforms and their special hats and…their bizarre slogans.' We are left to guess who 'they' might be. The wife tries to rationalise: 'How long will we keep running? They are everywhere and if we are to live among them all our lives, why not be calm and patient?' But the husband is haunted by the past: 'Do you know their history? They destroyed our houses, violated our sisters, tried to uproot us. And night and day they plotted to wipe us off the face of the earth. And you are pleading *their* cause?' Again, the wife tries to rationalise: 'All that is history. But I also know that personal experiences have no place in history.' Prodded by the wife, the husband goes to meet the neighbour and finds them to be ordinary human beings, like anyone else despite the 'signs' that were all around in their house. Yet again, it is the wife who soothes the husband by saying, 'The signs worry you because you've only seen them from a distance. Once you see them often, they won't frighten you.' And before they know it, the daughters of the two families become friends and the neighbours drop in for a chat. But the seeming normalcy of the situation is brought to a most unexpected crescendo when the neighbour, 'the one with the signs,' drops in a packet for safekeeping. The packet contains a brick: 'This brick is the reason why hot winds have been blowing incessantly and we have been obliged to stay cooped up inside our houses. This brick has been taken from the same building which ...' Again, much is left unsaid and we are left to guess where this brick might have come from and what that 'building' might be. At first, fearful and uncertain what to do with the brick, the husband and wife eventually decide to keep it in their house for it is, after all, nothing but a piece of earth.

From the city we move to the hamlet which still retains traces of a past that was multicultural, pluralistic and tolerant. That this too is under threat in the times that are a'changing is the subject of Tariq Chhatari's luminous story. 'The Line' (*Lakeer*) paints an evocative picture of Hameed, a Muslim boy, whose excitement knows no bounds when he is chosen by the local priest to dress up as the blue-skinned boy-god on the occasion of Krishna Janamashtami. Dressed in all his godly finery, the child rides a chariot at the head of a jubilant procession when a stone hits him. Chhatari writes:

> 'From the heart of this cacophony, a horrendous cry rang out as a stone, pelted from the direction of the mosque, hit Krishan Bhagwan squarely on the head and drew a blood-red line across his forehead. The blood from Krishan Bhagwan's forehead spurted, snuffing out the lamp in the ceremonial tray. The stone was aimed at Krishan Bhagwan. It wounded Hameed. And innocent Kanhaiya's blood snuffed out the lamp for the puja.'

But the blood that was spilt by the angry mob in that nameless hamlet somewhere in the dusty hinterland of northern India, was it Hameed's blood, or Kanhaiya's? Or was it that of *insaniyat*, humanity?

Zakia Mashhadi, a powerful writer from Bihar, takes us further into rural India, in fact, deep into its forested heart, with her story about wolf sightings and mysterious child abductions. A hungry wolf is on the prowl and small children are routinely being mauled and killed but rumour has it that it is showing a preference for victims from only one community. Angry murmurs begin to do the rounds of the village: 'This place is not a hideout for wolves … The wolves never came back after 1947-48.' Snide murmurs give way to rumblings of righteous indignation: 'We must respond with similar aggression – a tooth for a tooth, an eye for an eye. This is a grave failing on our part, that we Hindus suffer injustice and violence ever so submissively – as though we were drinking mouthfuls of nectar – without so much as hesitating to heave a sigh.' Tensions escalate amidst talks of secret agents from a neighbouring country being behind the dastardly acts when

Muslim women and children too are attacked and this time in broad daylight and a wolf is clearly seen. In order to establish its secular credentials, the wolf must attack and kill victims from both communities! And the story, called appropriately enough 'The Wolves are Secular' (*Bhediye Secular Hain*) concludes thus: 'In fact, not just that one – all wolves are secular. They do not kill on account of religious convictions.'

The analogy of the beast continues in Syed Muhammad Ashraf's 'Rogue' (*Rogue*) which, like the previous story, is set in a forest. At a time when communal passions are running high across the towns and hamlets of Upper India, an elephant has gone rogue. It mauls and kills humans and devastates human habitation. The forest ranger hires professional trackers and killers to find the beast and kill it. Written in the aftermath of the demolition of the mosque in Ayodhya and the sectarian violence that scarred the country, the story poses a question: is the rogue within or is it the one outside, is it the one we can see or is it a formless invisible entity that we cannot even identify? In placing the story right after Zakia Mashhadi's, I want to draw your attention to the beast – whether a wolf on the prowl or an elephant gone rogue – and the metaphor of the beast, any beast that fill us with 'a combination of horror, helplessness and embarrassment.'

Ajeet Cour's 'The Wail of the Black Breeze' takes us to the year 1984 when the beast was let loose to walk the streets of Delhi shortly after the assassination of the then Prime Minister Mrs Indira Gandhi by her Sikh bodyguards: 'Those were black days, bloody days, full of a strange fear of death. A choking sensation rose from the earth to the sky, like a black cloth smothering all... It was the month of November, the beginning of the month. The year was 1984. The city had been in shock, stunned, since the 31 October.' Cour's story reminds us that the Muslims – India's largest minority – are not the only ones who have faced the brunt of communal violence. Told in the first person, like an autobiographical account, it cannot be called a 'story' in the conventional sense, but it is nevertheless one of the most searing narratives in this collection.

With Asghar Wajahat's 'I am a Hindu' (*Main Hindu Hoon*) we return to the provincial backwaters of Upper India, undistinguishable by any landmarks yet deeply scarred and divided. A city is under curfew and its Muslim neighbourhood, a ghetto at the best of times, is viewed with extra suspicion by the police, in this case the notorious and much-disliked PAC (Provincial Armed Constabulary), an armed police force of the Uttar Pradesh police that was usually deployed in curfew-hit areas, with Hashimpura being by far the blackest chapter in their history. As the curfew drags on and on, sapping everyone of their religious zeal, one day when the curfew is relaxed for a few hours, the PAC guarding a Muslim neighbourhood come across a Muslim boy insisting that he is a Hindu. The boy's family takes him home, telling the PAC that he is 'soft' in the head, before he can create a scene. But the boy, teased and taunted by his Muslim neighbours, is convinced that a terrible lot will befall him if he is caught by the Hindus. In his simple way he has figured out the simplest way to fight his nightmares: declare himself a Hindu! 'I am a Hindu' is a caustic look at the majoritarian discourse, one that is now making demands of *ghar wapasi* and *shuddhi* ceremonies. Is the erasure of differences the only answer for peaceful co-existence? Is there no place for minorities in modern India? Will the talk of Muslims wanting to create 'mini-Pakistans' in their ghettos continue to be given validity? And will there be no more Hashimpuras if Muslim youth start declaring that they are Hindus, after all?

Deepak Budki's 'At the Zebra Crossing' (*Zebra Crossing Par*) deals with the loss and alienation experienced by the Kashmiri

Pandits who were forced into exile from their beloved Valley. In cities that are hostile and alien to them, many of whom have never set foot outside the Valley, they remember the beauty and plenty they have left behind as they eke out their days in want and deprivation in rehabilitation camps. '… brooding and thinking endlessly about his glorious past, insecure present and unknown future,' a young man probably lost in his thoughts as he crossed a busy road in the new city, is run over by a truck. His grieving father finds himself immobilised at a zebra crossing in the same city: transfixed by shock and grief over the loss of his son and, incapacitated by the heat and thirst that compounds all his other losses, he wonders why the city is so 'apathetic and undemonstrative,' why it makes him feel like a 'foreigner' in his own country? Mulling over the utter futility of his situation, the man at the zebra crossing wonders: 'How do I call this country my own? The country which neither gives me security nor sustenance? Does one become a refugee in one's own country?'

The sense of despondency lifts somewhat and the pall of gloom parts in M. K. Mahtab's sunny story about hope and resilience. 'Flowers of Mustard' (*Sarson ke Phool*) is set in the high noon of militancy in the Punjab. A journalist from Delhi is touring the troubled state. Daunted by the many stories of police encounters and abductions by terrorists who have free run in the countryside, he meets a beautiful young woman on a bus. He is struck not so much by her beauty as the air of simplicity and innocence about her. Guileless and hospitable, she offers him a night's shelter in her home even as the man from Delhi is besieged with worries about bombs going off and passengers being pulled out of buses and shot. In her home, he meets her brother Surjit, '… an enormously tall and well-built Punjabi sardar, with a black beard and a face as red as a blazing oven and ferocious-looking eyes' who turns out to be exceedingly welcoming and hospitable to a perfect stranger. Mahtab's story shows us how misleading stereotypes can be and how the human spirit survives intact and unharmed in the most trying of circumstances. It is also the only story in this collection that is unadulterated by darkness in its insistence that the clouds *will* part when the sun comes out, dark days *will* end and the flowers of mustard *will* shine bright and happy in the fields of the Punjab as they always have.

Tarranum Riyaz's 'Soil' (*Mitti*) is set in Kashmir, a land in the grip of insurgency like the Punjab before it. House-to-house searches, police encounters, bombs, violence and inhumanity mar the even tenor of day-to-day life. Talk of subsidies, appeasement and disloyalty further deepen the divide between the state and the people as does the constant presence of armed forces among civilians. Young Hilal Ahmed, an engineering student can take no more of the trauma and humiliation; a drop-out and missing person he ends up in jail where he hears the 'other' side of the story: 'All are the same … donning loose and long clothes … they commit crimes and then get away … where does one find them … often, they run from one lane to the other and then they are caught … there are so many lanes and we are strangers. What can we do?' And Hilal's side: 'If we had a leader then we would not have gone astray like this … the people we trusted broke our trust. They were merely concerned for a secure future for their generations. Otherwise, we never had a soft corner for the people on the other side … we wanted to lead normal lives … But …' And the 'but' is left dangling mid-air with no resolution in sight except for a vague promise of better days.

With Joginder Paul's 'The Last Lesson' (*Aakhri Paath*) we are back in the Punjab and on the familiar terrain of murder and mayhem. Armed assassins are sent to kill a village headman who counsels those Sikhs who have chosen the wrong path. Santa and

Banta – the archetypal comic duo who have been immortalised as the Abbott and Costello of modern India through countless jokes – are here transformed into two hired guns. One is a trigger-happy tough nut, the other plagued by doubts. If blithe wilful ignorance is one way of retaining one's sanity in a world suddenly gone mad, surely asking questions must be the other way? Santa rues a world where asking questions means showing fear and showing fear is a sure way of getting killed: 'What kind of a life is this? One's own people have become such strangers to such an extent that no one even steps forward to even try and speak a little sense and make others understand.' An argument breaks out between the two as they are on their way to kill the village headman causing their motorcycle to skid and both end up lying injured and broken on the road. As they lie there, dying in the middle of the road, Santa gathers his broken breath and whispers, 'Bantaya, many gods have put the human race on the wrong path!'

Jeelani Bano, the veteran writer from Hyderabad, locates 'The Culprit' (*Mujrim*) in a city divided along communal lines. A writer of long standing, she finds a place in this collection because she has been an active writer for nearly five decades and her pen has not stopped writing about the world and its affairs with passionate intensity. Distrust and disarray, suspicion and subterfuge cause the sanest of people to lose all sense of proportion; they begin to view the world with paranoia and see themselves as victims. A friend's call on a curfew-bound night causes alarm bells to go off:

> 'Why did Venkatesh call me so late in the night? Why did he want to know whether I was home or not? From what was being shown on television about the riots, it seemed as if he had instigated it. People are looking at him with

> hatred and wanted to seek revenge. No matter where the riots or who the people, Nisar always saw himself in the role of a culprit.'

What a sobering thought it is, then, to realise that poor Venkatesh thinks exactly the same: he thinks Nisar views him with suspicion and holds himself responsible for all the tension in the city as though *he* is the culprit. And how ironic it is that the same doctor has prescribed identical medicines for their stress-related ill health!

Ratan Singh's delightfully punchy little story 'Another Great War' (*Ek Aur Jung*) is a parable with no names and no places, for none are needed when it comes to universal follies. A war has broken out, not between emperors or nations, yet is greater than the First and Second World Wars; this war is between two beggars. But the problems are the same: 'The issue was of one's survival, to keep one's existence intact, to preserve the pride in one's ego … In the same way that two countries sometimes come to loggerheads over some trivial issue, the root of their differences was also a petty issue.' And what is the issue for the two beggars sitting side by side on a pavement with their begging bowls in front of them? A rich man, passing by, tosses a rupee coin which ricochets off the bowl of one and reaches the other. The question now is: who is the rightful owner of the rupee coin? The one in whose bowl it was tossed, or the one who reaches out and grabs it as it rolls off the rim of the other's bowl? 'And in the way that war breaks out between the armies of two countries, a bitter battle ensued between the two … But this war was not between two strong forces; it was a fight between two people who had been enfeebled by poverty.' And, as is usually the case with these futile wars, the effect is equally bad for both: 'In these twin attacks there was such fire and so much smoke that their little world was being scorched … They were breaking and scattering into little pieces but both were unwilling to withdraw from the battle lines. They were facing each other with the greatest determination.' While the two are locked in a bitter battle, a rich man comes by, distributes his largesse to the other beggars on the footpath and ignores the two squabbling beggars. 'Just as nations who are engaged in prolonged battles get poorer and poorer still and the rows of beggars become longer and longer in their cities, the same happened to these two beggars.' I included this story here – though not about communalism per se – because it seemed to contain a lesson for communities that live together yet engage in futile squabbling and bickering. And when they are equally poor, as is often the case when riots break out in densely packed shanties and hutments, the consequences are equally bad for all concerned.

Shaukat Hayat is a writer of great perception; his story, 'Pigeons of the Domes' (*Gumbad ke Kabootar)* carries the analogy of mindless violence to its logical conclusion. A man nurtures a '*gamla*' garden in his balcony with great tenderness. He has created a haven of calm and beauty in the midst of an urban jungle; he watches over it with great diligence and is fearful that its tremulous beauty will be marred, the tender flowers and buds nipped by callous hands, the birds and bees that have taken to flitting among his flowerpots will abandon his oasis, and someone or something will ruin his hard-won serenity. His worst fears come true when the neighbourhood children trample and maul the pots and plants leaving him devastated. Again, as in much of contemporary Urdu fiction on the subject of inter-communal violence, here too analogy and abstraction are used instead of directness and candour. The little garden, the marauding children who have suddenly become 'so venomous and barbaric,' the pigeons that have been rendered homeless since the destruction of the 'domes' – evidently these are metaphors. It is left to the reader to understand what they might allude to. And the only witnesses to this destruction are the pigeons: 'Up above, the flock of those warm-blooded pigeons from the domes was continuously hovering around in search of a home, desperate to say something, to just speak out.'

Khalid Jawed, an eminent name in contemporary Urdu fiction, uses the modernist approach in making a telling point about the 'bad times' the country is passing through even though it seems almost incidental to the story of an elderly invalid man, confined to his bed and rendered almost incapacitated by disease. His story, 'Hysteria' (*Hizyan*) is an oblique statement on the helplessness and despair of an entire society even though it is told from the point of view of one man, who is lying in bed and keeping vigil through the endless night knowing full well the futility of the vigil: 'There was complete silence outside. But then the siren of a police van from afar passed by, highlighting the dreadful night. Presently the country was passing through a bad phase. The city was under curfew. All night the CRP patrolled the city and police sirens blared.' 'Hysteria' is a dark story, full of existentialist angst, of looking for meanings knowing fully well that possibly none exist.

Noor Zaheer teases out the inconsistencies in the argument for living together separately and the arrogance and bull-headedness of those who shun multiculturalism and pluralism in favour of homogeneity. 'A Life in Transit' details the travails of Shabnam, a single Muslim woman living in a housing society where she is viewed with suspicion bordering on outright hostility when her Muslim identity is revealed by virtue of her Muslim-sounding name despite her otherwise 'normal' outward appearance. Shabnam's Hindu friend urges her to take the first step in being sociable, for: 'People get to know each other only if they spend time together. Your neighbours need to learn that there is no difference between the yearnings and aspirations of well educated, progressive Hindus and Muslims.' The attempt, however, backfires in the face of ignorance and prejudice and ends in fear and, yes, the same hopelessness that Khalid Jawed had alluded to in 'Hysteria' and the sense of victimhood that Jeelani Bano had described in 'The Culprit.'

Khurshid Akram's 'Blank Call' (Blank Call) is a close, hard look at communal violence: how it erupts over the most trivial of issues and how it spirals out of control because: 'Collective pride, collective obstinacy and collective rage can become dangerous.' Fear and fury make a deadly Molotov, causing a Domino effect with far-reaching consequences. As arson and violence rip through a city and curfew is imposed in an attempt to control if not douse the fire of hatred that has fuelled it, inflammatory exhortations by newspapers and community elders further divide their respective communities along sectarian and outright communal lines. 'Blank Call' ends with an unexpected spin to the slogan 'The Personal is the Political' for, here, it is when the perpetrator of hate crimes is personally inconvenienced that the consequences of hate are brought home fully.

Keki N. Daruwalla's story, 'Bars' is different for two reasons: it is the only story in this collection originally written in English and it has been written especially for this collection which also makes it the most topical and, as it were, the 'latest' story in this anthology. Daruwalla's has long been a powerful and fearless voice against bigotry and communalism; here, he gathers the strands of several recent concerns: charges of alleged proselytising against Christian missionaries and invocations of 'anti-conversion laws' in certain states, Muslims being rounded up and put behind bars on unsubstantiated charges of being 'terrorists' and the psychological trauma endured by law-abiding citizens who are cooped up with hardened criminals on trumped-up charges. The last is especially galling since, 'We in the jail know that between what the police and the courts say and the jailbird's version there's not just a gulf but an ocean.' Daruwalla also picks other motifs that have been in the news recently, '... denigrating Gandhi, extolling Godse, the majority being asked to produce more children, the division of people into legitimate and illegitimate people.' And it is these discordant noises that produce a clamour, a clamour that has long-term consequences.

It seemed appropriate to end this selection with a story that gathers up several motifs that the astute reader will find scattered throughout this anthology: animals, the world of nature, the allusion to blood and gore without any descriptions of physical violence and bloodshed with anything close to the bloodthirstiness of the Manto generation and, worst of all, a self-centredness and deliberate heedlessness to the consequences of such wilfulness. Ali Imam Naqvi's 'The Vultures of Doongerwadi' (*Doongerwadi ke Giddh*) draws our attention to a terrible aberration in the natural world and the time-honoured food chain. Two pall-bearers at a Parsi Tower of Silence are perplexed to find the corpses lying untouched and the sky empty of the vultures that are supposed to be nature's best scavengers. Instead of picking the bones clean from the corpses in the *doongerwadi*, the vultures are busy having a feast in the city streets that are piled with corpses. The Parsi *biradari* is assured by the police commissioner that the vultures will return once the riots are over and the streets have been cleared of the corpses. But the pall bearers still fret: 'So what if the roads clear ... will the vultures return ... After all, this is India ... there is a riot here every day. Everyday there is burning and arson, everyday people die ... What then ... what the hell ... will the vultures ever return?'

An anthology such as this takes a long, long time to come to fruition. Many, many people help along the way with ideas and suggestions. I am deeply grateful to Rajen Prasad and friends and fellow travellers at SAHMAT with whom I first discussed this anthology some time ago when dark clouds were gathering and we had a portent of the changes that were looming ahead.

Rajen gave me a copy of the excellent selection edited by Asad Zaidi and Vishnu Naagar, entitled *Aaj ka Paath* which, in many ways, showed me the way. Ali Javed, as always, has been supportive and encouraging. So has Tariq Chhatari of the Department of Urdu in Aligarh who has, as in the past, taken the trouble to find stories, scan them and email them to me in Delhi. Khurshid Akram proved to be a very useful sounding board for ideas and, given his vast knowledge of contemporary Urdu fiction, has been a much-valued guide all through the making of this book. Others who have offered help in different ways include: Madhu Prasad, M.K. Raina, Rahul Verma, Ruchira Gupta, Kanishka Gupta, Moonis Ijlal, L.K. Sharma, Praful Bidwai, Tarun Saint, Anita Samkaria, Akhlaq Ahan, Zakia Mashhadi, Syed Muhammad Ashraf and Indira Varma. Javed Akhtar gave a patient hearing as I discussed my ideas for writing the Introduction as well as the title of this collection.

As in all my literary endeavours, my mother Mehjabeen Jalil has been a source of immense inspiration and comfort. And as in all anthologies of translations, it is the individual translators who have finally helped in putting this book together. And it is to them and their selfless love for literature that I dedicate this collection of short stories. As well as to those writers who will continue to contest communalism and continue to write stories of hope and conflict. As Faiz Ahmad Faiz ended his own 'Dedication' I will end mine with his words:

Aane wale dinon ke safiron ke naam
Voh jo khushbu-e-gul ki tarah
Apne paigham par khud fida ho gaye.

In the name of those harbingers of the days to come
Who, like the scent of the flower,
Are willing to die for their own message.

Rakhshanda Jalil, New Delhi, August 2015

FEAR

GULZAR

His nerves were on edge. Even as he sat, hunched, his legs were trembling as though he was in the grip of an epileptic fit. The riots had been going on for the last four days. The curfew would relax for a short while both in the morning and in the evening. Some people would quickly buy essential commodities as soon as the curfew was relaxed. Some others would equally quickly indulge in violence – hit, set fire to things, kill, loot and plunder, before the curfew would be clamped again, to return and bolt themselves inside their houses. The streets of Bombay were overflowing with hot news and hotter blood. But the television and radio were constantly announcing that the situation in the city was under control and fast returning to normalcy.

Just to prove that the situation was normal, local trains were also plying till late at night. Most of the coaches were empty, but one could see the lights running on the track, which could dispel the darkness. The stony silence that had engulfed the *bastis* on both sides of the tracks was shattered briefly with the passing of trains, reviving the hope of some activity. Yaseen would listen to the sound and get up to check if the train had started to move. The next day would be the fifth day that he had been missing from home. By now, they must have given up waiting and started the search. His patience gave way by the end of the day. As the evening curfew relaxed, he reached Andheri station. The platform was deserted. But the train arrival time was flashing on the indicator.

Unlike other days, the train entered the station very quietly. As if it was intimidated, as if it too was scared and nervous. There were one or two people in the train. He couldn't make up his mind, if he should enter, or not. The Hindus have the number. People were huddled together in groups of twos and fours. He waited at the platform and leapt into a carriage when the train moved. He chose a vacant compartment. It seemed empty. He went and sank into the corner-most seat of the last berth. He could keep an eye on the entire compartment from here. He heaved a sigh of relief as the train picked up speed.

Suddenly, a head bobbed up from the other side of the compartment. Yaseen sat stiff, paralysed with fear, his knees jerking epileptically. He doubled to such an extent that if anyone were to come near, he could hide under the berth. Or stand upright, taking a position.

The door was not far. But jumping off from a running train would only lead to one fear, the singular fear of death. Even if the train slowed down, that man was still there. Suddenly, that man stood up. He looked around as he stood in his place. There was no trace of fear on his face. He was definitely a Hindu; this was Yaseen's first reaction. That man walked up to the first door of the compartment. His muffler was swaying like a tattered flag in the breeze. The man kept looking outside. And then, it seemed as if he was struggling with something. Yaseen could see clearly from where he was sitting. He was pulling at something. He would press, or pick, or pull. Yaseen thought he was trying to pull something apart. All of a sudden, the rusted door shut close with a loud bang. It was fortunate that Yaseen did not let out a scream, unnerved as he was by the sound. The man looked around. He kept staring at the place where Yaseen was hiding. Yaseen thought maybe he had seen him. Or heard him. Yaseen was even more scared, seeing the strength of that man. Would he be able to fight him, if they came face to face? The man went to the other door and stood there. The train crossed the isolated station of Jogeshwari. Had the train stopped, Yaseen could have got off. But the area was under curfew. So, the train didn't stop there. The area under curfew would have been safer. At least the police would have been there. And by now, the army too had been called. Army trucks were seen patrolling. The police was redundant by now. People were not afraid of them anymore. Mobs would fearlessly attack them with stones and soda bottles. Even with acid-filled bulbs. If the police threw tear-gas shells, the mobs would pick them up with wet handkerchiefs and lob them back at the police. What had the police done when the bakery at Sakinaka, where he used to work, was burnt down? The police had just stood and watched from a distance. Trying to save themselves, people ran through narrow lanes and reached the garages where the dented and scratched frames of cars were piled. He and others had run to hide, to save their lives. They were about eight to ten people. May God bless Bhau, whose *gamcha* he had held on to. Bhau had pulled him inside a shop. Bhau knew he was a Muslim. But Bhau was a Hindu! Why was he running? Bhau answered: when the mob is in a frenzy, they do not stop to ask names. Their thirst is quenched with blood or fire alone. Burn them, kill them. Finish them off. Their anger is subsided only when nothing is left.

A rattling sound at the other door alarmed him. The man had closed both the panels of the door on his side. And he kept staring at the place where Yaseen was hiding. Fear engulfed Yaseen yet again. Why was that man bolting the doors of the compartment? Would he kill him and get off at the next station, leaving his bloody and lacerated body behind? The train was slowing down … Some station was coming … The man seemed more confident now … He was slowly walking towards him. Yaseen's breath grew heavy. He felt trickles of cold sweat on his forehead. It was fear. His breath was getting knotted. He was unable to swallow his saliva. What if he sneezed? Or coughed? Here, hiding under the berth. The train stopped. Some station had come. That man came up and stood at the door on the side of the platform. One of his hands was in his pocket. He could have a weapon in his pocket. A pistol? … A dagger? … Yaseen thought of running to the other side and jumping off the platform. But that man would rip open his stomach by the time he reached the door from the place where he was hiding. Why stomach? He might even slit his throat, so that not a sound came out. He peeped. The man was looking outside. There was silence on the platform. No sound at all – not even of any footstep. Yaseen hoped that someone would come. But who knows, who would come? Hindu? Muslim? Even if he was a Hindu, he might be a kind-hearted soul like Bhau. How Bhau had saved him, bringing him from the tea stall to his hut, making him wear his *janeu*! He had given him shelter for four days. He had said, 'Although I am a Maratha, I do not eat meat every day. I can get it for you, if you want some. I don't know how it would be. I do not know the difference between *halaal* meat and the other kind. And the condition outside is such that the vegetables are rotting in Andheri, but there is no one to sell them. One can just loot as much as one wants.' And the radio kept on saying that the situation in the city was getting back to normal. People are moving. Buses have also been plying in certain parts of the city. Yaseen was very worried about his family during these four days. Even his family members must have been worrying about him. He was afraid of one thing. What if Fatima went looking for him at the bakery. He could see the rail track from the room where he was hiding. He could even see some cars. But Bhau did not let him go.

The train started with a jerk, bringing Yaseen back to the present. That man was holding the rod with his left hand and standing very casually. And the right hand was still in his pocket.

The train had still not picked up speed. Why wasn't it picking up speed? There was no reason that it wasn't getting the signal! After all, there was no traffic on the rail tracks. No train had crossed from the other side till now … The train remained slow … Very slow. And it stopped at a bridge. Under it was the bay of the sea. The same bay which was in the news, from where many dead bodies had been pulled out.

Yaseen was feeling suffocated. It was difficult to survive in this fear. And why was that man not taking his hand out of his pocket? One could see it in his eyes … that he is about to attack. What will happen if he attacks? What will happen when he asks me to get out of my hiding space? Or will he drag me out, pulling me by the hair and slash my throat with his knife? What will he do? Why isn't he doing anything?

At that very moment, that man took his hand out of his pocket. He was again pulling at something. He was trying to close the third door also. Now there was no way to run away. And down below was the bay. Death was certain if he were to jump. By now his fear was at its peak. He felt as if he was trapped inside a cave.

Suddenly, he leapt out of his hiding place. The man was taken by surprise. His hand went to his pocket. God knows from where Yaseen got so much strength. Screaming 'Ya Ali …!', he grabbed the man's legs and threw him off the train. As he fell from the train, he heard the man scream, 'Allah …!'

Yaseen kept standing. The train picked up speed. He was surprised. 'Was the fellow also a Muslim?' By freeing himself from the claws of fear, Yaseen had escaped death.

That night, he told Fatima, 'If I had not done what I did, what proof did I have of being a Muslim? I wouldn't have got naked!'

– Translated from the Urdu by Saba Mahmood Bashir

THE ONES WITH THE SIGNS

ABDUS SAMAD

My wife said, 'Everything is fine. The house is fine. But do you know your neighbours?'

'Look, we just got here yesterday. We don't even know the ups and downs of the weather here. How could I know anything about the neighbours?' I spoke in a rather irritated manner. I had just arrived at the new house with the most recent load of our belongings.

'Better learn about them as soon as possible.' My wife seemed to be hinting at something; I could tell from the tone of her voice.

I didn't pay much attention to what she was saying and got busy with arranging the furniture. Having done all this, I considered my handiwork with satisfaction. The place had appealed to me when I had first seen it. Now it looked so good that I felt we could stay here for a long time. After a short while in this state of enchantment, I showered and feeling refreshed had a cup of tea only to discover that I had become a hangnail in my wife's toe.

'What is all this about the neighbour?'

'All I am saying is that you had better find out more about the neighbours.' Once again my wife went back to harping on the old tune.

'If you know something, why don't you tell me?' With some difficulty I hid my anxiety behind a mocking smile.

'Our little girl said that they were the ones with the signs. My wife answered readily, contrary to my expectations.

'The ones with the signs!'

I shuddered. All those scenes that I had witnessed as a child swam before my eyes. All those stories echoed in my ears once again.

'What does she know? One shouldn't place blind trust in what a child says.'

I tried to suppress disbelief with belief.

'What do you mean! Can't she recognise the signs? On the roads – in school – here and there, amongst her friends … is there any place where she doesn't see the signs? And you are telling me ….'

My wife seemed to relish making fun of my naiveté.

'Still, a child is a child.'

I still had a ghost of a hope left.

'Then why don't you find out for yourself?'

This query ended the whole discussion of belief and disbelief and hope and lack of hope.

And now there was only one avenue open to me.

All night I heard shouts and screams and sounds of people trying to escape. I saw images of fires and bloodshed and murder and mayhem and signs of all sorts of destruction. Since childhood, I had feared the ones who carried the signs. The minute I saw their unique uniforms and their special hats and heard their bizarre slogans, I would run. And kept running and running. Because of all this running, I had lost all I had or, more accurately, everything was ruined. When my helpers and well-wishers saw me running, they felt sorry for me. They would give me pious advice. But the engine of fear that had started up inside me, showed no sign of stopping. I did my best to find shelter as far away as I could from even the shadow of the ones with the sign. But it was my misfortune that in a matter of days, I would discover that to my left or right, behind or in front, near or far, someone with the signs was always present. And then, the old engine inside me would start up again. If I saw someone with the sign coming towards me, I would change direction. When I learned of the locations where the ones with the signs assembled, I considered it a sin to go to those places. In spite of all these precautions, someone with the sign invariably showed up in some undiscovered corner of my life.

My sympathisers and well-wishers tried to make me understand.

'What's the use of running like this? If you keep running like this, you will die. What can you do? The ones with the signs are everywhere. How long will you run from them?'

What they said made sense and I understood them. But in a short while, if I happened to see someone with the signs, I forgot their words and once again the machinery of fear got going in my heart and under my feet.

And I had found this house in the hope that it would be a haven, a place of refuge.

My sympathisers had managed to convince me that I shouldn't divide a city into islands because, then, they can be identified easily and recognised. It is better for man to get so lost in a crowd that he can't even recognise himself. The people who live here do not have a sign. You need not be anxious about living among them … And now …

The first rays of the rising sun informed me that I had not slept all night. Whatever I had seen on the screen of my eyes was not a dream. And the eyes that had witnessed those scenes all night were bloodshot. My wife read what was written in my eyes and said: 'I should not have said what I said. It was a mistake. I was under the impression that you were quite calm now. How long will we keep running? They are everywhere and if we are to live among them all our lives, why not be calm and patient?'

I stared at her. She was telling the truth. I had burnt all my boats over the years and now I didn't know if I could plan anymore voyages.

'I'd like to suggest something, if you care to listen.' My wife looked at me. There was a glimmer of hope in her eyes.

When I remained silent, she picked up courage and delivered her precious advice.

'Go and meet the neighbours.'

Startled, I stared at her.

Her face was lit up with hope and confidence.

'Are you serious?' I rebuked her sharply, doing my best to keep my temper under control.

'Absolutely – this is my sincere advice. I just can't bear to see you so disheartened.'

I stared at her as though I would be able to see some sort of sign in her eyes.

'Look, they are our neighbours. We have no reason to suspect them. Moreover, our Maker has commanded that we love our neighbours. This will bring you closer to your Maker. After all, why should we entangle ourselves in all these doubts and suspicions?'

These were not the words of my wife. I felt as though some other woman had entered her being. And this other woman was tired of running alongside me.

'Do you know their history? They destroyed our houses, violated our sisters, tried to uproot us. And night and day they plotted to wipe us off the face of the earth. And you are pleading *their* cause?'

'Not them. But some misguided people who looked like them. Why punish them for the crimes of others? This is like saying, a thousand years ago …'

'Papa … Papa … the neighbour's daughter is asking me to come and play with her. Can I go?' My little daughter raised the question rather fearfully.

All this talk of signs and past grandeur was echoing in her ears and in the deserts of her being.

'Noooo.'

I yelled so loudly that my scream got stuck in my throat. This, my flushed face and the redness clouding my eyes, made my wishes plain.

'Why are you filling the child's mind with these sorts of ideas? Being on the run constantly – is this going to be her destiny too?'

'And those who would kill her in their house, poison her, make her disappear …'

'No, they will do no such thing. But even if they tried something like this, their daughter, who is the same age as our daughter, would definitely save her.'

I sensed total confidence in my wife's tone.

'So now you have forgotten all those scenes, all those anecdotes, all those stories.'

'No, I have not forgotten them. All that is history. But I also know that personal experiences have no place in history.'

'What do you want?'

I was weary of arguments.

'Go and meet the neighbours.'

She was stuck on this point.

'But I don't know them. Moreover, they could come over, couldn't they? Is this duty mine alone?'

I tried to battle with her on her own turf.

'It makes no difference. They are older residents. They have been here much longer than us. In a manner of speaking, they are our seniors and obliging a senior …'

It was useless to argue. But when I found myself ringing the bell of my neighbour, I can say with confidence that this was my own decision.

My feet had brought me here. This was my decision and mine alone.

The door opened. A head appeared and then disappeared. 'Perhaps these people don't want to meet me,' I told myself. But then the door opened again and I saw a smiling face.

'Forgive me. I was busy with my prayers. Come in, please.'

I entered hesitantly.

'By counting fewer frowns on your forehead, can I tell you?' My wife was very happy. I kept sipping tea silently. Having finished the tea, I had just extended a hand towards the packet of cigarettes, when she jumped up and grabbed it.

'Not yet … tell me all the details first.'

'Nothing special. He met me as though I were a long lost friend. His wife and children surrounded me.'

'You must have been scared.'

My wife smiled triumphantly. I felt a bit embarrassed.

'No, there was no reason to be afraid. They are human beings just like us.'

'Yes. They are definitely human beings. The only creature one need fear is the beast that hides inside human beings.'

'Now you are using my language.' I had my chance to be sarcastic.

'You haven't heard the whole story. I wanted to say that without being aware, we hold the chain that binds this beast.' My wife completed her sentence.

'Well, anyway, they treated me to delicious food, and gave me some sort of sweets …' I stopped, tongue-tied for some reason.

'What?' Her curiosity got the better of her.

'Perhaps they were the sweets from a temple altar, offerings. They made me eat them.'

'And you ate them?' My wife was openly teasing me now.

'What could I do? They actually ...'

'It makes no difference. I'm telling you there is no difference between sweets from the altar of a temple and the ones locked inside the sweet-maker's cabinet.' Her tone was placating.

'Temple offerings!'

'This is a matter of individual belief. They look on them as temple offerings and you consider them sweets. Look, your faith was not injured or insulted in anyway and their beliefs were never challenged either.'

It looked as though my wife did a great deal of thinking when I was not around.

'But I saw the signs everywhere in their house. How can we be friends with them? Visiting them once in a while is another matter.' I said, anxiously.

'The signs worry you because you've only seen them from a distance. Once you see them often, they won't frighten you.'

My wife spoke as if this was something unimportant.

'I am not going to visit them again and again. I went once upon your insistence. That's it. I will not go there again.' I tried to wreck my wife's calm with my sharp remark.

'But in response to your visit, they will come. Then in response you will have to visit them and then they will come. And so this process will continue.'

Her calm remained undisturbed. She was smiling perhaps because she could see me crumbling inside. But outwardly, I stayed unperturbed. I had just resolved to tell her about my unshakeable decision when my little daughter came into the room laughing, her arm around the waist of another little girl.

'Papa, this is the daughter of the uncle who lives next door. Her papa told her to come and play with me.'

My daughter informed me innocently. Perhaps she had come to know of the change in the circumstances. Only a few days ago, I had told her …

'Well, what do you think?' my wife said, fixing her eyes on mine.

'Fine … go play.'

I told my daughter, acting as though I had not heard what my wife had said.

'Good. Now we will be able to live here for a while in peace and quiet. Our exile is finally at an end.'

My wife was trying to comfort me. When the little girls had left, I addressed her sarcastically, 'But when you hear a bomb go off somewhere, then you'll see how this temporary friendship will turn into enmity.'

'When we have rid ourselves of doubt and suspicion, perhaps friendship won't change into enmity.'

I don't know what my wife was thinking of. She was so full of hope. There was no way I could shake her awake from this dream.

Seeing him at my door suddenly one day, I got a big shock. He wasn't alone. His wife stood next to him, all smiles.

'Aren't you pleased … ?'

Perhaps he had noticed my startled look.

'No, no. I'm delighted. Come in. Believe me, I'm very pleased to see you.'

Perhaps my words betrayed my hidden feelings. Actually, my drawing room was in a state of disarray. The children's clothes were strewn all over the floor. Their shoes were on the sofa. The wife's lingerie was draped over the arm of the couch. I was in a shapeless pyjama and vest. I had opened the door unthinkingly, assuming that the milkman was there to settle his accounts. Thank god, the wife was in the bathroom and the children, though back from school, were out playing. Quickly, I flung the clothes aside, cleared some space and asked them to sit. They thought for a moment and then after still hesitating a bit, they sat down.

'Where is the lady of the house?' he asked, looking around with great curiosity.

'She is having a bath. She should be out any time now,' I responded with some hesitation.

'Why are you so upset? Why don't you sit down?'

His wife read my state of mind and tried to put me at ease.

'No, I am not upset. What is there to be upset about? You are here in my house. This is indeed an honour. I'm sorry the house is a bit disorganised. I was out and have just returned. My wife and children …'

'Don't worry. That's how it is. It is the same story in every house.'

He did his best to put me at ease. Just then, my wife opened the bathroom door, peeked out and asked, 'Who is it?'

I ran to her and in urgent whispers told her to come out. 'The neighbours are here, both husband and wife,' I said.

'I'll be there in a minute. Just fetch my clothes. They are in the closet.'

I gathered the clothes she had selected in a hurry and placed them in her hand. She got dressed and was out in a couple of minutes. And then the two ladies got going, and chattered away oblivious of the husbands. They talked about their houses, the neighbourhood, the children, the whole world.

'My dear, are you going to keep on talking or do you plan to offer some refreshments to our guests.'

Meanwhile, my neighbour and I had not been entirely silent. Still, in comparison to our wives, we had said little. Nevertheless, my wife got up right away.

'No, please don't bother. Today we are fasting. We decided to come on a whim.' They offered by way of excuse.

'Come, come. This won't do. You have come to our house for the first time. A glass of water, at least ...'

'No, no. Nothing … next time, promise …'

Both of them got up. And after inviting us to visit them, they left.

'Did you see how he slapped my face and left?' I was livid.

'Why do you say so? If they were fasting, how can they accept our hospitality?'

The slaps had no effect on my wife.

'Why did they come if they were fasting? If you go to someone's house, he will at least offer you a glass of water and if you don't accept it, it clearly means that …'

I was babbling from the hurt. My wife tried to rub a soothing salve on my wounds.

'This was their first visit. Just think, even though they are the ones with the sign, they still came to our house. Perhaps this was some sort of an experiment for them. We have the time to wait. So we'll wait for them.'

'If I go to their house now, only then will they be able to come to ours. And we will eat everything in their house, even if they give us temple offerings.'

My wife burst out laughing at my sarcastic tone.

'Okay, you can also refuse to eat at their house the next time. You can say you are fasting.'

'These things that you consider of little importance are actually very important. Whenever you make friends, there has to be an equality in that friendship. Remember that, always.'

I was quite serious; in fact, in my heart of hearts, I was quite sad. I don't know why I kept thinking that they had insulted me in my own house. I was going over their antics in minute detail.

The way they had hesitated before they had entered my house, and the slight delay in their movement. Then, the critical glances they had cast on the clutter in my house which only I was aware of. Their refusal to partake of anything and the breezy manner in which they left.

Fabulous! How skilfully they had managed to slap my face in my own house! Without leaving a mark! And my wife? Poor thing! She is such a self-contained little creature. When her hands and feet begin to stir, they only wander within the limits of her private world. Whenever her thoughts take wing, they come up against the ceiling of her house and then fall back. She does not want to see her home ruined. This is her only wish. She does not want to go about looking for another house. Somehow, she wants to settle down.

Whereas I have many other weighty matters to ponder and not just these light, unimportant trifles! For instance: History, Politics, Geography, Literature and Journalism. I look at life from top to bottom, from side to side and from front to back. Daily incidents and events, passing moments are all in front of me and I cannot hide from them. And this wife of mine, the only thing she cares about is her home. Her entire world is limited to this small, unsafe, fear-ridden rented house. And to keep this world intact she has crushed and broken and teased me. She has destroyed my self-esteem. What did I get from visiting this fellow with the sign?

After the lesson I learned today, I am not about to enter his house again. As for him, having seen my filthy, disorganised house, I don't think he will dare show his face here again. Good riddance, I say.

The days went by. And so did the nights. The weather was warm sometimes and at times cold. Then suddenly an imbalance became apparent in the cycle of winter and summer. Winter vanished altogether and the hot weather began to dominate. All around my rented house, the heat became so intense that even though we kept the doors and windows shut tight the house was getting hotter and hotter and we were starting to burn up.

I couldn't think of any way out. No remedy offered relief from the heat.

We could not sleep. We were no longer hungry or thirsty. Our faces had lost their colour and were looking more and more pallid. Not a whiff of cool air came in from the outside. Nor was there any glimmer of hope that might serve as balm for my wounds. It became imperative that I come up with some plan to escape from the heat. At last, I got pushed into making a final firm decision.

One sweltering night, when the heat had almost rendered us senseless, there was a knock on the door. My daughter raced to open it.

'Stop …'

I went up quickly and caught her. 'You should never open the door like this, so carelessly! Haven't you learned anything yet?'

'Why are you getting angry with the child? How would she know? Why don't you find out who is there at this hour?'

My wife always wants to be very brave and take the prize from me. At that time she was telling me very sweetly how I could get myself nailed to the cross. The knocking was starting to get louder. And it went on and on. There was danger in opening the door and also in not opening it. Of course, I had to open the door. I tried to open it slightly and look out. The second the door opened, a quick, strong arm pushed it ajar. Our neighbour came in, looking worried and distressed.

'What the hell, brother? Why did you take so long to open the door? I've been standing there forever.' He spoke incoherently. He had a little bundle in his hands, all wrapped up in a piece of cloth. Hearing the noise, my wife joined us. And I don't know out of what kind of shared apprehensiveness, neither I asked him in nor did my wife extend the customary invitation.

'Is there some crisis?' I blurted out involuntarily.

'Look, brother, I have come to ask you to do me a favour. You are the only person I can ask. I can turn to no one else. You are my neighbour. (We had only visited each other a couple of times.) We are like brothers. (This was the man who had refused a glass of water in my house.) No one can help me as much as you can at this time. (Now you're begging because you need me!)'

A million questions flickered in my eyes and in those of my wife.

'How can I explain? I am in a state of confusion. But I do have to tell you. If I don't, where else can I go? You are the only person to whom I can tell all this. I thought and examined the whole thing for a long time and finally came to the conclusion that from you … I mean the connection that neighbours have is very solid. On the basis of this connection, I have the right …'

We stood there trembling with anxiety. The door that had been shut all morning was now wide open.

'Whatever you want to say, say it without any hesitation. You considered us your kith and kin and that is why you came to us at this ungodly hour …' I said this to him very gently, even though we still had not asked him to sit down.

'Look, it's like this …' He was not able to utter the words. I felt like pushing him out and closing the door. For no rhyme or reason the door was wide open because of him. After a longish while, I heard a familiar sort of sound. My neighbour shoved his bundle at me. 'Keep this. Our house might get raided. They might already be there. This will be safe in your house. No one will suspect you. Because of our connection as neighbours … I must go now. I'll see you later.' He finished what he had to say and moved away rapidly. The bundle he had given me was in my hands. I hurried to close the door and placed the bundle on a nearby table.

'I wonder what's inside?' My wife looked at the bundle with anxious eyes.

'Whatever it is, it does not concern us,' I spoke rather casually.

'What could it be? Something that is safe in our house but not safe in their house. Surely, this is something to ponder over. It is quite possible, it may be …'

My wife spoke as though she were talking to herself. Even now, she was worried about her home. Her own house was looking unsafe to her now. Otherwise, this is the same woman …

'Could be anything …' I was totally worn out.

'A bomb … or something like that!' She was the one who had uttered those words, but it was as if exactly the same bomb had exploded inside my head. I cast a fearful look in the direction of the bundle. It was a plain, small, very ordinary-looking bundle.

It looked very innocent. But who knows what …

'This is exactly why I used to say … I went to his house for no reason at all. Just one visit … and now I wonder what he has deposited in our house?'

The bundle sat on the table and all of us looked at it fearfully. Suddenly my daughter piped up, 'Last time when bombs exploded in Delhi, they said on Television that whenever you see an unfamiliar object, you should call the police. Don't accept anything from a stranger. Now Uncle never told us what is inside this bundle. This is why we should contact the police right away.'

'Yes, that is correct. We should seek the assistance of the police.' A look of satisfaction flashed across my wife's face. It was as though all her problems had been solved.

'And what will we tell the police? How did this object come to be in our possession? Obviously, the neighbours will say they don't know anything. Then who will end up getting trapped?

Them or us?' With a single sentence, I wrecked all their hopes. Then suddenly my wife remembered something.

'It is possible that he left this here with us because he also feared a police raid. I am sure this bundle contains something that … why don't we open it and see?'

'Never make such a blunder, Mummy. What if it contains a Time Bomb?'

Even at such a tender age, my daughter knew all about bombs.

'Then it is even more necessary that we examine it before it is time …' I opened the bundle even as I was speaking. Under three layers of fabric, neatly wrapped in paper, I found a brick. It was an old brick, but in good condition. It was the type of brick that ancient monuments had been built with.

'You know what? This is like digging up a mountain only to find a mouse.'

My wife laughed when she saw the brick. But then noticing my grave demeanour she fell silent.

'What is it?'

'This is not what you think. You didn't dig up a mountain and find a mouse. Instead …'

There was something in my voice and manner that silenced everybody. In the quiet ambience, this silence was creating a strangely meaningful mood.

'Do you have any idea what this is?' My eyes were starting to burn.

'This brick is the reason why hot winds have been blowing incessantly and we have been obliged to stay cooped up inside our houses. This brick has been taken from the same building which …'

'What are you saying?'

My wife's eyes were wide with disbelief. 'And he has left this brick in our house … that is to say, he left the snake that poisoned an entire era, in our house.'

'In his estimation there could be no safer place than our house,' I responded with utmost calmness.

We were caught in a strange dilemma. The neighbour had felt very confident leaving this thing with us without telling us what it was. Now if policemen went to his house – and they were there already most probably – what would they find? And they would never suspect us, not even in a million years. Our neighbour had surely displayed amazing far-sightedness and cleverness. I applauded his intelligence.

'What are you thinking about? Get rid of this horrible thing as quickly as possible. Is this the reward we get for all the kindness and affection we showed him? You were quite right …'

My wife's manner and tone revealed a range of emotions: regret, shame, loss of trust, fear.

'Get rid of it … do you mean throw it away … you simple woman, if this brick leaves our house it will fan the flames that are all around us and if nothing else happens, our house will certainly be burnt to cinders.'

'Why should we stay here? Now I will tie my legs to yours and run with you.'

My wife's defeat was worth seeing. I never thought that she would accept defeat so meekly and that too at my hands. I laughed at her.

'Will my legs be capable of this? Now listen to me … Tell me what should we do?'

'If we want to keep this in the house then we have to think … if this remains in our house … we have to destroy it …'

She seemed to have made a decision.

'But I think it should stay in this house now. By chance, it has reached the most appropriate spot.'

My wife was startled at my earnestness and looked at me as though I had lost my mind.

'In this house … this thing … I can't understand you. What are you saying?' She was yelling now.

'Yes, in this house. Just think. What did the monument this brick come from mean to us and still means to us? And for them also …'

I tried to make her understand. Lack of trust still lurked in her eyes.

'But of what use is this to us?' She asked this just for her own satisfaction.

'Many. For example: performing any ritual purification without water.'[1]

'What if he asks for it back?'

'If he makes a big fuss we'll give him half, but certainly no more than that.'

My determined tone silenced my wife. She was starting to think of our small rented house as a place where she might have to spend the rest of her life.

– Translated from Urdu by Javaid Qazi

1 In the absence of water, Muslims can perform the prescribed ablutions before namaz with any piece of earth.

THE LINE

TARIQ CHHATARI

Just before setting, the sun had hung peculiar banners in the clouded sky. These banners were red and also yellow. The sky seemed to be divided into twin-coloured bands. A dark line could be seen where the two colours met. If you looked closely, you could also see some white shadows lurking close by. With even the slightest quiver in the white shadows, the red and yellow colours seemed to darken and a strange primeval fear seemed to percolate in the atmosphere. Never before had such strange white shadows appeared in the sky above this hamlet, nor had they ever managed to so neatly divide the sky into red and yellow bands. But today …

This fearsome evening had not had an ominous morning. Though the sky had been overcast from the start, the clouds were not dark. As the day wore on, a large white cloud, which was white on the surface but hid an inky blackness in its bosom, had drifted up from the west and spread itself gradually over the entire sky. Till then, small tufts of clouds had been frolicking among themselves, just like the Hindus and Muslims, who hopped and skipped across the line of communal differences, lived and played together in the hamlet. It was the seventh day in the month of *Bhadon* and the temple was being decorated for tomorrow – for Krishna Ashtami, the birth of the Lord. In the small room below the temple, the idol was being dressed in all its finery and put in the gaily coloured and brightly festooned little crib. The Lord would be born at the stroke of midnight – everyone knew that, Hindus and Muslims alike.

'No, no, Hameed … not so high,' squealed Kusum, and Hameed immediately slowed the swing. Kusum was Pandit Brij Kishore's darling daughter. As she got off the rope-swing dangling from a branch of the neem tree, Hameed took out a handful of ripe neem berries from the pocket of his kurta and gave them to her. She loved to eat those luscious berries, almost as much as Hameed loved to play the flute. Pandit Brij Kishore turned around as the first notes of Hameed's flute reached his ears. Kusum was filling a brass pitcher with water and Hameed was sitting at the edge of the well playing the flute with his eyes closed. Panditji smiled, got up and walked to the well. Placing his hand on Hameed's head, he said, 'Truly, you are Kanhaiya … my Kanhaiya. This time, I will dress you as Kanhaiya and make you sit in the Janam Ashtami procession.'

And Hameed felt as though he was sitting, not beside the well, but in the golden chariot playing his flute, and all around him were the fair maidens of Brindavan. He searched the crowd for Kusum. He looked again and saw a group of women wearing silken *ghararas* and dupattas reciting a *milaad*. Kusum was sitting beside his Ammajaan. When several women started singing together, he could see Kusum's lips also moving. She seemed to be singing along with the other women. The flute still rested on his lips. Was he playing the flute or was it the sound of Kusum singing the *milaad*? He didn't know. Then there was a clamour – inside him and outside. It was the sound of children's voices. Perhaps school had just gotten over and the children were scrambling home. Hameed suddenly came to his senses and began to walk behind Pandit Brij Kishore.

Hameed was the son of Faqir Muhammad. He had run away from his school at the mosque to sit in his neighbour Pandit Brij

Kishore's *pathshala.* Pandit Brij Kishore loved him dearly, more than all his other pupils, and affectionately called him Kanhaiya. Hameed dreamt of Krishna and the Ashtami festival and rocked his thoughts like the idol of infant Krishna being rocked in its gilded crib.

Panditji was standing in the sanctum in front of the image of Krishan Bhagwan. Hameed paused at the doorway and looked closely at the Lord with the flute at His lips. Panditji offered water to the deity, lit the lamp and closed his eyes in prayer. Hameed said his own prayer: 'Please, Allah Miyan, let the Ashtami come quickly, let me wear the tiara and become Kanhaiya and play the flute …' He crossed his right foot over his left and stood on tiptoe. He felt like taking the flute from the idol inside the temple and resting it against his own pursed lips. But his heart was aflutter. He could hear the sound of distant thunder. He looked up and saw banks of dark clouds rumbling and growling in the sky. Soon it would rain. It was only appropriate that it should, for hadn't Kanhaiya been born on just such a dark, rainy night. Soon the women of the hamlet would go for a ritual washing of His soiled diapers.

At last, night had come. How eagerly he had been waiting for it! Tomorrow was Janam Ashtami. His uneasiness left him and he felt light and joyful. Night fell. The sleep from Hameed's eyes changed magically into the lilting notes of Krishna's flute. The flute played on and on all night long and Hameed hopped and skipped in the temple courtyard like the playful waves of the Jamuna River. The premises housed the temple itself, a courtyard and a high-roofed veranda. In a corner stood a gleaming palanquin mounted on a brass-plated chariot, an elaborate four-legged affair burnished with ornate, beautifully embossed brass plates. Hameed danced over and stood close by the palanquin. He sat down and felt the aeons passing by. He felt as though he was growing taller and bigger and mightier. On his finger was a chakra that whirled with amazing speed. Hameed could feel his own being dissolve and merge with every atom, every particle of the universe. His eyes were wide open. He could see everything in the world – the bright rays of the sun and the dense blackness of the night. Slowly, the night seeped into his eyes. As the cattle made their way to the fields with bells tinkling around their necks, and the muezzin in the mosque and the bells in the temple began to herald a new day, Hameed ran to seek shelter and sleep in Pandit Brij Kishore's lap.

In the morning several well-meaning people from the hamlet assembled in the temple courtyard. Bakhshiji, a pillar of the local community, asked Panditji, 'So, who have you chosen to be the Child this time?'

Hameed's innocent pranks and guileless face danced before Pandit Brij Kishore's eyes. He said, 'Kanhaiya will be Krishna.' People looked at each other. Vaidji stuttered, 'Who? Kanhaiya?'

Panditji shook himself and said, 'I mean Hameed.'

'Hameed?!' Several people objected simultaneously. Then there was silence. Someone broke the silence. 'But the child must be a Hindu!'

Before Pandit Brij Kishore could answer, Bakshiji pounced, 'But this is unheard of … how can you have a Muslim child as Krishanji on Ashtami?'

Seth Dungar Mal cleared his throat and said, 'It is all very well, Panditji, that we must abolish these differences of caste and creed, but …'

After a great deal of debate, the matter was settled. Hameed was chosen. But some people left the temple courtyard to show their displeasure.

The preparations began at noon. Panditji bathed Hameed, and then began the elaborate ritual of dressing him. First a light dye made of indigo was patted all over his body. A lead oxide that gave off a faint effulgent shade of pink was soaked, then ground to a paste and rubbed on Hameed's face. As the paste began to dry, a pale blue and pink powder was dusted over it. A glittering belt encircled his waist, a necklace gleamed around his throat, and a brocade tiara glowed on his head. There was also a flute in his hand and a multi-coloured *chunri* was looped from his left shoulder to his waist.

Pandit Brij Kishore had transformed his Kanhaiya into the real Krishan Bhagwan. Hands folded, he bowed before his Lord.

And then the wheels of the chariot began to move. At the head of the procession walked six groups of singers and beside the palanquin Panditji himself, holding a tray of offerings. The devout came in hordes, with offerings and flowers, clamouring to touch the Lord's feet and receive His blessings. By the time the procession wound its way through the narrow paths and alleys and reached the mosque, the sun too had nearly finished its trek across the skies. The muezzin was waiting for the procession to pass before he called the faithful to the evening prayer. The procession stopped beside the mosque. The *kirtan* singers sang with gusto. Panditji blew the conch shell with all his might. At the sound of the conch, the drummers stepped up the tempo. From the heart of this cacophony, a horrendous cry rang out as a stone, pelted from the direction of the mosque, hit Krishan Bhagwan squarely on the head and drew a blood-red line across his forehead. The blood from Krishan Bhagwan's forehead spurted, snuffing out the lamp in the ceremonial tray. The stone was aimed at Krishan Bhagwan. It wounded Hameed. And innocent Kanhaiya's blood snuffed out the lamp for the puja.

Chaos broke out. Loud, hysterical voices crying for blood besieged the homes of Muslims. People swarmed towards the mosque. Pandit Brij Kishore plunged through the crowd to find a young man hacking away at the door of the mosque with an axe. He snatched the axe away. The air was rent by the cry: 'Nara-e-Takbir … Allah-o-Akbar!' He ran towards the sound and saw Seth Dungar Mal and Ramanand trying to pacify the crowd. 'Brother, what is this? We are brothers, aren't we? We were born on this soil and we shall …'

'And we shall die on this soil!' came the scream. Brutish rage and terror took over. Seth Dungar Mal and Ramanand were killed. Now there was no stopping the mobs. No one knew what would happen next. Panditji ran towards the house of Banda Khan from where he could hear jubilant cries of 'Jai Bajrang Bali.' He found Banda Khan's doorway spewing flames and heard the piteous cries of women and children trapped behind that wall of fire. Panditji looked at the mob. Fear and horror were in their eyes. They seemed to be asking: 'What's happening? This shouldn't be happening.' But still, it was happening. It was as though something was going on right in front of their eyes without their wanting it to. But how? And why? What was this force that was invisible yet caused all this …

In the midst of it all, Panditji noticed that several people were looking up at the sky. The sky that sheltered them was today adorned in the most peculiar colours. It was streaked with red and also yellow. A dark line could be seen where the two colours met. If you looked closely, you could see some white shadows lurking close by. The red and yellow colours seemed to darken with the slightest quiver in the white shadows and a strange primeval fear seemed to percolate in the atmosphere. Never before had such strange white shadows appeared in the sky above this hamlet, nor had they ever managed to so neatly divide the sky into red and yellow bands. But today …

Pandit Brij Kishore ran towards the palanquin. A man had picked up the axe from beside Krishan Bhagwan – the ceremonial axe with which the Lord slew Evil – and he stood waving it before a terrified Kanhaiya. Every year, the sharp-edged axe was kept in the palanquin and, at the end of the Ashtami procession, Krishan Bhagwan slew the evil Kansa, thus symbolising the victory of good over evil.

A muffled cry escaped Panditji's lips, 'What is this … this is Krishan Bhagwan … our Kanhaiya.'

Har Prasad had just sung the *aarti*. Now he spoke in a dull, flat voice, 'No … this is Hameed. Faqir Muhammad's son.'

Several people spoke up, 'Yes, yes, this is Hameed, the son of a Musalman. They have insulted our Krishan Bhagwan. They threw a stone at the palanquin. It hit Bhagwanji. Look at the blood dripping from his forehead. And now these cowards are hiding in their homes.'

The man with the axe swung it in the air and roared, 'We will avenge this outrage. Today we will …'

'No …' Panditji shouted and lunged at the axe. The man threw Panditji down from the palanquin and struck Hameed a mighty blow.

Resplendent, glowing, Krishan Bhagwan fell … scattering the shining tiara, the spangled necklace and the glittering waistband. A thin red line formed on the ground. Some people stood on one side of the line, some on the other. There was clamour on both sides. It was difficult to tell whether the noise was greater on this side or on the other.

– Translated from the Urdu by Rakhshanda Jalil

THE WOLVES ARE SECULAR

ZAKIA MASHHADI

'Hey you bitch, you offspring of beggars! How much longer will you linger on, making excuses about the child? Will your father come and wash the utensils for you?'

A perceptibly shaken Saroja patted the child gently, scrambled to her feet and hurried inside. Three month old Mahesh had just fallen asleep. One could not fathom what troubled the child – whether he suffered from gripes or some other disorder. He had been restless all afternoon. Saroja had had to do all the work holding him in her arms. All the while, her mother-in-law sat comfortably, drawing on the hookah, cursing Saroja's family because they had foisted such a slovenly, abusive and slothful girl onto her family.

As she dashed into the house, Saroja glanced quickly at the child. He seemed composed. It was evening now. Inside the houses, the lamps had been lit, but everything outside was engulfed in the calm of a hushed darkness. On the veranda lay Saroja's rope cot. A pregnant buffalo was tethered beside it. On the opposite side was a bamboo door.

Saroja entered the kitchen, layered with the clean mud paste and gathered up the wicker basket laden with fresh *bathwa* greens. Picking the leaves from their stems is a time consuming job; besides, the leaves require a thorough wash, else the little particles of mud that remain behind, leave a gritty taste in the mouth.

Once, Saroja's father-in-law had tossed out his plate of food because some of the muddy residue had gotten in his mouth. Saroja had to make the chapattis after putting the pot of herbs on the stove to cook – at least twenty-five chapattis. She also had to grind chutney from red chillies. If the child slept soundly, she would manage to do all this peacefully. That afternoon, she had had quite a rough time. The buffalo's fodder had to be prepared; the chapattis also had to be made before the men left for the fields. Having picked the leaves from their stems, Saroja cast a sidelong glance at her child as she went past to wash the greens at the hand pump outside. He was sleeping soundly; both his fists were closed and his tiny legs were partially arched in the manner of little babies when they are fast asleep.

Having washed the *bathwa* leaves, Saroja implored silently on her way back to the kitchen, 'Dear God! Let him sleep soundly for some more time.' Before she could get to the stove, a mysterious shadow-like creature lunged forward from behind the hand-pump. Its dark skin-tone seemed to blend so naturally with the dusk gathering around that, had someone been there, he could only have sensed a movement, and not seen what it was that had moved in the dark. Abruptly the buffalo stopped chewing its fodder; its tail too stiffened – as though it had turned to stone. Precisely at the same time Saroja placed the basketful of dripping wet greens onto the floor and intuitively turned around, her maternal instinct having warned her, but by then the shadow had already vanished into the dark, as swiftly as lightning, holding the child between its jaws in a vice-like grip.

Saroja's reaction was very similar to that of the buffalo. She was transfixed – as though under a spell. Nevertheless in the flash of an instant, she let out an ear-piercing scream and ran in the direction of the movement. Calling out to her husband, she wailed, 'My son … *hai re daiya*! My son …'

By daybreak, the entire village was abuzz with the news that the first-born son of Panchoo had been carried away by a she devil.

Probably she had devoured the child by now – bones and all – as though she had been munching on a tender laddoo. The villagers tired themselves out hunting all over the fields but there was no trace of the child's body. Only a talisman resembling the one he wore round his neck was found somewhere. However, even Panchoo was sceptical whether it was the same one worn by his son because several people in the village wore similar talismans, provided sometimes by Maulvi sahib or sometimes by Ram Sanahi Ojha. Both the men gave more or less similar-looking talismans. Whatever minimal difference there would have been was erased because now, sullied in the mud and crushed by the creature's hooves, it had lost its identity.

Thereafter, during the next four months, three children from the village were picked, one after the other. Coincidentally, they were all boys. People began to assume that the evil spirit was eyeing only boys. She did not want the village boys to survive.

'Oh yes! No one can bring the girls to any harm. How they dance the jig upon our chests! This third daughter of mine grows by the minute, even though she does not receive the full quota of milk. Despite contracting pneumonia she bounced back to health after some minimal amount of affliction,' said Saajapuri Chachi, who had got her name because her paternal home was in Shahjahanpur. She was appointed the Village Level Midwife and had been given strict instructions to ensure that the villagers did not discriminate between girls and boys.

Since Saajapur-wali was not a native of the village, she was decorated with quite a few personality traits. Some even credited her with having a black tongue. In one instance, she cursed little girls and in the other, the potter Bansi's six-year old daughter was carried away.

Often, large kilns were lit in the precincts of the potters' residences to bake the mud vessels. Bansi had placed his cot out in the open at night in order to ensure that the fires did not die out. His family was very fond of their daughter because the six elder children were boys. The little girl too, was much attached to her father. She awoke in the middle of the night, and began to insist upon going over to sleep with him. After a hard day's work, the mother was overcome with fatigue and slumber. She spanked the girl and shouted, 'Go out and drop dead! Your father is outside, near the furnace.' She was a petite child, giving the impression of being a couple of years younger than her age. Rubbing her eyes drowsily, she went out in the open. It was pitch dark. However, the fire in the kiln could be seen from a distance. On the way to the furnace, several large, unbaked earthen pots were kept under a shed, waiting to be baked the next day. Behind the pots a pair of eyes shone as brightly as the live coals in the fires. The little girl shuddered just a little, near one of the pots. She tried to call out to her father – 'Bapu' – but was scarcely able to articulate 'Ba …' because her neck was seized in a vice-like grip. Her face lost its radiance and her bright eyes were soon as lacklustre as the darkness into which she had unwittingly stepped. Paradoxically, content that her daughter was fast asleep with her arms around her father's neck, the mother slept soundly through the rest of the night.

The little girl's half eaten body was recovered in the vicinity of the bamboo thicket. Most of the village believed that a she-demon dwelt in the thicket.

About seven years ago, the village herdsman, Ram Babu's youthful, hale and hearty wife, Phoolmati, had been killed by the co-sharers of the property and interred in the bamboo thicket. Ram Babu had been in possession of five *bighas* of fertile land and three cows of good breed. The cows had been delivering calves quite regularly. However, Phoolmati had not had a child even after twelve years of married life. Ram Babu was not very worried about this. He had left everything to God's will and was quite content with looking after his land, his cows and his beautiful wife. His co-sharers, too, were quite pleased with the fact that Ram Babu did not have any child. Conscious of her own limitation and apprehensive about the intent of the co-sharers, Phoolmati had insisted upon marrying Ram Babu off to her younger sister, Parvati. Eager to punish her for the crime she had committed, the co-sharers conspired with the Ojhas of the village, accused her of being a demoness, had her put to death and buried her in the bamboo thicket. A few days later, not only the co-sharers but also the rest of the village was abuzz with the rumour that Phoolmati, in fact, had been a demoness. Her sister had become pregnant soon after her death.

Ram Babu was impotent. The village medicine man had pronounced this fact and it had been reiterated by the village Ojha. His first wife had slept with him for twelve years but nothing had happened. How then, could her younger sister whom she had brought into her own house as a co-wife conceive so soon after her death? Either Ram Babu was not the father of the child or Phoolmati had impregnated herself into her sister's womb in order to avenge her murder at the hands of the co-sharers. One day Phoolmati's ghost manifested itself upon the wife of one of the co-sharers and announced that Ram Babu was so barren that he could not be expected to father even a clod. How could his second wife become pregnant? Obviously, it was Phoolmati who had descended into her sister's womb! Now it was out in the open for everyone to see – she would be reborn and settle scores with each one of them.

The villagers hatched yet another conspiracy. After a great deal of persuasion they were able to inveigle Parvati to accompany them to the bamboo thicket. They had already slit a hefty bamboo so as to make a wide noose-like cleft in it. They forced the eighteen year old pregnant girl's slender neck into the opening and pressed the two halves of the bamboo so forcefully that her eyes bulged out and became the very picture of shock and dismay. The poor girl's bulging eyes seemed to be asking, 'Why? Why?'

In addition to the noose-like cleft they made in the bamboo, they also dug a pit in the thicket. Parvati was interred beside Phoolmati. By now, Ram Babu had lost his sanity. Instead of tending to his cows whose udders were swollen with milk, he kept making the rounds of the bamboo thicket where his wives were buried. He began suffering from hallucinations, imagining songs being sung to the accompaniment of the flute; he also began to imagine the sound of an infant's babble which sometimes questioned, 'Why? Why? Why?'

Nobody dared give his daughter in marriage to Ram Babu after this. His co-sharers warned the community and the residents of the neighbouring villages that were anybody to marry their daughter to him, she would be killed by the *churails* or, alternately, the *churails* would seek sanctuary in the girl's womb. After all, now there were two of them! It was they who had driven Ram Babu barmy.

Every time the wind blew through the bamboo thicket, it seemed as though someone was wailing. Now even other people began to hear the sound of sad songs being sung in the vicinity of the bamboo thicket, quite like the dirges that are sung during the month of Muharram. Phoolmati would begin the song and Parvati would continue the strains from where her sister would trail off – exactly in the manner of *Nauhas*. Just then a *papiha* would tweet *pi kahan* and those passing by the bamboo thicket would shudder and scurry away. As time went by, people began to avoid the place. The village women, in particular, never went past the thicket after dusk. And now, it was from this very bamboo thicket that the half eaten body of potter Bansi's tiny, delicately-built daughter was recovered.

The *churails* had become far too active.

The district administration had an altogether different view. So many children had disappeared that the news was splashed all over the newspapers and the television. The administration dispatched a team to the village, to conduct an investigation into the incidents. It included two huntsmen who had lived in regions which were inhabited by wolves. Nevertheless, when an investigation was conducted, it became apparent that in the past fifty years, no incident involving wolves had been reported from this village.

The oldest resident of the village Allah Diya said that, when he was a young boy, the village was assailed by packs of wolves. They picked so many sheep, goats and hens that the farmers were devastated. The wolves had not tasted human blood but the loss of animal life had been so large that the administration had announced an award for anyone who would kill the wolves. During those days, the award settled by the officers for killing one wolf was forty rupees and that was believed to be quite a hefty sum of money. Allah Diya's Bade Chacha, Allah Rakha, had participated in the Second World War. Although he had served in the Supply Section, he had been trained to shoot. He had retired by that time but was still quite robust and courageous. He shot four wolves and created a record.

'Four in one blow?' interrupted somebody. 'No, one after the other; over a span of one or two months.' He was awarded for each kill. During those days one could buy one *tola* of gold for eighty rupees. He used the prize money to purchase big earrings for his wife and had his picture taken with his leg atop the carcasses of the wolves.

When he had killed the fourth wolf, the Deputy Commissioner Sahib shook his hand.

'Do you have those photographs with you?' asked one of the huntsmen.

'Let's talk business, old man!' interrupted the leader of the team who was a Class Two officer in government service.

'One day, beside herself with anger, Chachi tore the pictures and threw them away.' He was about to launch into a detailed account elaborating the cause of his elderly Chachi's annoyance, but was stopped midway by a gesture signalling silence.

'Tell us when the wolves were seen again!'

'In 1947, a wolf had ventured into the populated areas of the village. An alarm was raised but many people thought that a riot had broken out; after all, the atmosphere was quite charged with communal tension. Later, we learnt that it was a wolf. After this nothing was heard about them.'

A number of village dwellers had gathered by now. A middle-aged person spoke up with considerable bitterness, 'After this, violence was unleashed against our community. At night when people raised an alarm, most people thought that a wolf was on the prowl. Meanwhile, the assailants conveniently massacred about twenty-five or thirty people and took off. At that time, one of my chachis was a newly-wed bride. She jumped into the well.' Overwhelmed with emotion, the middle-aged man became quiet.

'I think you people will not permit us to do our work. Get out of the way. Go home.' The officer spoke so crossly that the villagers felt intimidated – as though a wolf were growling in their midst.

Regaining control over his tone, the officer addressed an elderly person, 'Yes, you tell us. Were wolves ever seen again in the populated parts of the village?'

'No, Sahib. It has been a long time now … during the period between 1947 and 1950, people killed countless wolves in order to receive the prize-money of forty rupees. They combed the jungle. Had any wolves remained, they would certainly have fled for fear of the threat to their lives or continued to live in obscurity in the thick of the jungle.'

'Once in a while, the woodcutters have chanced to see a lone wolf or two in the thick of the jungle but none has come this way. Why should they come this way now?' Another person, unable to exercise control over himself, spoke up. He was a well-built man with a dark, tanned complexion. He wore an undersized dhoti and sported only a vest to cover the upper part of his body. He spoke in the *Purbi* dialect. His countenance wore a hardened look; his voice was laced with anger. He put forth his point without much ado.

'There is only one thing I do not understand Chacha Allah Diya. All these boys that have disappeared belong to the quarters inhabited by the potters and the fishermen. Not a single boy belonging to your community has been abducted. Even the goats that were picked belong to an old woman who is a Brahmin. Do you have anything to say that can shed light on this phenomenon?'

'Son, I had never given a thought to this idea – that even a wolf …'

'Have you seen the wolf, Chacha?' he interrupted.

'No, I have not seen the wolf, son. But evidently these are the doings of wolves, aren't they?'

'That is not the case. Answer my question. It is not yet apparent whether a wolf has killed the children or someone else.'

'What can I say that will answer your question appropriately? You have thought of something quite awful.'

'Why would you think of that?' Having said this, the man cast a sidelong glance at Allah Diya and smirked in such a sinister way that the elderly Allah Diya began to scratch his head awkwardly. Then he addressed the team, 'You have conducted a close investigation into the matter. Somebody covered a distance of about six miles from the jungle and pilfered Dharmindar Mishra's goat which was tethered to a stump. Now, don't you see that only "our" animals are being picked? The following day, according to the buzz, lots of people were invited to a sumptuous feast at Manzoor Mian's place. There was pulao. Mutton stew was prepared in a large vessel.'

'Now look here, you are talking about something quite different,' said one of the government employees. 'We are not concerned with personal rivalries among the villagers, neither with thefts and burglaries nor incidents of animal thefts. We are here to resolve the larger issue at hand – that of young children continually being killed in the village.'

'But there are no wolves and that is a fact,' said another man with a great deal of conviction.

'Maybe not wolves – it could have been a cheetah, a leopard, a hyena or any other wild animal. We need your cooperation to resolve the mystery.'

'Cheetahs and leopards do not inhabit these regions – we may presume that it is a wolf. But even wolves have not been seen in the village for the last fifty years.'

'Trees are being felled and the jungles are disappearing; the villages are gradually extending into areas that were once a part of the jungle. The wasteland was never so big, was it?' said Asha, who ran the village Adult Education Centre, and had universally been nick-named 'Nurse didi' because she was a trained midwife. She was only too willing to offer her services if she were called to assist in the delivery of a baby.

Bhagirath glared at her and mumbled loudly enough for her to hear, 'She is modestly lettered but the wretch thinks she is a scholar.' Asha felt intimidated by Bhagirath. In fact, even the elders of the village were in awe of him. The poor woman stood no chance. Quietly, she covered her head with the *pallu* of her sari and slunk away in the direction of the Centre.

The hard work of the next three or four days did not yield anything fruitful. The huntsmen continued to scour the jungle, the villagers continued to be cross-questioned, the sites of the tragedies continued to be probed. However, Bhagirath's stark remark questioning the fact that not a single boy belonging to Allah Diya Chacha's community, i.e. Muslims, had been abducted, began to spread like jungle fire in parched grassland. People began to discuss this brand new implication with a great deal of enthusiasm.

One woman claimed that one night as she walked towards the *sarkanda* bushes on her way to the fields after nightfall, a dark shadow had lunged forward from behind the bushes and disappeared. She swore that the shadow had pounced on two legs and was enclosed in a black sack-like overcoat.

'On the basis of Lajwanti *behen's* claim it is quite evident that it was a woman clad in a burkha.'

The story of the burkha-clad woman, who was kidnapping children, also began to do the rounds. From the potters' quarters, it travelled to the cobblers' settlements, then resting for a while with the Kayasthas in their part of the village it passed through the orchards of the Thakurs to reach the mango groves of the Brahmins where it finally sat comfortably.

Bhola Singh observed that, earlier, he would not have perceived the incidents of the burkha-clad woman and the kidnappings as connected to one another, but of late the situation was developing in such a way, that he too was obliged to put two and two together. One day it was getting dark by the time he had returned from the meeting of the panchayat regarding the boundary wall of the graveyard. Night had fallen by the time he walked past the local *nullah*. On the opposite side of the *nullah* were the dwellings of the Muslims. In the distance, coming from that direction, he had heard the piercing sound of laughter. It was such a dreadful and ominous a laugh, that it could well have been that of a hyena. His hair stood on end. Just then he recollected that Majeed, the madman, would laugh in exactly the same manner. It must be him. Simultaneously, he saw a burkha-clad woman dart out of the lane stealthily and disappear in the direction of the mud path that led towards the thakurs' establishments. Underneath the head gear, her head moved from side to side, as though she were taking in the details of the surroundings despite being in a hurry. That night, the watchman Ballabhdhar's six-year old son, who was asleep under the thatch in the Thakur's fields, was abducted from his rope cot. The father had been a little distance away, relieving himself. He ran with all his might but by then the dark shadow had disappeared into the night. Armed with pick-axes and iron rods, a number of young men launched a search in several directions but the lost boy was not to be found.

Now people passed by the Muslim quarters of the village either looking suspiciously and gesturing among themselves, or murmuring softly while they stood and watched. The residents became anxious. Only a few days ago, the matter concerning the boundary wall of the graveyard had been resolved after much deliberation. With great difficulty, they had managed to prevent it from escalating into a serious controversy.

The eldest *thakurain* of a Thakur household was seriously considering doing away with the services of Isa Bo, whom she had employed to clean the grain and perform other odd jobs. Overnight, she had become quite indifferent. However, none of the women in Isa Bo's household wore burkhas. These were women who toiled for long hours under the sun weeding people's fields, or working on hire, exerting hard labour by means of the sickle. Only women of wealthy households could afford to wear the burkha. Isa Bo too heard the story of the burkha-clad woman and was as frightened as anybody else. She had begun to sleep on the veranda, letting her daughter-in-law sleep inside, in the only room of the house, along with the two little granddaughters. She had also issued strict orders to her daughter-in-law to latch the room securely from inside. Her son worked in a cloth manufacturing mill in Kanpur; Isa Mian had died several years ago. Isa Bo could not comprehend what had come over the genial *thakurain* who always had a kind word for her and who often sent fruits and other goodies for her grand-daughters.

It was around this time that the armed huntsmen, who had been scouring the Sakhu jungle, shot a wolf – a healthy, dark brown, female. They also picked up adolescent cubs from its hideout. The bones that they recovered were so worn out and broken down that it was difficult to make them out at a cursory glance. However, in all likelihood they were human bones, apparently of little children. These were gathered together in a bag, for forensic examination. The cubs were confined in a cage, in order to be sent to the zoo and the carcass of the female wolf was paraded in the village. People heaved sighs of relief.

The team that had been sent by the administration was given a grand send off. Nevertheless, quite a few people were still puzzled as to why not a single child had been lifted from the Muslim quarters of the village. Surely there was some mystery behind this. How could it be ascertained whether the wretched female wolf was actually carrying away the children; whether the bones recovered from its lair were in fact the bones of children and not the young ones of rabbits, deer, sambar or any other animal? How could one depend upon the government employees? They could make any claim in order to close a file!

After about a week, the gardener, Mansa, came over to the *thakurain*'s place and informed her that on the previous night while returning home, he had seen a dark shadow on the prowl. He was so frightened that he did not dare look back; he took to his heels immediately and did not stop until he got to the buttress surrounding the well in the garden. Only there did he catch his breath.

Isa Bo was busy at work, her head bowed low, pounding green gram in the stone *chakki*. She was quite hopeful that today, the *thakurain* would certainly give her some of the crushed dal. Chapattis made from the crushed dal are good to taste. Besides, they stay longer in the stomach and keep hunger pangs at bay. However, the *thakurain* emptied the powdered dal into the clay urn quite indifferently and tossed an instruction towards Isa Bo, 'Tomorrow when you prepare the silage for the cow, make sure you mix the powdered dal in it.'

About two months went by. No one's child was killed and nor were anybody's sheep or goat stolen. The wolf seldom figured in the conversations of the people now. Many of them were convinced that the brown, female wolf had been killing the children. After all, she was an animal. In any case, even human beings do not hesitate to kill their own kind if and when the need arises. Hadn't Ram Babu's co-sharers done away with both his wives and an unborn child? Neither had anybody raised a voice against the crimes nor had the police acted in order to bring the killers to book. Yet the entire village knew what had happened. Apart from that, when beautiful, young women are put to death so ruthlessly before biding their time, they are bound to take the shape of *churails* and demonesses and haunt the village. Everyone knew that too.

However, in the third month after the brown female wolf had been killed, the most appalling incident occurred.

Toilets were quite a rarity in the village. Women, especially, would go out to relieve themselves in the fields before daybreak. Quite often, they waited past midnight before they went out. Sukh Ram Pandit's newly-wed wife, who was suffering from an upset stomach, felt compelled to go out and relieve herself in the evening. At about midnight when she suffered from bouts of pain once again, she did not wake up her husband out of sheer embarrassment. After all, she was not a child. She was a robust, able bodied, nineteen-year old daughter of a farmer's household.

She took off her anklets and bangles so as to go out quietly, without waking up anybody. Gathering her sari around her and adjusting her nose ring, she set out to relieve herself behind the *sarkanda* bushes. It was an eerily quiet night but a full moon hung low in the skies suffusing the *sarkanda* bushes with a magical charm. It was the moonlight which prevented the girl from experiencing any fear. The next morning, Sukh Ram Pandit woke up to find that his wife was not by his side but he knew that she went out to the fields before daybreak. However, he was a little surprised to find her bangles and anklets lying on the bed. When she did not return even after sunrise, people went out in search of her. They found the lota lying upside down in the *sarkanda* bushes and the body of the girl lay a little distance away. A large portion of her thigh had already been devoured.

This was the first incident of an adult's killing, on a moonlit night.

'The wolf was killed. Now whose handiwork is this?'

'Surely, there can be more wolves!'

'This place is not a hideout for wolves' said someone seething with anger. 'The wolves never came back after 1947-48.'

'This time, too, the wolf has brought harm upon *us*.'

'Yes, this is an issue that requires solemn deliberation. How much longer can we shut ourselves out from this matter?'

'We must respond with similar aggression – a tooth for a tooth, an eye for an eye. This is a grave failing on our part, that we Hindus suffer injustice and violence ever so submissively – as though we were drinking mouthfuls of nectar – without so much as hesitating to heave a sigh.'

'Ah! The waters are flowing well above the danger mark now. These government employees will do nothing. They have killed a hapless female wolf and packed off its poor little cubs to the zoo – to suffer life-imprisonment. Such severe injustice! Ram, Ram, Ram!'

All the village folk had gathered round the partially-eaten body of the young woman. Isa Bo was also hanging about in the vicinity. Settling her dupatta on her head and shaking her head from side to side she observed in quite a philosophical manner, 'My mother would say, "Whether he kills or not, it is always the wolf who takes the blame."'

'Last year, during the Ram Naumi procession, her son stood in our midst, holding a glass of jaggery sherbet. He puts on a charade of friendship and wields the knife on the quiet. Every evening, I go to the village *chaupal* to read the newspaper. These days, our village is making news. It is alleged that undercover agents belonging to the secret agency of the neighbouring country are roaming about in our midst. It is due to protection from people such as these that they find easy passage. How else would it be possible for them to find their way in?'

Once again, Isa Bo could not understand what had transpired among the people – words like neighbouring country and secret agency too, were beyond her comprehension. After all, she was both foolish and a little hard of hearing. She stood there in a daze for a while, then wobbled away to do her work. Nevertheless, she felt uncomfortable. She had not grasped the full meaning of their words but there was something sinister in their attitudes that language could not articulate – and Isa Bo could not miss that.

However, before the scheme to slit open Isa Bo's throat could be hatched, something bizarre happened. This time two children were lifted within a span of twenty-four hours from the Muslim quarters of the village.

One evening, having cut the grass, Abdul's seven or eight year old daughter was on her way back home, accompanied by her mother and some other women. Abdul earned his livelihood by picking *mahua* during the summer and plucking water-chestnuts from the ponds during the winter months. That day, Abdul's daughter was running a slight temperature which had risen by the evening. She was trailing behind her mother and continually being reprimanded for lagging behind. It was getting dark and a chilly wind began to blow. All of a sudden, as they neared the mango grove, the girl was pounced upon. The women turned around and created such a din that the animal let go of the girl and darted off. Nevertheless, due to the creature's vice-like grip around her neck and probably due to the severity of shock, the little girl had died by then.

The next day Mukhtaran *bibi* was attacked during the day in a most baffling manner. She was walking down the thoroughfare carrying her child on the waist and a basket over her head. Despite the atmosphere of fear that assailed the villagers, life seemed to be moving at its own pace (besides, fear had become quite ubiquitous by now!). It was daytime; gathering up the livestock droppings for preparing fuel while walking down the mud path, she had wandered off towards the bamboo thicket. All of a sudden, a full-grown, healthy wolf pounced upon her from behind the bush, grabbed the child in the batting of an eyelid and disappeared into the thicket as fast as lightning. Owing to the attack, Mukhtaran *bibi* suffered deep gashes on her arms and around her ribs. By evening they were able to recover the half-eaten remains of the child's body a couple of kilometres away. This was the first time somebody had actually seen the assailant in broad daylight and identified it. It was a wolf alright. Whether it was male or female could not be discerned in the flash of an instant – but without doubt, it was an incredibly secular wolf.

In fact, not just that one – all wolves are secular. They do not kill on account of religious convictions.

– Translated from the Urdu by Fatima Rizvi

ROGUE

SYED MUHAMMAD ASHRAF

The sun had set some time ago, or maybe it had just gone down, when the station wagon slowly took a sharp right turn on the path that headed towards the jungle. The vehicle had not even picked up speed when a woman, dressed in an overcoat, appeared on the culvert, and raised her hand in a bid to stop the car. Her other hand clutched the right hand of a small boy.

As a natural response, Nadeem screeched the car to a halt. This threw up so much dust, that for a few moments the woman's ankles and the boy's knees were not to be seen.

By the time the dust settled and the engine stopped making noise, Nadeem heard three phrases in the car and felt a bit ashamed.

Dr Wiqar had picked up the rifle in his hand and spoken in a rushed manner, 'Why have you stopped the car? The DFO would be getting anxious waiting for us at the Ranger's office; as it is we are late.'

Asif lowered the window, peeped out, pulled his head in and said with a smile, 'Headed to hunt a rogue elephant, one turns a hero on seeing a woman.' Feeling both inquisitive and concerned Rashid said, 'Let us at least get out and ask who she is and what she wants.'

Nadeem stepped out. The December chill was in the air as he headed towards the woman. 'At least close the door, you devil.

It is very cold; it seems to have snowed somewhere close,' Dr Wiqar muttered.

Nadeem returned to the wagon, shut the door and as he tried to address the others he realised something and re-opened the door. The anxiety of the door being slammed on her face gave way to relief and the woman relaxed.

'Actually, this woman is carrying ten thousand rupees,' Nadeem said but stopped abruptly as he realised that what he said sounded awkward and out of context.

'What is this? To whom does this money belong? And why does this woman have so much money … that too here in this jungle …'

Nadeem interrupted Dr Wiqar with casual confidence and carried on, 'She has got this money from the Agarwal trader of village Baroli who trades in katechu. She is here from Canada and is a resident of Lucknow. She had lent this money to Agarwal so that she can take it back when she is here. She has to reach Lucknow tonight; the kid is her nephew, Raju. Today, there is a strike of bus operators; she came to know this only after she had left and she does not want to return because not a single house there …'

Suddenly aware of the presence of Dr Wiqar's compounder Ramesh who was seated quietly on the back seat holding on to his single-barrel gun, Nadeem did not complete what he was about to say.

At times it does not take long to figure out the scenario.

'Let us take her to the Ranger's office, from there we shall send her with the DFO to Bahraich; rather, we shall ask him to drop her at the bus stand in Bahraich.'

All the tension that had crept in since the car had stopped seemed to ease out with this one sentence and everyone seemed satisfied.

Dr Wiqar picked up his rifle and moved to sit on the seat behind, next to Asif. Holding the steering with one hand and leaning out and holding the handle of the open door with his other hand, Nadeem stuck his face out and called out to the woman.

'Come along, why are you standing? We were trying to make space for you.' The men inside the car heard the lie and seemed satisfied. Nadeem opened the door on the other side. She first got the child in and then placing her shoe on the board she too hopped in. She was wearing high boots. Right from climbing into the car till settling in her seat – all of them managed to get a good look at her. When she was standing a little away at the edge of the road, staring at her had seemed awkward.

She was a tall and attractive woman. Looking at her glowing cheeks and flawless skin, Nadeem guessed that she lived on a healthy diet of fresh fruits. It is quite possible that others too thought the same.

She slowly ran her hand over the pocket of her overcoat as if feeling for something, and then without turning her head she softly whispered 'Thank you' to everyone. Quickly again she repeated loudly, 'Thank you all for your help.'

By now it had grown dark and it was difficult to say what was growing in the fields next to the road. The barrier indicating the jungle post lay ahead.

The car had just slowed down in front of the barrier when an untidily dressed guard approached and, shading his eyes from the headlight with his hands, he recognised the car and lifted the rope to allow it to go through. They had barely moved ahead, when Asif said to Nadeem, 'Stop for a moment … just a bit!'

'The same movement, the same fragrance, isn't it?' asked the Doctor.

'Yes,' Asif agreed.

Asif and Dr Wiqar stepped out. The air that came in from the open door seemed to be from another planet. The car was now well inside the forest.

Asif and Dr Wiqar leaned against the car and drew in long breaths. Nadeem had opened his side of the door. He too turned his face towards the jungle and drew in long breaths and tried to absorb the fragrance with keen interest. He thought the air carried the smell of the huge elephant-ear like leaves of teak, the sharp smell of the bark of the *sakho* tree, as well as the scent of a variety of grasses that grew in the forest along with the smell of the skin and hair of the many creatures that lived here. And because it was dark the eyes were not able to do their job; hence the forest had to be sensed entirely through its many smells. At times the vast forest, which is so quiet, makes existence seem so meaningless, and at other times it becomes pregnant with meanings. When the shriek of a bird or the roar of an animal breaks this silence, it seems that that part of the forest has lit up.

At first the child seemed disinterested in his surroundings, but gradually he started paying attention.

Nadeem wondered. Can light transform into sound the way in which sound, at times, transforms into light? He wanted to take this thought to its proper conclusion when Dr Wiqar shut the door and stretching himself on his seat announced, 'What a beautiful and quiet jungle this used to be! This mad elephant has spoilt everything.'

There was a change in the posture of the woman and child when the mad elephant was mentioned.

'What fun it used to be, Wiqar Bhai, when we used to come and live in this jungle for days! There was never any danger. Last season we walked in the moon-lit night from the Ranger's office all the way to the river Gerwa and lay on the sand watching the crocodiles; what fun! We also spotted those rare deer,' Rashid reminded.

'Nowadays we cannot even enter the forest after sunset,' Ramesh whispered from the back seat.

As Nadeem closed the door and started the car, he saw that the child was clinging to the woman and hiding his face; he was probably crying.

Looking at the woman he asked the kid, 'What's the matter?'

'The elephant story has scared him,' she clutched the child close to herself and replied, 'I mean hearing about the mad elephant … what is the matter, has an elephant turned rogue?'

'Yes, for some time there has been a rogue in this jungle and we are on our way to kill that beast.'

By now the kid was grasping the woman tightly around her waist; though his face was hidden, he was listening to Nadeem.

By the time they reached the Ranger's office he had told the woman that this rogue had claimed many innocent lives, one of its tusk was broken and there was an injury mark left on its belly by the bullet of a villager, the forest officer of this district had sent his report to the chief wildlife warden and got the elephant declared a rogue and Dr Wiqar and Asif were given the permit to kill the elephant. Earlier, there had been a few instances but gradually the havoc created by this rogue had increased. The matter had first been discussed at the village council, then the block and later the matter went to the provincial assembly. Since forest and wildlife are a central government issue the matter was also discussed in Parliament. On being asked by the woman why there had been a delay in killing the elephant, Nadeem told her of the difficulty in identifying the rogue. As it is, government matters took long because of the ways of officialdom; on top of that, the area was so large …

The Ranger's office was still far, time was at hand and the company was charming; so, Nadeem went on to explain at length that the resources of the government are limited. In such sensitive matters, the government contacts private individuals and gives them the responsibility of tackling the rogue. For example, the actual order to eliminate the elephant is in the name of the DFO but he is a government official. He is not very dependable: this is known to all the high officials and the ministers too know that the name of the DFO on the permission order is just a formality; actually it is Dr Wiqar and Asif Bhai who have to carry out the order.

The woman addressed Nadeem but was actually telling everyone that she had been in Canada for many years where her husband was a doctor and that she visited her parents in Lucknow every two years, and she had gone to Canada for the first time when Raju was just a one-year-old, whereas now he was in the sixth standard. She also said that she could have easily come on her own from Lucknow to Baroli but her parents thought it improper that she travel alone so they sent a man along to guard her. She had glanced at her nephew with a smile while addressing him as a man. In spite of the fear created by the elephant story, Raju looked pleased and also a bit shy. She went on to say that her parents had asked her to be back at any cost by sunset because these days in that area … She had to abruptly stop here because Dr Wiqar loudly took Ramesh's name and started a pointless conversation with him. Meanwhile, Ramesh too confessed that ever since peace had vanished from the Terai he too was scared and had stopped travelling on the highway at night because last Sunday a bus had been stopped near Puranpur and …

As they carried on, the woman kept explaining things to the child bit by bit. In a bid to share her burden, Nadeem gradually tried to win over Raju's trust and was happy to notice that, thanks to his efforts, the lady seemed more at ease and had relaxed somewhat. He continued talking with greater enthusiasm with the child as he informed him, 'We may need many rifles to kill this elephant.'

'Do you have many rifles?' the child asked.

'We have one rifle and two guns, but the bullet of the gun does not cause much damage to the elephant. For an elephant, one needs a big bore rifle.'

'Are there many types of rifles?' the child asked.

'Yes, rifles are of various types, based on the weight of their bullet and the range it fires, like a 30 Springfield, or 315 carbine.' Seated behind, Rashid could make out that though Nadeem was addressing the child he was actually talking to the woman, and was trying to impress her with his knowledge.

Nadeem continued, 'The rifle we have is a 375 magnum. The weight of its bullet and velocity has matchless proportion.'

'What do you mean by proportion?' the child asked.

'Proportion … Proportion, meaning ratio.'

'Ratio is in Arithmetic,' the boy said.

'The same ratio is in other things too.' Unable to explain further, Nadeem was frustrated.

'What if, while firing, the rifle does not work for some reason?' the child asked.

'Think positive, friend.' Asif interjected.

'In such a situation we can fire from the other gun and scare the elephant away,' Nadeem explained.

'But what if he does not run away?'

'Then we light a big fire to scare him away.'

'He is scared of fire?' asked the child.

'He is scared of light in the dark,' this time Rashid answered instead of Nadeem.

'You have something to light the fire?' the child asked.

'Yes, we have this,' smiling, Dr Wiqar showed a matchstick and lit a cigarette.

Hearing this answer, Raju kept staring at the matchstick for some time.

Meanwhile, the woman said that her parents had cautioned her that this area was very notorious, thieves and thugs roamed freely here and so she must get back before dark, especially as she had cash with her.

Nadeem felt ashamed upon hearing this. So while driving, he jogged his memory and tried to recall what he had read in English magazines. Collecting his thoughts, he addressed the woman, 'Quite often we get worried about our fellow countrymen who are living in Canada, as skinheads are known to cause harassment and disgrace people from the Asian community.' He emphasised *disgrace* while making that statement. The woman understood his smartness; keeping the delicate situation in mind, she slowly explained, 'Such gangs are usually in places like London; Canada has other kind of problems.' She went on to discuss these at length.

Nadeem felt embarrassed at his ignorance and started speaking about the damages caused in the forest by rogue elephants. Firstly, all work inside the forest comes to a halt. Workers who are supposed to repair roads run away. Women who pick leaves stop coming. The contract to cut grass from the jungle also stops as no one is willing to endanger his or her life. Honey pickers also leave work. Officers are unable to keep an eye on the thieves who steal wood from the forest. 'We can't even go poaching as who knows from behind which tall grass or bush a red-eyed ferocious elephant may come charging at us with its trunk raised.'

Just before reaching the Ranger's office the headlights lit up a wooden pillar, which said in Hindi: 'Beware, elephant crossing area.'

Raju also read this and snuggled closer to his aunt.

All of a sudden, Nadeem switched off the headlights and shut the engine. The car came to a shuddering halt. The stillness of the jungle was heightened and everyone was disoriented. 'Elephants are crossing the road ahead,' Nadeem whispered. Everyone held their breath and saw hazy black figures slowly crossing the road. It was absolutely still within as well as outside the car. After some time Nadeem started the car and drove at some speed to the Ranger's office at Nishangada. Stopping the car he looked at the woman and the scared child and before getting off he told the child that a rogue is never in a herd. Herd elephants are usually harmless. A rogue is always a loner.

At the Ranger's office many people were huddled around a bonfire warming themselves. Seeing this, Raju regained the colour of his skin which had tuned pale. Stepping out of the car he asked, 'If many rogue elephants come together won't that be a herd?' What ridiculous thoughts this kid has, wondered Nadeem as he shut the car door. The Ranger was in uniform and was shaking hands with everyone. He asked Nadeem, 'Is he your son?'

'No sir! We met them at Baroli,' he then explained the entire matter.

'There will be some problem. DFO sahib has had to go to Nepal via the Motipur road, as one of our men has been held there at the customs post.' Hearing this, the woman turned helplessly towards the others, as though asking them what she should do.

'I will send a wireless message to Lucknow and someone will inform your people that you are safe,' the Ranger offered.

'But how will she go home?' Dr Wiqar asked.

Nadeem came towards the woman and said, 'You rest at the Ranger's house; his wife is a very nice person, and she treats us all like we are her brothers.'

The woman was confused. Adding to her confusion, the Ranger said that his family had left for the village two days ago. As there was widespread terror because of the rogue, his wife's father had come and taken the daughter and grandchildren away.

The scene right now was such that the red building of the Ranger's office was circled by barbed wire and there was a bonfire around which the entire range staff was huddled, along with two motor cycles, a station wagon, the hunters from Bahraich, as well as the woman and the child … All of them looked like strange creatures against the glow of the bonfire as their shadows danced along with the length of the flickering flame.

In the background, the forest stood still, its majestic *shishum* and teak trees enveloped in fog. In this forest, many animals must have been sleeping or quietly grazing or drinking, or perhaps standing in herds and rubbing their horns against their mothers, or the mothers licking their offspring. Some others may be stalking and others may have attacked their prey.

The woman looked helplessly around her. She realised that tears were welling in her eyes.

'We are getting late,' Dr Wiqar broke the silence. 'Any news today?'

'Yes,' said the Ranger. 'Today, pug marks were seen at plot 1955 in the teak forest near the old guest house in Motipur block.'

Asif smiled and said, 'Today you are speaking the language of a tiger hunt.'

'No, not that, but it is true that everyone here is extremely scared. If they see him they will pass out in sheer terror. All the families who were living here have left the Ranger's compound and fled. Since the day he entered the compound and trampled the chowkidar it has been like this. Today, you must leave only after exterminating him.'

'God is the saviour,' said Dr Wiqar. Coming close to Nadeem and the woman he said, 'What have you decided?'

Nadeem stood there silently looking at Raju who was trying to light a small fire with a matchstick. The woman spoke softly but with confidence, 'Send information to my family and take me along . Don't leave me here in the Ranger's compound.'

'Better think about it, you have a child with you, you may both get scared seeing the rogue.'

"We'll see; I am not afraid of animals in the wild. After our marriage we had gone to the jungles of Africa … hunting in Zimbabwe … for our honeymoon … we had taken a permit … I had myself killed a bison.'

Nadeem was surprised as well as relieved on hearing this.

'But Raju …' Nadeem said.

'I will take care of him,' she replied.

The car was refuelled. People sat around the fire, ate sandwiches, drank tea and lit up cigarettes. One last round of the washroom was made and the rifles and guns were checked again.

'The strategy shall be the same: if we get a close shot then we will fire; otherwise we shall scare him by firing the guns, because if we injure him he can do anything,' Dr Wiqar told Asif and Nadeem.

The Ranger's staff and Ramesh were busy cleaning the windscreen that had accumulated a thick cover of frost. It was so cold that every two or three minutes a layer of frost would form on it. 'Have you checked the searchlight?' asked Dr Wiqar.

'Yes sir,' replied Ramesh, squeezing water out of the rag.

'This fog shall spell trouble. Closed windows in the car shall cause frost on the inside as well,' Dr Wiqar voiced his misgivings.

'There is no remedy for this; it had to be so cold and foggy today,' Nadeem mumbled.

A light appeared on the mud road leading to the Ranger's compound and then one could hear the light rumble of a motorcycle engine. The motorcycle neared the little group beside the bonfire and stopped. Two men who looked confused alighted. One of them was armed. 'Who is the Ranger, Sir?' asked the man who was not carrying the gun.

'I am,' said the Ranger stepping forward and looking concerned. Having stayed in front of the fire, his forehead was moist with perspiration and he looked uneasy. 'Has the rogue …?'

'No sir. We have received news from Bijnor … that the rail coach in which your father-in-law and family …' Their voice was lowered to a whisper. On hearing of his children the Ranger got hysterical and started to cry loudly. Seeing his condition, Dr Wiqar raised his voice and tried to intervene, 'Let us listen to the whole thing calmly. Has there been a casualty?'

'We were unable to listen properly as the voice on the phone was faint and garbled,' one of them said.

'Is it a matter of dacoits and thieves?' the woman asked Nadeem anxiously.

'I don't know, they are saying that the phone was not clear.'

'These days those kind of riots are also going on in this area,' Asif said in a low voice.

'Maybe it is the Terai issue,' Rashid said thoughtfully.

'Terai is far from there, my friend.'

'What is the use of such senseless guessing? You all talk a lot,' Dr Wiqar's tone was horror struck. All of them looked askance at him.

Regaining control, he said, 'You should leave on the motorcycle for Bahraich. On reaching there, call Bijnor to find out about the situation. Only after you have heard from them, make any plans to travel ahead. Take someone along with you and do not drive by yourself.'

After the Ranger had left, there was silence for a long time. The crackling of firewood was the only sound.

Dr Wiqar faced the fire and stretching his palms towards its warmth said, 'The thing is that these days everywhere … meaning in all regions … I mean amongst people …' then again after some silence he continued, 'Let us take the name of Allah and start the work, which we have come to do. Come, let us get into the car.'

Dr Wiqar sat next to Nadeem on the front seat. Behind were Asif, the woman with Raju and Rashid, and on the last seat sat Ramesh with his gun. Rashid felt that the woman was turning around and staring at Ramesh and his gun. Rashid tried to smile but by the time he could do so he too got worried and he too started stealing glances at Ramesh.

Asif remembered that when the news of the Ranger's family was being conveyed to him how Ramesh's face had turned red.

Someone from the Ranger's staff had whispered to Ramesh that these days those kinds of conflicts were taking place near Bijnor. Who had said it, the staff there or Nadeem? Or had none of them said it? Had he just imagined it? Or, had he himself said it? Asif's mind stopped working.

The car started. Dr Wiqar loaded the bullets in the magazine, bolted it, readied the rifle and sat alert. Asif also loaded his gun and sat close to the window.

Rashid tightly held on to the handle of the searchlight and fixed his eyes on the windscreen. The woman tightened the belt of her overcoat and brought Raju close to her and clasped him. Ramesh too loaded a bullet in his single-barrel gun and sat alert next to his window.

'I request none of you will make any noise now; elephants have very sharp hearing,' said Dr Wiqar softly.

'We are still far from that spot,' said Nadeem.

'Still, what is the harm in remaining silent?'

Nadeem pulled out a cloth from the dashboard and cleaned the windscreen from the inside. But there was fog outside. When he put the wiper on he realised that there was moisture on the inner side of the glass as well. Visibility was very poor outside. Only the beams from the two headlights could be seen.

Nadeem said, 'If we open the windows the moisture inside shall disappear.'

'That will not be correct. I mean it is dangerous in the present situation,' was Dr Wiqar's reaction.

'But then it will remain foggy inside and nothing will be visible,' Rashid said anxiously.

'There is no other way,' Dr Wiqar said with a touch of finality.

Asif ran his eyes all around the car, 'There is nothing to be seen from the side and the rear window.'

'There is no light here … I mean headlight,' said Rashid.

'The fog will only increase as we get closer to the river Gerwa,' Nadeem muttered.

The car was moving slowly and one could see the smoke-like swirl of the fog in the beam of the headlight. Apart from this swirling fog, nothing was visible in the jungle on either side of the road.

'Is that a cheetal in front?' Nadeem stared hard at the road and asked Dr Wiqar.

Dr Wiqar too peered closely and said, 'My friend that is a rabbit. In such dense fog all things look larger than they actually are.'

The loud noise of the car had made the hare stop in its path; when the lights hit its eyes, two blue bulbs lit up in them.

'Hey, look at those shining eyes,' screamed Raju.

'Shhh … Stay quiet,' Dr Wiqar scolded him and then extended his hand backwards to pat his shoulder. It was then that Ramesh realised that everyone sitting in the car except Raju had stared at him in a strange way. He looked at each of them, one by one.

Everyone except Raju was now aware that Ramesh was looking at him or her in a strange manner. Inside the car it wasn't so dark and everyone's eyes were by now used to the darkness.

There was a strange restlessness amongst all except Raju. He raised his head and slowly asked, 'Aunty … who killed the Ranger's wife and children?'

Nadeem hit the brakes and the car came to a jolting halt. He switched off the lights and whispered, 'The rogue is standing in front.' He could say no more.

A wave of horror engulfed them all. 'Where is it?' Dr Wiqar whispered so softly that for a moment he thought that Nadeem had not heard him. He removed the safety latch of his rifle. 'I think he is coming from the right side of the road towards the left. Or from the front he was coming to the right or to the left,' said Nadeem.

'Nadeem, lights … How will we see him?' Dr Wiqar said.

'He is behind, right near the car.'

All of them turned around to see. There was something on the dark road. Asif suddenly raised his hand and pressed Dr Wiqar's shoulder. 'Here it is … on my side near the window … Very near.' All of them stared hard across the window; they felt a massive shape standing in the mist. Their heartbeats were racing.

'It kept its trunk on my window,' Rashid whispered. Outside his window a long winding object had been felt.

Nadeem signalled everybody to stay quiet and said, 'I think the rogue on my side is still standing there.'

'Can you see it properly and take aim?' asked Dr Wiqar.

'No, not very clearly, the glass is hazy. Should I roll it down?'

'Not at all … If you do that, he will be able to hear even our breathing.'

The woman turned to look at the child whose face had turned pale with horror. Snuggled close to his aunt he was trying to stick his neck out and look outside the window. She wiped the sweat from her forehead and dried it on her overcoat.

'He is slowly moving in this direction,' said Ramesh, sounding scared. He was sitting with his nose stuck to the window. Looking at their side of the window Asif and Rashid also said the same thing. Filled with a mixture of horror and confusion Dr Wiqar said, 'See which one has a broken tusk … that one is the rogue and only he is the dangerous one.'

All of them looked hard outside their windows and claimed that the one on their side seemed to have a broken tusk.

'Are there many rogues?' Dr Wiqar questioned himself and looked at the woman who had just peeped out. She seemed to agree with him. Her eyes were filled with horror.

Dr Wiqar felt a push from his side of the window, or was it the beat of his heart or the butt of his rifle that had been struck by his shoe? He once again looked out into the darkness. He could make out that the eyes were red, a tusk was broken and the trunk was rising up.

He said in a sombre manner, 'No one will fire. We cannot kill so many together. Rogues have surrounded our car on all sides. We are lucky that the windows are rolled up and our voice is not reaching them, otherwise they would have crushed us by now.'

'What do we do now?' asked Nadeem. All of them were experiencing a combination of horror, helplessness and embarrassment.

'We can wait till daybreak,' the woman said softly in a broken voice.

All of them seemed to agree, but at that very moment, the child drew something in his hand out of his pocket and fell unconscious …

Nadeem didn't look at the others. He turned around, stretched his hand out and opened the boy's closed fist. And saw it. He thought for a moment, closed the boy's fist again, and turned away. Like all the others, he bent his head and waited in silence for daylight.

– Translated from the Urdu by Sohail Akbar

THE WAIL OF THE BLACK BREEZE

AJEET COUR

Those were black days, bloody days, full of a strange fear, the fear of death. A choking sensation rose from the earth to the sky, like a black cloth smothering all.

It was the month of November, the beginning of the month. The year was 1984. The city had been in shock, stunned, since 31 October. The woman who had ruled the country for so many years, the woman who had launched an attack on Harmandir Sahib at Amritsar like Abdali, the woman who had treated the country as her private property, that most exalted empress had been assassinated.

Of course assassination is deplorable. Reprehensible. Particularly of that woman who also had several sensitive layers in her soul! The woman with large eyes which seemed to announce that she was in control of the universe, the woman with beautiful little feet and nimble hands, the stunningly beautiful and intelligent woman who made friends with Castro and any American President with equal aplomb, the empress of her times.

But in this country it has not been uncommon for kings or queens to be assassinated. Here a king has been known to imprison his own father and murder him, or chop up his own brothers and then proceed to rule the country.

This country has also witnessed the assassination of the man who was popularly known as the Father of the Nation, a secular nation.

But after any such assassination, death did not hover over the defenceless and innocent citizens of the nation.

This time in the Black November of 1984, people were being killed openly, out in the streets. Hordes of people, instigated and guided by their leaders, roamed the streets and by-lanes of the city, shouting slogans. Hordes of people hunting for men of a particular community and slaughtering them. Raping their women in open streets! With their children looking on in dumb horror.

Homes were looted, burnt. People slaughtered.

All this had happened before too. Exactly like this. When the father of this empress had agreed that this country be partitioned, cut into two, and that too with a blunt knife. Then also, a savage madness had the people in its grip. Then too homes had been set afire, like now. Then, too, people had knives driven into their abdomens. They were disembowelled. Their intestines pulled out of open gashes lay in blood-soaked puddles, or were scattered on the naked roads, in the fields and on footpaths.

Then too, fear, like a vulture, had hovered and circled over the cities and the villages.

Today, thirty-seven years later, the same thing was happening all over again.

I had closed all the doors and windows of my house and had sat inside with my daughter, Arpana, on 31 October, and the first three days of November.

Our neighbours destroyed the name plate hanging on the gate downstairs. They telephoned to reassure us, 'Don't worry. We are here to protect you.'

But when thousands were being murdered in the colonies across the Jamuna, it was not possible to remain locked up, like cowards, in the house.

It had been announced on the television and on the radio that the army had taken charge of the law and order situation in the city. But if the army was guarding the city, how would we be able to leave the house? We would have to cross the bridge over the river to get there. Surely we will be stopped. They will ask what business we have there …

We should try. We could see how far we could get. We could not remain holed up, cowering inside, while people were being killed on the streets, their heads bashed with iron rods, drenched in petrol and set on fire, alive. Being burnt with kerosene-filled rubber tubes and tyres around their necks. Their homes torched.

When women were being smoked out of burning homes and sexually assaulted right there, next to the bodies of their sons and husbands. Right there on the naked streets, covered with blood and mud, these atrocities were being committed.

Entire crowded *bastis* were being devastated. Already in the grip of death and poverty there was no recourse for them.

In the midst of this murderous outrage, to think of our own safety alone was immoral. Unethical.

On the television and the radio there was a constant replay of the last words of the slain empress: '… Every drop of my blood … Blood! … Blood! … Blood …!'

We, my daughter Arpana and I, set out from the house. The driver was a bold neighbour Manoj, a Hindu, and I felt that the fact of his being a Hindu would be a protective shield for us.

That year winter seemed to have set in early. We decided to take some food with us – packets of tea, sacks of sugar, milk powder, and some blankets. We turned towards Azad Market to get the blankets because that is where the thick army blankets are readily available.

As we were about to turn into Paharganj from Chitragupt Road, right in front of Paharganj Police Station, we saw a large mob shouting in frenzy. The slogan they were raising was, '*Khoon ka badla khoon!*' – Blood will be avenged with blood!

As our car crawled past this crowd, I felt choked as though a lump of ice was stuck in my throat.

This was terror!

A primeval fear!

The fear of death …!

A numbing fear that my daughter, sitting beside me, could be dragged out by the hooligans …

Having got the blankets, we crossed the bridge across the Jamuna. We saw no soldiers, nor any police. There was no official there. No army, no police! Nobody in uniform!

Nor could we see any turbans. There was no Sikh out on the road.

Proceeding slowly, we reached Gandhi Nagar School. A police truck was parked outside the gate, and there were two or three policemen relaxing in it, drinking tea, gossiping.

Inside the gate there was a flood of people. So many people! All of them huddled inside the school building! So tightly packed that a needle couldn't have got through. Terrified, they stood in stunned silence. They were crowded in tight bunches, filling all corners, crammed in that dust-laden space with their backs to the walls.

Women, children, men, old people.

It seems someone deep in the crowd recognised me. He raised both his arms, and in a tearful trembling voice said with a heart-rending cry: 'Bibiji! Not wail of blood! Now there are wells full of blood.'

Perhaps he had read my article after the attack on the Golden Temple – 'Puddles of Blood.'

Hardly five months had passed since then.

And now …

There was no room for the car, but they insisted, 'Bring the car inside, just inside the gate. Who knows what will happen outside? Someone will set it on fire …'

They squeezed closer together, everyone shrinking back perhaps an inch, till there was enough space for the car.

What amazing people! They had lost everything themselves and yet they were concerned for the safety of my car.

We unloaded the provisions. They said, 'There is no need. A *langar* is constantly going on. We have enough to eat. You shouldn't have taken the trouble ...'

Behind the school building, in what used to be the playground, huge fires were burning under large *choolahs*. On one, daal was simmering, and on the other rotis were being made.

'But how do all these provisions get here?'

'Oh! There is one Kishenlalji. Morning and evening he brings sacks full of daal and *atta*. All the shops are closed. But they say he begs or borrows, or just breaks open the locks of shops and brings the stuff. We have to survive somehow ... and there must easily be ten to fifteen thousand people here! Kishenlalji has taken it upon himself to see that we have enough food.'

Human beings were being slaughtered, but humanity still survived.

In the playfield at the back, some fifteen or twenty badly wounded persons, mostly with burn injuries, were lying on the bare, dusty earth. Only one person had something under him – his wife's dupatta. She herself, her head uncovered, sat huddled next to him, hugging her knees to her chest, sobbing.

In the morning these people had been taken to a hospital in the police truck but the hospital authorities had refused to admit them saying, 'Those hooligans will burn our hospital down.' *Those hooligans*, meaning the attacking mobs.

There were some with severe burns on their legs and arms. Others had their heads crushed, and yet others had broken limbs. It was a terrifying sight. There was a strange helplessness. A shocked, numbing fear. An abject resignation.

We came back to Connaught Place. Bought bottles of Dettol, bandages, tubes of antiseptic creams, and returned to do whatever we could to clean and dress their wounds.

And then, for the first time, I felt a revolting stench in the air as the wind changed direction. Obviously all these people, having been cooped up like so many chickens in a basket for so many days, had to relieve themselves somewhere. The building was enclosed from all sides apart from the gate which was open, but no one had the courage to go out.

This was a ghetto! This is how those Jews must have lived, hiding like frightened rats from the atrocities of the Nazis, and taking refuge collectively in derelict towns in Poland and elsewhere. Terrified of death, they had sought shelter in underground sewage pipes, or in manhole tunnels, or in deserted attics.

When it became dark, we left that place to drive straight to Khushwant Singh's house. It was 9:30 pm. No relative or friend is allowed in Khushwant Singh's house at this time. His home is closed for visitors after 9:00 pm.

But this was a day of doom. The day all rules and laws are set aside.

Khushwant opened the door.

I don't cry in anyone's presence. But that night … the shock of the whole day, the helplessness, the fear, the horror, they all poured out of my whole body, shaking with tears of heavy grief. Heavier than any burden human endurance can carry! With my head resting on his shoulders I sobbed loudly, helplessly. And Arpana silently wiped her eyes with her dupatta.

I told Khushwant everything. He listened in stunned silence. I suggested to him: 'Next to the Gandhi Nagar School building, is the building of Shyam Lal College. All schools and colleges are closed. If you can speak to the Lieutenant Governor and ask him to get the College premises opened, these thousands of people will get some space to sit, or even stretch out.'

Khushwant said he had been trying to reach the Governor for three or four days. But these days, whether it is a minister, a police officer or any government official including the Governor or the President of India, there is a stock reply: 'Sahib is not available.'

These days no one was available, anywhere. No one seemed to exist. The secretaries repeated like parrots, 'Sahib is not available. Gone for a meeting.'

And that was the truth. The whole country was caught in the eye of a storm. A swirling, black whirlwind.

It was not dust that the wind whipped up, but blood.

The sun had vanished. And the sky itself was hiding behind a bloody veil.

'I'll try again,' Khushwant said. 'I'll phone again at night. I'll call his residence. Can they possibly do anything worse than what has already happened? And what do I have to lose? For two days I took refuge at the Swedish Embassy, with my entire family … We returned home today because the government announced that the city has been put under military rule, and nothing will happen now …'

'Military rule? We didn't see any signs of the army the whole day! Hardly a furlong away from Gandhi Nagar School, a mob killed twelve people! We were witnesses! Helplessly looking on from a distance! And something must have happened in Paharganj too, because a bloodthirsty mob had collected there. We passed by them. We crossed the Jamuna Bridge four times … and there was no military presence anywhere. Take care! Keep the doors and windows closed.'

It was about 2:30 pm that night when it occurred to me that an extremely nice doctor, a top cardiologist at the Medical

Institute – Harbans Singh Wasir – was the personal physician to the President of India, Giani Zail Singh. It doesn't matter how weak a person is, or how blinded a person can be because of his rank and position, he still cannot ignore his doctor.

So I called up Dr Wasir. 'Please tell Gianiji to at least get Shyam Lal College opened for these refugees. And, Harbans, if possible, please ask him to get fifteen or twenty temporary lavatories built. And the same number of cleaners … Let them at least dig pits in the ground. There is a real risk of cholera breaking out. Can you send an ambulance there? Some people are wounded. Just lying there in the dust with open wounds … They could develop gangrene! The wounds will certainly turn septic.'

I don't know whether it was because of Harbans' efforts or Khushwant's influence, but on the third day the rooms of Shyam Lal College were opened, temporary lavatories were built, and the cleaners were also deputed.

For the wounded, Harbans sent not only an ambulance but also a team of doctors.

Some artists, social workers, and theatre people came together to form a group. They would meet early in the morning in Lajpat Bhawan which was a central collecting point for food, clothes, shoes, blankets and quilts. They would sort them and send out vans with the provisions to different make-shift camps in the city.

Arpana and I also joined them. The group worked systematically, and the service and help they rendered was therefore more effective.

None of these people were sentimental or emotional. They were motivated by a deep compassion for their fellow human beings. They didn't weep or cry like me. They were like soldiers in battle. Leaving the comfort of their homes, away from their loved ones, they were committed to the common cause of safeguarding humanity from the onslaught of barbarian bloodthirsty hooliganism.

The gates of Shyam Lal College were opened. The rooms were also unlocked. But no one was willing to go there, leaving the safe haven of the school and stepping out onto the narrow street between the school and the college. To step out on to that street was to step into the dark kingdom of death! To go out on the street meant that they would be at the mercy of the murderous mobs. To be out on a street was to invite danger! To walk into a seething cauldron of trouble.

What a strange age! When men should be petrified to go out in the street, just outside the place they were huddled in!

'Let's break down the side wall of the Gandhi Nagar School, and make a corresponding opening in the side wall of the College, so that people don't have to cross the road,' I suggested.

'But the police …?'

There were two policemen sitting on the raised platform under a tree in the backyard of the school. I took them aside and spoke to them. 'We have to do this! How much money will you want?'

They hesitated slightly. They didn't speak for about five seconds, and kept looking at each other. 'But what if the school and college authorities object later...?'

'Don't worry about that. It is my responsibility to have both the walls repaired.'

I paid them. Then they said, 'What if you don't get them fixed?'

I showed them my Press Card and also gave each one my visiting card.

'Do me a favour. The police truck that is parked at the gate, please park it at the head of the street. We will close the gates of both buildings. Should any attackers come, they will have to come from the lane, and you will be guarding the opening there. Then there won't be any danger.'

I knew very well that in those days the biggest danger was from the police itself, because every bloodthirsty mob was accompanied by a protective unit of police. It was in such police jeeps that jerry cans of petrol and kerosene were carried to those settlements where the mobs set people on fire and burnt down homes. Policemen too were among those who looted and raped.

In fact in some places the police had gone in first and collected all arms – mostly *kirpans* and sticks and occasionally a revolver or gun. They said that it was in the interest of keeping peace. When the people had thus been disarmed, the screaming mobs attacked ...

The massacres were done in the style of Ghengis Khan or Taimur with the knowledge of the police and with their blessings.

But what blessings? They said these were the orders they had received 'from above'! But then in this country there is always a reward for any favour done. From the constable to the minister, from the peon to the Prime Minister, everyone dispenses favours to those in need, and collects their own share. Showering favours! And grateful thanks given for every such consideration!

These attacks were different from the attacks of earlier times – whether Ghengis Khan, Taimur or Nadir Shah. Those people were fired with personal ambitions! They were conquering kingdoms, expanding empires, extending their territories – even though they, in the pursuit of glory and victory, marched through rivers of blood.

These attacks now, merely displayed naked savagery, and were proof of their own basest beastliness.

In the depths of my being I felt historical memories being revived. These attacks, these murders, were like those committed by the Nazis, methodically, and in cold blood. Armed with lists of names, they used to ferret out the Jews. They pulled out people – men, women, children who hid like mice – from gutters and manholes, and then separated them on the basis of their usefulness. And then sent them to concentration camps and gas chambers accordingly.

Six million Jews were murdered.

And today, when I write after years of the bloodbath of November 1984, hundreds of thousands of people are being killed in Bosnia, Sarajevo, Rwanda, Iraq, Afghanistan! It has been going on for years.

And in my own country, the blood-soaked pages of Bhiwandi, Malyana, Gujarat, Mumbai, flutter before my eyes, the pages of which history will always be ashamed.

And in Punjab and Kashmir, and Assam and Bihar – everywhere it is overcast with dark red clouds of blood.

And the soul-shuddering memory of Nagasaki and Hiroshima still makes our hair stand on end.

Man! The supreme creation of God! In whose heart the barbaric animal is still alive, screaming for blood!

Anyway, the walls of the School and College buildings were broken to give those people a little bit more of space. Even so, there were still about fifteen families in each room. They spilled over into the verandas too, and into the open compounds as well.

For almost a month, we – Arpana and I – stayed there from morning till midnight.

On the seventh day, Mother Teresa's missionaries brought tins of milk powder and biscuits for the women and children.

They spent the entire day, day after day, feeding the hungry children and tending to the sick.

On the tenth day a tent was pitched. And a short, fat man, an officer of the government, occupied it. Half a dozen policemen hovered around him day and night.

The first thing he did was to put a lock on our store room. The room in which we put the things we ourselves had bought, or collected from friends, relatives, and neighbours. Things like blankets and quilts, stocks of food and medicines.

We got to know of it at nine at night, the time that we would go from room to room and distribute blankets and quilts as required. It was done very systematically. First lists were made. Then blankets collected from the store would be distributed. Groups of workers were in charge of separate wings. Each of them was responsible for taking care of the refugees in his wing.

When the lists were ready that night, we went to the store to find it locked, and an armed policeman guarding it.

'Who has locked this?' I asked in shocked surprise.

'Sahib has.' The sahib's agent said arrogantly.

'Sahib? What Sahib?'

'He joined duty today. He is a Government Sahib.' He offered casually.

'Where is he?'

'Find out from his office.'

'Where's the office?'

'There, in the tent.'

In the tent another couple of armed policemen were relaxing, their legs stretched out resting on a tabletop, as though they had come to a wedding party.

'Where is Sahib?'

'He must be somewhere around!' they replied nonchalantly, as though to say, 'Get lost!'

'Around, where?' I was beginning to get angry, and a little bold too because some of our people had also reached there.

They whispered in my ear, 'Be careful! These sons of bitches can be nasty … they could also throw us out. Those who get people killed, can do anything!'

'All they can do is kill. So, a few more will get killed!' I was furious.

I shouted: 'Tell us where he is! He is not in the camp … we have just been around it.'

'Then he must have gone for dinner. It's dinnertime. He has to eat, doesn't he?' one of them snapped back.

We waited for two hours for him to return. When he came, he was chewing paan and reeking of liquor.

'Are you the in-charge? The new in-charge?'

'Yes. I am!' he thundered at us.

'And where were you till 11:00 pm?'

'I'm not answerable to you,' he replied in English.

'No. You aren't answerable to anyone! You are the government. The government is …'

'What do you want?' he snarled.

'Why have you had the store locked?'

'Why shouldn't I lock it? I am in charge of this camp.'

'That's obvious. With all the security you have for yourself! You must be a senior officer. Have you inspected the camp? Have you done any good to anyone? Have you registered a single complaint, a report? Have you appointed anyone to trace the missing members of any family? Nothing! All you have done is to lock the store …! And you have come after TWO hours, chewing paan ...!'

'I'll have you arrested for insulting a government officer …'

'Yes. Why not? You can arrest me, you can get me liquidated – in jail or outside! I am fully aware of your power. You can do what you want, but right now unlock the store.'

'The store will NOT be opened!'

'The store will definitely be opened, and NOW!' I retorted and produced my trump card – my Press Card. 'Here! You can note down my name and address. Arrest me whenever you want. But first open that lock. Not even a pin there belongs to the government. Everything in it has been bought by our own money, money earned by our own labour, not bribe money!'

He looked a bit shaken as all this went on in front of his subordinates. He had the lock opened, but said softly, 'I'll get back to you later!' It sounded both a threat and an embarrassed repartee.

In this camp there were ten to fifteen thousand people who had ten to fifteen thousand stories to tell. And there were as many stories from the camps at Trilokpuri, Uttam Nagar, Shahdara and their adjoining colonies. I will tell you only three of them.

One woman sat in the corner of one room, her four children huddled around her. Whenever we urged her to go to the *langar* for her meals she would simply shake her head.

'Food for the children? Milk?' The response was the same dejected, 'No.'

One day passed. Two days. Three days went by.

By that time she was no longer sitting. She had sunk to the floor, lifelessly, helplessly. Her children clung to her legs and belly, digging their knees into their stomachs, their heads drooping.

'She doesn't eat herself, nor does she allow her children to eat. What should we do?'

We brought in people from other rooms to find out if anyone knew her. Perhaps someone from her own colony would recognise her. At last we found one man, who went and sat next to her and talked to her: 'Bibi, get up. Have courage. You are not the only victim … everyone has been hurt.' The woman opened her eyes a little, and then started crying uncontrollably, loudly, helplessly.

'Let her cry. If she cries, only then will she be able to see her children. If she cries, only then will she think of feeding them.'

Then that man told us that on the night of 2 November the mobs had attacked her colony.

'They had dragged her husband out into the street, hit him with iron rods and then put petrol on him and burnt him alive. His shrieks pierced holes in the sky. Her eldest son remained inside, hiding behind a big tin trunk. 'She took the other children and ran out into the street … The neighbours pulled her and her children into their home and hid them.

'The mob then set fire to her house. She was frantic and tried to open the door again and again. "Where is my Sohan? Let me go! Let me go and get him … they'll butcher him …"'

'When the mobs departed shouting in victory and intoxicated with glee, the neighbours brought all of us, including this woman and her children, to this camp …

'She had gone in the middle of the night to her house looking for Sohan, her son. There was still smoke coming from the house which looked like a gaping hole, burnt to ashes.

'In the compound she had found Sohan's half burnt body. She thought that the dogs would find it and eat it. So she spent the rest of the night pulling down the remains of half-burnt doors and windows, and tried to burn the corpse of her son.

'We heard of this later when our neighbours told us she had gone to them to borrow kerosene oil and matches.'

This poor woman who pulled out bits of half-burnt wood to cremate the body of her half-burnt son! What else can happen to her?

The woman continued to sob uncontrollably. We brought water for her. She drank it. We put a plate of food before her. She broke a morsel with her trembling fingers and put it in her youngest child's mouth …

I'll tell you the second story.

In the veranda, there was an imposing, handsome, middle-aged man. Next to him was his pretty, plump and impressive wife, and a young son whose hair was cut like grass. This is the Sardarni's story.

'The factory was burnt. The house was robbed and then burnt. The neighbours hid us. When they brought us to the camp they begged me: "Bibiji, save your son's life! Cut his hair." So I cut his hair with these, my cursed hands …'

She wept bitterly.

Then wiping her tears with her dupatta she continued.

'The factory and the house don't matter. The Guru bestowed them, and He has taken them back. He knows best … He will look after us. He will grant them again. But Kaka's hair! *Haaye!* How I used to take care of it! Washing it with fresh curd ...! So beautiful, so thick, so silky. Such lovely golden brown hair!'

The third story is about a very old man who sat in one corner of the veranda. He had sat there for almost a week. Sometimes he would doze off leaning against the wall, his mouth slightly open, his white beard quivering as he shivered with cold. His eyebrows were shaggy and white. He was wearing an old kurta pyjama and his head was bare, covered with white hair.

We tried talking to him but he kept his eyes closed. At times though we could hear a soft murmur, 'Wahe Guru. Wahe Guru.' And he would sigh.

We found out that both his sons were auto-rickshaw drivers. They didn't come home for two days. When his colony was attacked, he brought both his daughters-in-law and their children to the camp somehow – hiding and running to evade the attackers.

After two days the daughters-in-law left, saying they were going to look for their husbands.

'And the children?'

'I don't know whether they've taken them along, or left them with somebody. How to find them in such a crowd … ?' And his voice faltered.

At that moment I thought of Darji, my father. If he were alive he too might be sitting in a corner, just like this. His white beard would be trembling just like this old man's. I thanked God that he had passed away before he could see all this!

'Bapuji!' I touched him gently, 'Please take this blanket. It is cold.'

'No. Give it to a needy person.'

'But what if you catch cold and get fever?'

'It will be good. I have nothing to live for.'

I left the blanket next to him anyway. The next day it was exactly where I had put it. We tried our best but he would accept nothing, neither clothes nor the blanket.

On the seventh or eighth day I took a white turban for him. For a minute he looked at it. Then he looked at me. I don't know what it was about that look but I felt a searing heat. Even now sometimes at night I feel it shooting through me.

He accepted the turban with trembling hands. Slowly he unfolded it and, crumpling the width of it with both hands, started tying it, one fold after another.

When he had finished he looked at me again. Two tears spilled over from his eyes. They trickled down the creases in his cheeks leaving a trail of wetness, and disappeared into his beard.

– *Translated from the Punjabi by Satjit Wadva*

I AM A HINDU

ASGHAR WAJAHAT

A scream to make the dead stand on their toes ... The sound came from somewhere close by. In these times ... I sprang up in my bed. The sky was still studded with stars ... it was, perhaps, three past midnight. Abbajaan had gotten up too. The scream came again. Saifu was lying on his coarse string cot and screaming. Beds had been laid out in the courtyard from one end to the other.

'*Laahoulvillaquwwat* ...' Abbajaan muttered.

'God knows why this boy screams in his sleep,' Amma said.

'Amma, the other boys rag him mercilessly all night ...' I tried to explain.

'Don't those fellows have anything better to do ... here we are cowering for our lives, and they can only think of their fun and games,' she said.

Safiya poked her head out from beneath the sheet and said, 'Tell him to sleep on the roof.'

Saifu had still not woken. I went up to his bed and peered to look closely at him. His face was bathed in sweat. His breath was coming fast and shallow and his body was trembling. His hair was dripping wet and some strands were plastered across his face. As I looked at poor Saifu, a terrible anger gathered inside me against those wretched boys who terrified him so.

Those days, the riots were not like they are now. There has been a sea change in the politics, pace, perspective and policy of riots. Till about twenty-five to thirty years ago, people were not burnt alive during riots, neither were entire neighbourhoods laid to waste. Nor did rioters have the blessings of the powers that be. Riots were usually orchestrated by small-time, local leaders with short-term, immediate greeds and concerns. Business rivalries, land grabbing, garnering the Hindu or Muslim vote in the municipality elections – these were the usual compulsions behind most riots.

Saifu was woken up. He looked all around like a lamb searching for its lost mother. The youngest child of Abba's stepbrother, Saifuddin, aka Saifu, saw himself surrounded by all the other family members and jumped to his feet in abject consternation.

I still remember the postcard with its bitten-off corner that came with news of Saifu's father, Uncle Kausar's, death. People from his village had given not just news of his death but had also informed us that Uncle Kausar's youngest child, Saifu, was now all alone in the world. His elder brothers had refused to take him with them to Bombay. They had made it abundantly clear that they could do nothing for him. And now, save for Abbajaan, there was no one for him in the whole world. Abbajaan had sat silently for a long time, holding the postcard with the bitten-off corner. After many bitter quarrels with Amma, he had left for his ancestral village, Dhanvakheda, sold off the pitifully few acres of land left and returned with Saifu in tow.

How we had laughed at our first sight of Saifu! But then, how else would you expect a boy studying at the Aligarh Muslim University school and a girl like Safiya from the Abdullah Girl's College school to react? It was clear on the first day itself that Saifu was not just an uncouth village lad; he was simple to the point of being a half-wit, almost a moron. We would tease him and pull his leg in a hundred different ways each day. This had one unexpected fallout: he made a place for himself in Amma's and Abba's heart. The boy was a veritable model of hard work. He would never tire of hard, physical labour. It especially endeared him to Amma. So what if he ate an extra roti or two; he worked like a slave all day long.

As the years went past, Saifu became a part of our lives. Gradually, we softened towards him. If some boy from the *mohulla* called him mad, I would be ready to claw his face. 'He's my brother,' I would say, 'how dare you call him mad?' But inside the house, it was another matter; we alone knew what Saifu's standing was in our family.

The riot had started in our city as it usually does in most small cities, that is, a parcel of meat had been found inside a mosque and without so much as inspecting the meat, it had been decided that just because the parcel was flung inside the mosque it must necessarily contain pork. In direct retaliation, a cow was slaughtered in Mughal Tola and a full-fledged riot was stoked. A few shops were burnt; most were simply looted. Seven, maybe eight, people were knifed to death in scattered incidents but a sensitive administration had immediately clamped a curfew. It wasn't like today when even after thousands of people have died politicians go about smirking and saying whatever happened was just and right.

Since the riots had spread to the neighbouring villages, it was considered best to extend the curfew. Mughalpura was the biggest Muslim ghetto and so the curfew was at its strictest best here as was the jihad-like fervour among its youth. The *mohulla* was crisscrossed by a labyrinth of narrow, snake-like *gullies* but the experience of many recent riots had decreed the need for interconnecting passageways through the houses. Emergency exits, as they were called. And so, routes were planned over rooftops, inside homes, across walls that could take you safely from one end of the *mohulla* to the other. The *mohulla* was prepared for battle. It had been decided that even if the curfew extended for as long as a month, the necessities of daily life could be found inside the besieged neighbourhood.

Riots were a time for the neighbourhood boys to display a peculiar sort of excitement and valour. '*Arre*, we will make the Hindus bite the dust; what do those dhoti-wearers think of themselves?' ... 'Cowards, that's what they are!' ... 'One Musalman can outdo ten Hindus' ... 'Winning Pakistan was a Laugh/Now we will fight to win India.' All this was inside the *mohulla*; once outside they became timid as lambs. The PAC picket was posted at both ends of the *mohulla*. At some point or the other, most had known the taste of the PAC's boots and rifle butts, so idle talk inside the safety of the *mohulla* was one thing; anything else was quite another matter ...

Crisis teaches unity, unity creates discipline and discipline leads to practicality. Every household was instructed to give one boy for night patrol. I could no longer qualify as a boy, since I had already crossed the age of twenty-five, and so Saifu was the only one eligible for night duty. The nightly vigil was maintained on the rooftops. Since Mughalpura was on a relatively elevated spot, you could see the entire city from our roofs.

Saifu started going for these nightly vigils, which was actually quite good for us, for Abbajaan, Amma, Safiya and me. If Saifu hadn't been a part of our household, perhaps I would have had to volunteer for those wretched patrols. Because of his nightly duty, Saifu was granted certain 'concessions,' for instance, he was allowed to sleep till eight o'clock. He was exempted from the sweeping and swabbing jobs; these fell to Safiya's lot who hated them.

Sometimes, I too would join the gang on the rooftops. The boys from the *mohulla* ruled the roost on this sprawling kingdom. Bamboo poles, sticks, staves and bricks were kept in neat piles. A few boys could even boast of country-made firearms; most had knives. The majority of the boys were small-time daily wagers. Several worked in the lock factories nearby; the rest were apprentices with tailors or carpenters. Since the bazaar was closed these days, they were – almost every single one of them – without work. For most, the home fires were burning on loans from petty loan sharks. But they were happy. Perched on the safe haven of the roofs, they would either pass 'expert comments' on the riots or hurl abuses at the Hindus. The choicest invectives were saved for the PAC. They would listen to Radio Lahore at low volume and could reel off entire programmes aired by Pakistan Radio from memory. A few who had travelled to Pakistan were treated with the reverence that is usually reserved for those who have made the Haj pilgrimage. Going by their stories about Pakistan's super-fast train 'Tezgaam' and the 'Gulshan-e-Iqbal Colony,' one would be forgiven for thinking that if ever there is heaven on earth, surely it is in Pakistan! When they had had their fill of singing paeans in praise of Pakistan, they would turn to teasing poor Saifu. One day, Saifu who had been listening ad nauseum to the glories of Pakistan, finally plucked the courage to ask, 'Where is Pakistan?' Gleefully, they pounced on him and teased him mercilessly for this innocent query. Saifu still wasn't sure where Pakistan was.

The patrolling boys would take turns pulling Saifu's leg and scaring the wits out of him: 'Look here, Saifu, do you know what will happen to you if the Hindus catch you? First, they will strip you naked.' The boys knew that despite being a half-wit, Saifu considered nakedness as something awful and *bad*. 'Then, they will rub oil all over you.'

'Why? Why will they rub oil over me?'

'So that when they beat you with canes, your skin will come off. Then they will scorch you with burning rods ...'

'Noooo,' Saifu could not believe this.

The nightly stories of violence and terror preyed on his mind. Sometimes, he would come to me with his garbled stories. I would snap with irritation and tell him to shut up but his questions didn't go away. One day he asked me, 'Do they have dirt in Pakistan?'

'Why? Why wouldn't they have dirt in Pakistan?'

'Because roads aren't like roads … you can get terylene there … everything is so inexpensive …'

'Look here, someone has been feeding you a lot of rubbish. Don't listen to everything that Altaf and the others tell you,' I tried to explain.

'Do the Hindus pluck our eyes out?'

'What rubbish! Who told you this?'

'Bachchan did.'

'He's wrong.'

'You mean, they don't even skin us alive?'

'Ufffff … what is this … run off … scoot …'

He fell silent but a hundred questions swarmed in his eyes. I went out and he went to badger Safiya with his questions.

The curfew was extended. The nightly vigils continued. Saifu continued to represent our household. And, then, a few days later, Saifu began to scream in his sleep. The first time it happened, we had been startled and worried, though it didn't take us long to figure out that the nightly terror spiels were behind all this. Abbajaan was furious. He had even spoken to a few of the *mohulla* elders, but nothing came of it. Boys – that too, *mohulla* boys, starved of fun – were not likely to let go of easy game such as Saifu.

I hadn't realised that things had gone so far till the day Saifu asked me with complete earnestness, 'Shall I become a Hindu?'

The question left me stunned, but I quickly gathered that it had been caused by the nightly terror sessions. My first reaction was anger, then I rationalised that little purpose will be served by getting angry with my dull-witted cousin. I tried to make him understand. I asked, 'Why do you want to become a Hindu?'

'I will be saved,' he said.

'That means, I won't be saved?' I asked.

'You too become one,' he answered.

'What about your uncle,' I asked, referring to Abbajaan.

'No, he, he …' He stopped; perhaps he got tangled in Abbajaan's flowing white beard.

'Look here, the boys have been telling you a lot of tall tales. They want to mislead you. They have been telling you nothing but lies. You know Mahesh, don't you?'

'Yes, he comes on a scooter …' he cheered up a little.

'Yes, yes, the same.'

'Is he a Hindu?'

'Yes, he is,' I said and watched a frisson of disappointment flicker across his face as he became quiet.

'All this is the handiwork of hoodlums … it is not Hindus or Muslims who fight with each other in these riots … the hoodlums do the looting and the killing. Do you understand?'

The riots stretched on and on like the devil's entrails and people began to tire – *Yaar*, if you count the Hindu and Muslim thugs in the city, how many would there be? A thousand, all right, two thousand at the most. And these two thousand people have managed to make the lives of thousands upon thousands of god-fearing law-abiding citizens a living hell. And what are we doing about it? Nothing. We are sitting in our homes like scared mice. Doesn't it remind you of the time when ten thousand Englishmen ruled over millions of Indians? And who is the beneficiary in these riots? Beneficiary? Why, who else but Haji Abdul Karim who is fighting the municipality election and will bag all the Muslim votes. And Pandit Jogeshwar who will mop up all the Hindu votes. But what about us? What are we? You are a voter – a Hindu voter, Muslim voter, Harijan voter, Kayastha voter, Sunni voter, Shia voter. Will it always be like this in this country? Yes, why not? Where people are illiterate, where you can get guns on hire, where politicians orchestrate riots to keep their seats of power, what else do you expect? *Yaar*, can't we educate the people … bring about greater awareness? Ha-ha-ha-ha. Who are you to educate the people? The Government will do it – if it wants to. You mean, if the Government doesn't want to, nothing will ever get done in this country? Yes … that is what the English have taught us … That is what we are used to … All right, let it be … So, the riots will go on happening for ever … Yes, they will … Suppose, all the Muslims in this country became Hindus? … *Lahoulvillaquwwat*! What are you saying! … All right, then, suppose all the Hindus in this country became Muslims? … *Subhanallah*! … *Wah*! *Wah*! What a thought! … Will that stop the riots? … It's worth a thought! … Look at Pakistan – the Shias and Sunnis are forever at each other's throats! … And in Bihar, the Brahmin shrinks away from the Harijan's shadow … Maybe mankind as a species is destined to fight with its own kind … Look at Maiku and Jumman – they are such close friends. Shall we also become Maikus and Jummans? … I mean … I mean …

I was twisting the radio's ears early one morning and Safiya was sweeping the courtyard when Raja's younger brother, Akram, came running. Half out of breath, he blurted, 'The PAC-wallahs are beating Saifu.'

'What? What are you saying?'

'The PAC-wallahs are beating Saifu,' this time he spoke clearly.

'Why? What has happened?'

'I don't know … There … at the corner …'

'At the corner picket post?'

'Yes.'

'But why …' I knew that the curfew was relaxed between eight and ten in the mornings and Amma had sent Saifu at eight to fetch the milk. Even a halfwit like Saifu knew that he had to return as soon as possible, but it was almost ten by now.

'Come, let's go and see …' I left the house without bothering to fix the crackling radio. Why are the PAC-wallahs beating a halfwit? What could he have done? What can he possibly do? He is so scared himself that he can't hurt a fly. Why beat him? For what possible reason? Money? Amma had given him two rupees. Would the PAC-wallahs beat him for two rupees?

At the corner, beside the police picket on the main road, people were clustered on their rooftops, watching the spectacle below. Saifu was standing before a cluster of PAC-wallahs. He was screaming at the top of his lungs, 'Why did you hit me? I am a Hindu … a Hindu …'

I stepped forward. Saifu saw me but didn't stop shouting, 'Yes, yes … I am a Hindu …' He was trembling and tottering on his feet. A drop of blood had trickled down from his mouth and come to rest on his chin.

'Why did you hit me? … I am a Hindu …'

'Saifu, what are you saying … Come on, let's go home …'

'I … I am a Hindu …'

I was stunned … Was this the same Saifu?

I could feel the people gathered on the rooftops tittering among themselves. It made me angry. Didn't they know he was mad?

'How is he related to you?' one of the PAC-wallahs asked me.

'He is my brother … he is a little off … a mental problem …'

'Then take him home,' a soldier said.

'He has been driving us crazy,' another spoke up.

'Come on, Saifu, let's go home … The curfew has begun …'

'I won't go … I won't … I am a Hindu … a Hindu …'

Suddenly, he began to cry like a baby, 'They hit me … beat me … I am a Hindu … a Hindu …' Then he slumped to the ground. Perhaps, he had fainted.

Now it was easier for me to lift him and carry him home.

Translated from the Hindi by Rakhshanda Jalil

AT THE ZEBRA CROSSING!

DEEPAK BUDKI

To cross or not to cross? That was the question which had baffled him for the past one hour. Puzzled and petrified, he kept helplessly watching the speeding vehicles passing by. Road etiquette demanded they should stop or at least slow down at the very sight of the zebra crossing and let the pedestrians cross the road but none of them showed any signs of responsibility. Why should they? There were neither policemen nor traffic signs to regulate them. Self-discipline is something unknown in this country. Everybody wants to rush past the other.

In Delhi, usually the pedestrians throw caution to the winds while crossing the road. They tarry a while, watch the flowing traffic and at the first available opportunity push forth to make way for themselves. But his case was different. He was not able to muster enough courage to cross the road while lorries, motorcars, jeeps, motorcycles, scooters and auto-rickshaws mercilessly sped past him. He feared that one of them might crush him to death in the same manner they had crushed his son only a day before. He was aware of the liabilities he had and, therefore, did not want to die a violent death.

Stripes of black and white on the roads for pedestrians to use were hardly seen in the place from where he had come, or more appropriately, had been forced to come. In the entire district one could notice just a few zebra crossings in some specific areas which practically had no use whatsoever except that it was an indication that the area was posh. One could walk across any road anywhere and at any time. The vehicles would slow down automatically and even stop to allow you to cross the road.

However, in bigger cities the black and white stripes are an open invitation for a person walking on foot to cross the busy road assuring him precedence and a safe passage. It is the duty and responsibility of every driver to stop while you are walking over the stripes.

'Duty! Responsibility! Good gracious!' he felt nauseated and reacted instantly, 'Who cares about duties and responsibilities? Everyone wants to outwit everyone else. Even if it takes a toll of a few men it does not matter because human life has lost its value in this overpopulated country.'

At that very instant, a Mercedes sped past him leaving a gap of just a whisker. Shivers ran down his spine. He withdrew both his feet from the road immediately for fear of being run over. He was reminded of the death of his son a day before. His son had also attempted to cross a road when he was run over by a speeding truck. His body had lain in a pool of blood the whole night till it was noticed the next morning. The police registered a case against an unknown driver, conducted a post-mortem of the body and at the end declared the case as untraced. It would not have been difficult for the police to trace the murderer had they pursued the case sincerely but they were not willing to shoulder additional responsibility. The police believed that they were already overburdened with cases especially those with VIP tags. The police had found a diary on the dead body which helped them trace his house and hand it over to his parents. Otherwise, the body would have been consumed as unclaimed.

House! Was it worth calling it a house? A tattered canvas tent, repaired at several places giving it a patchy look where the family of six had huddled up to spend their allotted days. Their real house was left behind by them in Anantnag. A building of three storeys with a foundation made of flawless green stone drawn from one of the most reputed quarries; walls made of high quality bricks; ceiling, doors and windows made of deodar and inclined roofs covered with Tata corrugated galvanised iron sheets which did not permit snow to stick to them for too long. The building was surrounded by lush green meadows and paddy fields which extended right up to the foothills on the far side. At a short distance from the main door of the house one could see a large stone mortar placed permanently under a magnificent walnut tree. Four feet high wooden pestles were kept in the cowshed nearby for use by the women of the household for pounding paddy, red chillies and condiments during the autumn season. The pounding was accompanied by melodious Kashmiri songs. Behind the house grew almond, plum and peach trees, the blossoms of which would enchant the passers-by. The family got their requirement of grain, lentils, vegetables, fruits and marigold flowers for the entire year from their own farm and did not make any additional purchases from the market.

Many a time he thought of going on pilgrimage to the four *dhams* across the country before his mortal self would breathe its last but his ties with the family prevented him from doing so. All his life he had not ventured out of his nice little town except on a few occasions when he had gone to Srinagar where tongas were yet to be replaced by minibuses, tempos and taxis. He saw the train for the first time after migration from the Valley.

'What a fool I am! What wild thoughts besiege my mind? That house is a lost dream now. Never to be seen again.' He laughed at himself, 'They call this suffocating torn tent a house. My cowshed at Anantnag was bigger than this tent.'

Suddenly, he recollected the face of his lost son. A tall fair and handsome youth with apple red cheeks and sky blue eyes that fairies would yearn to possess. He was intelligent as well as sharp in his studies and used to get excellent reports from his school. Yet one thing that differentiated him from his class fellows was his compassion and sentimental behaviour. Of late he had started brooding and thinking endlessly about his glorious past, insecure present and unknown future. Most probably he may have been lost in his thoughts at the time when he crossed the road and was therefore run over by the truck.

'Brooding has become a permanent feature of these afflicted people coupled with hypertension and diabetes. Nobody is able to escape. This is what they will leave as heritage for their coming generations till they become extinct and part of history,' he shook his head briskly as if he was trying to get rid of all his painful thoughts. Then he fixed his gaze at the zebra crossing in front of him. It was as expectant as ever, shining bright under the scorching sun. The vehicular traffic too was as brisk as before.

He gathered courage and moved his right foot forward to walk over the stripes. At that very moment a speeding motor bicycle passed by, almost touching his advanced foot and leaving him no option but to pull it back hastily. The biker turned round and spewed abuse on him calling him blind. He was at a loss to understand as to how to make his way across under such circumstances.

It was the month of June and the sun was shining bright overhead. His family had cautioned him about the high temperature outside but being a villager he was confident of his physical fitness. He had no choice but to leave his home to collect his rations and the relief for which he had to traverse a distance of about ten kilometres. Earlier he was entitled to sixteen hundred rupees but after the death of his son he could only draw twelve hundred rupees as relief.

His son was a great asset to him. He would do all the work such as collection of rations and relief, purchase bread and vegetables, take his parents to the doctor and get them the prescribed medicines. But now the entire burden had fallen on his shoulders.

Being a peasant, he was entirely dependent on the relief provided by the government unlike government servants who were assured of their salaries, work or no work. Worse still, in Anantnag he lived jointly with his two brothers but at the time of migration the three fled in three directions and nobody knew where the other person had gone. Anyway he was successful in taking his family safely out of the Valley which by itself was a great solace to him. He had rescued his wife, a son and two teenage daughters not knowing that Death awaited his son at one of Delhi's highways.

'Relief of just twelve hundred rupees and rations for the family every month plus a tattered tent to huddle under,' he lamented. 'Neither a roof overhead nor a piece of land to stand on. Over and above, so many mouths to feed. What a contrast! There was a time when everything was in plenty. Money, foodgrains, dry fruits, and spices. We used to expect one or the other guest in our home and cook food for one or two extra persons daily. What a turn the wheel of fortune has taken! We have to live from hand to mouth now. Out of twelve hundred rupees, the clerk in the relief commissioner's office takes away one hundred. What remains is just eleven hundred to feed four mouths, purchase their apparel and pay for their education. My wife is illiterate and unskilled and cannot get a job. She had never anticipated such a plight. My only hope was the son who was snatched away from me from the jaws of death even before he could complete his studies. Now all that is left is two daughters who are studying in school.'

All of a sudden he remembered that his wife wanted him to return home before lunch. She had given him a small towel wetted with ice cold water which by now had dried up. He turned round and enquired about the time from a vendor of drinking water nearby.

'It is quarter past one,' sharp came the reply. The vendor had been curiously watching him all the time he stood there and had felt pity for him. 'Babuji, you have been standing in this scorching sun for the last two hours. Pray tell me where do you want to go?'

'I want to cross this road but this uncontrolled traffic does not allow me to do so,' he said.

'So many people have crossed since the time you stood there. What are you afraid of?'

'No no, the traffic is so much and so fast that anyone may crush me. Then where will my family go? They should at least have some consideration for those walking on foot. Nobody is bothered. Brother, it is not so in our town. Neither so much crowd nor so much speed. No, not at all. In our place, if an old man is unable to cross the road on his own, people will go, catch hold of his hand and help him till he reaches the other end. I have done so myself so many times when I was young.'

He started thinking as to why people in this city were so apathetic and undemonstrative and then laughed at himself. 'What a fool I am! Which place am I claiming to be mine? If that is my town then what am I doing here under this scorching sun?'

'Babuji, please have this glass of water. You need not pay for it,' the vendor said while handing over a glass of ice cold water to him. 'You seem puzzled. Are you a foreigner.'

'Foreigner! What makes you think so? No, brother, I belong to this very country called India. I am no foreigner.' He drank the water in one gulp and requested the vendor to wet his towel if possible.

Having said so, he suddenly felt speechless and again started thinking, 'Belong to this country! How? How do I call this country my own? The country which neither gives me security nor sustenance. Does one become a refugee in one's own country?'

'Babuji, it seems you wanted to say something but stopped short.'

'Brother, what can I say? There is nothing left for me to say. I have been made a refugee in my own country.'

'Babuji, it seems the traffic has thinned out. This is the best time to cross.'

He looked at the road in front of him. It was really free from heavy traffic. Possibly the traffic had thinned down due to lunch time in the offices.

So he mustered courage and put forward his feet one by one on the black and white stripes. For a moment he turned round and nodded his gratitude to the vendor and then moved his feet briskly.

One … two … three … four … five … six … seven … and so on, till he reached the other end of the road.

Then he stopped on the footpath at the other end and heaved a sigh of relief. He wiped his sweaty face with his wet towel. His whole body had turned into a furnace by now. His head was reeling, his eyes became blurred and he could not see anything around him. With mouth frothing, he fell like a chopped tree right on the footpath.

The vendor whose eyes were fixed on him was shocked. He ran across the road carrying a bottle of ice-cold water and sprinkled it on his face but it was too late. The body was lying motionless on the footpath with white froth coming out of the mouth and the pulse had already stopped.

People started gathering around the dead body and soon the police came by and picked up the dead body and took it away in a van.

For the police, it was a simple case of heat stroke. That is all it meant to them: an addition to the statistics of death by sun stroke.

– Translated from the Urdu by the Author

FLOWERS OF MUSTARD

M.K. MAHTAB

The reason for the interest in Balvindar was not that this tall girl, who seemed to be the epitome of simplicity and innocence, was extremely beautiful too. Girls with ruby-red complexions like ripe pomegranates, long hair and wide eyes are often to be found in the villages of the Punjab. What had impressed me the most about Balvindar was her simplicity and large heartedness. This girl dressed in a pale pink salwar-kameez and clutching a leather bag in her hand, had no idea that a beautiful young girl like her should not be speaking so freely to an unknown man.

The evening shadows were lengthening. The bus travelling from Ferozpur to Moga was ready. I had hurriedly bought the ticket and sat down in the bus. Had I missed the bus, there would have been no other way of reaching Moga that night. Because the times were not good, the last bus would leave by six in the evening and I had already sent word to my friend, Ram Singh, that I would reach Moga by 8:00 pm. If I had missed this bus, poor Ram Singh would have been so worried. He might even have thought that I had been killed in some mishap, or caught by someone or become the target of some terrorist group or the other who were roaming around freely all over the countryside.

With all these thoughts going around in my head, I experienced a strange sort of peace when I sat down in the bus. As a result, I had not realised that in my haste and anxiety my pocket had become considerably lighter till Balvindar drew my attention to it. She said, 'Mister, you have forgotten your wallet outside.'

I raised my eyes and looked at the girl whose face radiated with light and colour and whose doe-like eyes were resting on me. Flustered, I could not understand what this Punjabi girl was saying. 'Perhaps you have left your wallet on the ticket counter,' she repeated. She was bending over me and the loose hair at the end of her long plait tickled my neck and caused a shiver to course through my body. I jumped to my feet and began to feel my pockets. Certainly, my wallet was not in my pocket. I was moving towards the door of the bus when Balvindar stopped me.

'Don't worry; I have brought your wallet.' And she took out my wallet from her leather bag and handed it to me. I was overwhelmed with gratitude. I didn't have words to thank her. What is more, I had never thought that one day I would meet such an open and good-natured girl, in a remote rural hinterland, who would talk to an unknown traveller with such perfect ease as though she had known him for years. I invited her to sit down on the seat next to mine and she accepted with alacrity. She put her small attaché case under the seat, took out a pair of knitting needles and began to knit something.

I was telling her that my oversight had been due to my fearful state of mind. I had come to tour these border areas and write about them for my newspaper. I had been told that these places become desolate as soon as night falls. The administration turns its face away and the anti-social elements have a free rein and if one misses the last bus then the Lord alone can help the traveller. And so I had taken a tonga from a neighbouring village and come dashing all the way here to catch the bus before it left.

Sensing the extent of my worry, Balvindar smiled softly and said, 'It isn't quite so bad. You people who sit in the glittering high-rise buildings of Bahadurshah Zafar Marg and Connaught Place are needlessly scared of the darkness of the villages.' And with her eyes lowered, she kept knitting.

Balvindar lived in a village near Moga. She was a teacher of History in the Government Higher Secondary School of Firozpur. She clicked away with her needles and I was creating the warp and weft of my report on the next part of my travels in my head. And during this time, we were taking the help of small talk to get to know each other.

The cold had intensified outside, and the windows of the bus had been closed. The darkness too was deepened and I was remembering those bloody incidents when buses would be stopped on dark nights such as this, innocent passengers pulled out and shot. Or a bomb would be flung at a bus. How would those innocent passengers have felt? And what would happen to us if someone were to abduct our bus and take it to some fields somewhere. The thought terrified me and I sat with my eyes clenched shut and my back pushed tightly against the back of the seat.

'You are scared! Where do you have to go?' she asked.

'I will go and stay with a friend in Moga. Will I get a rickshaw or a tonga at this time?'

'Why don't you stay with us? Our home is on the road, barely two kilometres before Moga. You can go in the morning.'

'But my friend will be waiting for me.'

'We can send word through a servant.'

This girl with the dulcet voice extended this invitation with such good-natured naturalness that I could not say 'No.' We got off the bus a little before Moga. It was bitterly cold outside. Sharp gusts of wind were numbing our face. My woollen suit could do little to protect my body. I felt life course through my limbs only after we reached her house. Balvindar had a bed made out for me in one of the rooms. The room had two chairs, a small table and a jug of water. I snuggled under the quilt and blanket and only then felt the day's tiredness and cold seep out of my body.

But soon I felt as though I was a fly trapped in a beautiful web. A bulb hung from the wall but its light was far too dim. Suddenly the door was flung open and an enormously tall and well-built Punjabi sardar, with a black beard and a face as red as a blazing oven and ferocious-looking eyes, wearing a white turban and a coloured shawl, pushed the door open with his strong hands and entered the room. One look at his massive build was enough to terrify me. Two blows from those enormous-looking hands would have been enough to pulverise me. Terror-stricken, I gathered the quilt around me and got up from the bed shivering from head to toe.

That terrifying-looking man was Surjit, Balvindar's elder brother. When he stepped forward to vigorously shake my hand I felt as though my arm would come out of its socket. Then he produced a bottle from the folds of his shawl and placed it with a loud thump on the table.

'You city-slickers won't drink the real stuff; so, I have brought some "English" liquor. Will you have salted peanuts with it, or shall I get a salad of tomatoes and radishes to go with it?'

Surjit took out two glasses from a cupboard and kept them on the table, broke open the seal of the bottle with a loud 'click' and poured two drinks.

'Wait, Sardarji, wait! Don't pour for me; I don't drink.'

'How can that be? Who doesn't drink nowadays? And then newspaper people are supposed to even drink poison! Tell me, shall I add water or will you have it neat?'

'Sardarji, I swear upon my father, I have never tasted alcohol,' I answered with some agitation.

'Well, never mind if you have not drunk before; have it now. The cold is so intense here during the night that your blood will turn to ice. And tomorrow morning your corpse will be found in the bed and the police will come and take us away accusing us of abducting a man from the city and killing him. Take the name of the Blessed Guru and pick up your glass! Or else place your hand on my head and swear that you don't drink!'

I placed my hand that was as limp and cold as a dead hen on Surjit's head. He poured the brandy from my glass into his own and said, 'Come clink your empty glass with mine and let us take a vow of friendship.' I raised my glass. Surjit drained his glass in two gulps and said, 'Surely you will have hot milk?'

'Yes, yes!' I said eagerly, to get rid of him. Surjit left the bottle, glass and peanuts lying there and went away to get the milk. I rubbed my hands between my knees and wondered how I had got trapped in a lion's den. Surely, by the time this man had downed half a bottle he would throw me to the ground and beat me to a pulp. All the of the Sikhs ire would be vented on me. How foolish I had been! I should have gone to my friend Ram Singh's house. I was supposed to have gone there and written a highly evocative description of the extremely dangerous conditions prevailing in this border area. But now I myself was in a dangerous situation. I could not hear Balvindar's voice and God knows what would happen to me by the time the sun rose the next morning.

Surjit, whose eyes were bloodshot, placed the glass of milk on the table. I was scared that he would finish the entire bottle as I sipped the milk. And then he would begin to curse me and start beating me. I said to him, 'Surjit, I did not listen to you but now you listen to me and have some milk with me.'

'I have a large heart, Bauji; I will not disappoint you.'

We sat there talking. He would mix his rum in the milk and drink it. He had reached home after driving his tractor for four hours. He was extremely tired. And as he was telling me rum was effective in making the tiredness go away. As soon as he had reached home, Balvindar had told him that a journalist from Delhi was staying in their home and Surjit must make him feel welcome. 'Had I known earlier, I would certainly have brought fish and paneer pakodas from the city,' he told me. And then he said, 'Why have you come to see the mess here and write about it? Why don't you sit in Delhi and find a solution? Take the fighting and the troubles there. You will find enough news to sell your newspapers. Why do you trouble us and yourselves like this? All we want to do here is work hard ploughing our fields with our tractors, have our rum and then go to sleep with the blanket pulled over our head.'

Suddenly the door opened and a smiling Balvindar, her younger sister and brother and father came in looking like the epitome of a happy family. They were talking to me as though some eminent person had come to their home from Delhi. And Balvindar's younger sister, Inder, was running around behind me, as though checking to see if journalists have a tail!

Dinner was ready, and they had all trooped into my room to call me. Plenty of fresh leafy vegetables, a gigantic omelette made from dozens of eggs, paneer, honey, pickles, preserves, butter, in short whatever they had in the house had been brought and placed on the table before us. Helplessly, I looked at Balvindar who tried to hide her pearly-white teeth with her rose-petal pink lips and seemed to be saying to me, 'Nicely caught, aren't you my friend?'

Balvindar's father, Daya Singh, patted my back and said, 'Son, why are newspapers published every day?'

'A daily newspaper should be published daily, Sardarji; yesterday's newspaper becomes rubbish.'

'But surely they should stop some days; they cause a lot of trouble to people hereabouts.'

I could well understand the sharp taunt hidden behind Daya Singh's words.

That night an extremely comfortable bed was laid out for me in that room. Soft mattress, a velvety quilt, it seemed as though a much-venerated Godman was being served by his disciples.

After some time, Balvindar appeared; she was wearing her night clothes, a comb was stuck in her long, open hair and she held a glass of milk in her hands. 'Are you bent upon taking my life?' I asked her laughingly.

'You yourself have written in your newspaper that every man fears for his life in these parts.' From the pocket of her gown, she took out the newspaper I had given her to read in the bus. And she put down the tumbler of milk on the table and laughed and went out of the door. Her long hair swayed past her waist like waves reaching out to the shore.

Snuggled under the quilt, I was trying to recall my dispatch in the newspaper, where I had written how explosive the situation was here and how people had lost all faith in life and how no one was willing to speak, let alone trust the other. I had written how dangerous it had become to travel around here. People would sit silent and stiff as statues in cars and buses, forever fearful that someone would get up and spray them with a sten-gun. No one knew when, or where, they might be killed. After all, the police patrols could not do much good, etc, etc. And I had followed this up with my interviews with people.

The next morning, I decided to set off for Ludhiana immediately after breakfast. Balvindar, too, got ready to leave with me. She had to go there for some errand to do with her school. Her mother said, 'She is a young girl; why should she travel alone. Let her go with Babuji; she can come by evening.'

We sat side by side in the bus. Fields of wheat and mustard stretched out on both sides of the road. The sun was out. In the bright sunshine, the fields too seemed wide awake. The fog that veiled the windows was beginning to drip down in lines of water. The scene outside was bright and clear. Balvindar sat close beside me. The biting cold had made her nose red. The heat from her body was piercing my clothes and crawling over my body like ice. I said, 'Balvindar, how lovely the scene is outside! How beautiful the mustard flowers look – as though someone has brought autumn to sit down on the earth. I had come here thinking that the fields would be desolate, the roads deserted and fountains of blood would be spouting from the earth.'

And that teacher of History answered thus, 'This is the earth; its nature never changes. From Kandhar to Kurukshetra, so much blood has been shed and so many times too. Who knows how many fires have blazed here? Or how many spears and lances struck in her bosom? Yet, mustard flowers as beautiful as ever continue to burst forth from her bosom. Because the earth never changes her nature.'

'Just like humanity,' I said.

And Balvindar looked at me as though she knew exactly what I was going to write in my next article.

– Translated from the Urdu by Rakhshanda Jalil

SOIL

TARRANNUM RIYAZ

'Will you give me a blanket?' Kishanlal looked towards Hilal Ahmed and asked in such a manner that his restlessness as well as earnestness, both, were evident in his eyes.

In this harsh beginning of winter if he had tried to show patience for a little more then he would not have dozed even for a moment as he was very tired and wanted to rest for some time. It was another matter that he was ninety per cent sure that his plea would be rejected. The rest ten per cent effort was made in a doubt – a doubtful hope that only a human being can have when it comes to another human being.

The severe cold had darkened Kishanlal's wheatish complexion and turned his lips almost black. His woollen jacket was buttoned to the neck and in spite of wearing a full-sleeved pullover along with a sleeveless one, he was shivering badly. It was only a few days ago that he had joined his duties as a new recruit and had been sent to this area which was experiencing tension. Unaware of the climatic condition of this area, he had soon fallen ill and was still not feeling strong enough.

Kishanlal pulled his long socks above his ankle but they came back to their original position as soon as his hands left them. He set the shrunken collar of his greenish-yellow uniform as well as his cap which was already covering his ears. While setting it right, he started looking towards Hilal Ahmed with impatient but unpromising eyes. Hilal Ahmed, too, was looking towards him.

Even in this harsh winter he had left his collar unbuttoned. As a result, the drops of blood that fell from his wounded lips froze on the hairs of his chest. He was sitting against a wall, his legs covered with a blanket. The length of the blanket was not sufficient to cover his tall body.

'You are saying this to me?' He said with an emphasis on 'you' and a look of shock on his face.

'Who is here apart from you?' saying this Kishanlal stood up and walked slowly towards the bars. He kept his hand on the bars and ran a searching glance inside. The bars were very cold. He thrust his hands back into his pocket.

'Why can't you see these two?' Hilal Ahmed said while stretching both hands and pointing them to the left and the right direction.

'Even you cannot see them … had you seen them you would not have pulled away the blankets from their bodies.' Kishanlal said while standing at the same place and hopping on one foot then the other.

'Is this a body? … you are calling it a body! The body has turned to soil long ago.' Hilal Ahmed was not able to suppress the pain in his voice.

'I know …' Kishanlal said softly.

'You know nothing – for knowing anything it is necessary for a man to be human. I cannot see any trait of human beings in you. You are no more than an unsympathetic beast … you are a stone … you all are stones.' He said with anger and hatred and turned away so quickly that his face was scratched by the stony wall.

It was a mere chance that he had been caught; otherwise, till date, he had committed far more dangerous acts and had always managed to reach his companions at his secret place without being caught. Today also he had been going towards his destination. He had stopped upon seeing a wounded traveller lying on the street. He had carried the wounded man on his shoulder and walked swiftly when suddenly a nervous boy of ten or twelve years came and caught his legs. Feeling scared, he brought the boy close to himself.

'Brother … save me … he will catch me …' He was so breathless that he was unable to complete the sentence. Meanwhile, many people with guns surrounded them.

It is another matter that the place they were taken to was not the destination of any of the three. This was not the path that Hilal Ahmed had chosen before he was caught. He was undergoing training in mechanical engineering. He, along with his parents, had long had this dream. He used to repair his tricycle and other mechanical toys ever since he was a child. When he grew up a little, he began to make a coop for hens, fix electric wiring and water taps, repair sewing machines and watches. He would repair all sorts of machines that were out of order and bring them back to working condition. His parents liked his interest in these things. He passed the entrance examination with flying colours and joined the college but …

The incident had occurred a few months ago. The trees were swaying after shedding snow from their fresh, colourful branches and the spring season had just begun. The almond trees, donning a veil of tiny green leaves and fresh pink flowers, were bowing with coyness. From where the birds unhurriedly fly and produce the sound of *tak-tak* with their long beaks on the hollow branches of the *chinar* trees; the sound that becomes a source of disturbance to the leisure of the tiny insects that dig up the soft ground; and again they take a long flight back to the blue coloured washed and bathed sky, fresh and clean, and again indulge themselves in the same activity. The soft sunshine, with its rays, tickle the lush green earth and the strands of grass spread their fragrance while dancing. It was late afternoon. From which direction the dark, dirty and thundering clouds came and covered the sky swallowing its pristine blueness? Although it was late afternoon, it seemed like evening; the ambience was filled with a dark, red and dirty light.

Hilal Ahmed returned from his college at that very moment.

'My darling has returned,' his mother said as she cracked her knuckles against her head in a gesture of warding off evil.

'Had you said that my Hilal has returned, then I would have felt that I have grown up!'

'I have said that only …' she said while pushing the locks of hair from his forehead.

'Hilal means moon … Your grandmother chose your name because you had a big forehead when you were born. She used to say that our Hilal will become a big name … he will shine like a moon … He will bring prestige to our family name … Insha Allah …'

'So, don't I know all this?' Hilal Ahmed feigned anger.

'Oh! I have forgotten that you know it,' and both burst out laughing together.

'Today I have got *bakarkhani* from Panpura for your salted tea,' his mother said.

'The condition there is …' His voice became a bit serious.

'It is better than yesterday … your father had to go there for some official work.'

Hilal Ahmed broke a piece of the *bakarkhani* and as he dipped it into a small, handle-less wide-brimmed cup of pink chai he heard a loud announcement that was being made from a megaphone. Hilal Ahmad ran out.

'All of you! Come out of your houses … There is a search on for some miscreants … All the houses will be searched … We are giving you five minutes!'

'Ya Allah! … here too …' his mother's face flushed a deep red with fear.

People hurriedly put out the fires in their hearth … uncooked food, utensils, work and rest – everything was abandoned. Hurriedly, they came out of their homes. In a moment, the entire neighbourhood was deserted. People gathered in the big ground in front of the colony; this ground had heaps of golden paddy and the open space was used for separating husk from grains by beating them against big stones and then filling them in gunny bags. Apart from beating crops the big mortars were used by children during their play and often, they would hide behind the big stones. During festivals such as Eid, people would collect in this big open ground and sing folk songs. During moonlit nights, groups of girls would come here and make merry, sing and dance.

Hearing the announcement, Hilal Ahmed, too, came out with his parents. The houses were being searched. The investigating team was moving from house to house. The uniformed man, who was going from one house to the other, had a golden chain that was hanging from the back pocket of his trouser. Perhaps, in a hurry, he had not put it properly in his pocket.

'That's mine … it belongs to my daughter. It is for her marriage,' Ghulam Hasan, Hilal's neighbour said in a loud voice and ran towards the man in the uniform. The girl followed her father slowly, and then stopped at a distance.

'Silence! Old man … traitor!' The uniformed man kicked the old man's weak and aged legs. The old man trembled and fell down. He caught the legs of the uniformed man. 'For God's sake … My daughter!'

'Leave it, Bastard … the free food has given you strength … you get subsidised ration … after all this you have the nerve to look us in the eye!' He said angrily and pointed his gun towards the old man, but he soon brought the gun down as perhaps he saw his officer coming from a distance. He hit the old man with the butt of the gun. The old man fell down and cried. The man in the uniform again lifted the gun. The daughter of the old man fell on her father … a lot of commotion ensued.

'Forgive him! Sirji … you may take it … whatever you like,' she started weeping.

'Are we thieves? … What shall we take? … What have we stolen?… Basta …' He pulled the girl by her hair and pushed her. She fell down. Her head hit the corner of one of the mortars. Her face became pale. She stuffed her dupatta in her mouth. Her fragile body made efforts to gulp down her rising hiccups. She was shaking like a ferry caught amidst a storm in a lake. The crowd stood numb. The children were shivering. The girls were trying to hide behind their relatives. The loud cries had been replaced by repressed hiccups.

'This … what is happening? … doomsday … doomsday,' Hilal Ahmed's father shouted. In that state of suppressed cries, his voice was no less than the sound of a blast.

A bullet hit his shoulder. He fell down immediately. Hilal's mother shouted in a voice that rent the skies, and fainted.

The uniformed men returned the same night. Whom were they searching for? … They had found no one there. Still, they stayed for hours in some houses. Ghulam Hasan has been spitting blood from that day and his daughter has not spoken a word ever since. She is always found hiding either in a corner or clinging to a wall. If someone calls out to her, she looks shocked, as though she has been electrocuted.

The remembrance of *maidan-e-hashr* was alive in Hilal Ahmed's eyes while he was returning after performing the last rites of his father. He was looking towards the sky and walking. He saw flames rising high at one end of the field. The smoke was spreading everywhere. The distant screams and cries of humans sounded like howling of animals.

Hilal Ahmed reached home but he was not able to say one sentence of sympathy to his mother. He held her head tightly – as tight as his mother used to hold him during his childhood whenever he was afraid. Perhaps, he wanted to take refuge in her affectionate lap yet again so he could forget all his sorrows and troubles. But, suddenly he pulled away from the arms of his mother. He took a few steps and then stopped. On reaching the door he stood still as if he was a statue made of stone. For a while, he stared at his mother with traumatised eyes and then walked away.

As he crossed the villages, that were near the field, he saw ashes of burnt houses and half-burnt dead bodies – a few completely burnt, some partially charred and some scorched portions of human bodies. It was as if a child had attempted to make human bodies with black clay and on being unsuccessful he had given up and thrown the unfinished bodies and body parts here and there.

Hilal Ahmed did not want to see more of this.

Engineering colleges, like other colleges, were open only for two or three days. 'Roll no 22,' a teacher called out as he searched the classroom for his favourite and most promising, student.

'He is absent, Sir,' a student stood up and spoke in a loud voice …

'What happened to him … he too … his future,' the teacher murmured as if he was talking to himself. 'What will happen to him? Such intelligent students are not born every day,' the teacher said and then fell silent.

Hilal Ahmed, R.E.C (Regional Engineering College), student of first year, roll no. 22, from the year 1991, is absent. Is he no longer a seeker of knowledge? Where is Hilal Ahmed? He is not at home. His friends from college hardly ever drop in at his home to enquire about him … Hilal Ahmed's mother runs out to the streets frequently. She stares at any boy wearing jeans and t-shirt … she asks about Hilal Ahmed, and then she becomes hopeless. She weeps and walks about in different directions. She knows many women who are like her … whose sons are missing, some of them have lost their husband … or whose children have become heart patients and whose daughters have become dumb.

Hilal Ahmed, too, has been missing. When will Hilal Ahmed's mother get a chance to see him again? Will she ever see him or …

His mother now is unable to do anything in her home. What can she do inside her home? The row of flowers, which flourished on the left side of the courtyard, has dried. The small vegetable garden, which was on the right side, has also been ruined. The trees are standing dejectedly in the corners. Now, the *bulbul* has stopped singing in these branches, and the *ababeel* has also stopped visiting.

Hilal Ahmed took a deep sigh and touched his wounded lips. His lips were bleeding again as his face had again been hurt by the stone wall.

'If we are stones then what evidence of humanity has been given by your people,' Kishanlal asked while continuously jumping from one foot to the other as he gave up all thought of sleeping on the duty chair.

'You have brought this day upon us,' Hilal Ahmed said in a depressed tone.

'You people started it … we are simply continuing it.'

'Is this your duty?' Hilal Ahmed said as he pointed his hand towards the lifeless body of the ten or twelve year old boy. 'What harm had he done to you? And these five young men … one of them was afflicted by polio. What had he done to you? In the report you will say that they were killed in an encounter. I know it … I was taking him away from the site of the blast. His leg was badly injured. He told me that his wife was so afraid of the sound of gunshot that even if she hears a distant sound of gunshot she faints for hours and does not open her eyes for days. He had a small child. He was carrying medicine for his wife … when … when I blasted the bomb … why have you punished them? You should have punished me. The child's neck was broken by just one slap from one of your men,' Hilal Ahmed's eyes became wet as he spoke and soon he began to weep so much that his voice choked and seemed stuck in his throat.

'It was an order from the higher authority … what could we do?' Kishanlal said softly while standing close to the bars.

'This was not the order … whosoever … whosoever is found … jail them … shoot them …' Hilal Ahmed's voice had a blend of helplessness and anger.

'All are the same … donning loose and long clothes … they commit crimes and then get away … where does one find them … often, they run from one lane to the other and then they are caught … there are so many lanes and we are strangers. What can we do?'

'It is a good method. If a criminal is not caught you can catch any innocent person even if he is unaware of the crime. You go to these sensitive areas without any prior knowledge … and … and …' Hilal Ahmed started walking impatiently.

'When the local administration was unable to do anything … then we were assigned duties … We don't have personal animosity with anybody …'

Kishanlal too started walking again. It was as though he was walking on a wide, well-lit and grassy road. The redness of his eyes spoke volumes about his fatigue. Actually, he had duties in the morning. In the evening when the duties changed then he handed over the keys to the next man on duty. As he was about to leave he heard the sound of a blast outside. The person in-charge of the night duty came running and told him that the blast was, perhaps, in the vehicle by which he came. His brother was going to another nearby place by the same vehicle. He ran out. In fact, all the remaining people also ran out. He was left alone. The man did not return; perhaps his brother was injured in the blast. Something must have happened, for nobody had returned till now. So far, Kishanlal had not felt the cold. Now, while walking, he was feeling cold. He also wanted to rest for a while.

'Hand over one blanket to me,' he said to Hilal Ahmed.

'Why do you need to ask? Open the room and take it,' Hilal Ahmed turned his face away as he spoke.

'I don't have the keys and many people have been assigned duties just like me. I don't know where the others are. I don't know when they will return. The storekeeper is also not here.'

'I know … if you had the keys you would have come inside and taken the blanket along with my skin. Who can stop you people from doing whatever you like?'

'It is not necessary that everybody is the same … if it had been so, I would have shot you dead and would have taken the blanket by breaking the lock … there are two dead bodies already … the number would have gone up to three. Moreover, the fear of anyone escaping would have ended too … but …' Kishanlal looked at him and left his sentence unfinished.

'Fine, you can fulfil your wishes … it is just that nobody would listen to us and nobody would question you. You are delaying. If your friends would have been here then they would have done this much earlier,' Hilal Ahmed said while looking towards him.

'Why have you people always regarded yourself as the "other" … and now …'

'We are considering ourselves as the other because you people have left us alone ... it has been fifty years since independence... There was a bridge which could have brought us together ... one ... I am giving you an example ... Was that built? ... tell me!'

'There is a way ... there is an airway.'

'Can the common man afford it? Don't you know the conditions of the roads? You have also come from there,' the expression on Hilal Ahmed's face was a blend of helplessness and curiosity.

'It is said that unlimited resources are needed for ... during every rainy season that bridge flows away ... How people ...' Kishanlal left the conversation unfinished.

'Unlimited resources ... Mahatma Gandhi Bridge is also very huge ... Was it not constructed? ... Don't we need roads and railway tracks? ... The majority of people here have seen trains only in movies ...'

'The railway tracks are there on the other side ... the same railway tracks in the entire area ...'

'This side ... that side ... all the facilities are available in other hilly areas ... but narrow-minded people ... they give step-motherly treatment on the basis of religion ...'

'You talk of the issue very lightly but it is very difficult ... there are various geographical as well as financial issues involved. This task is no less difficult than digging for a stream of milk.'

'Why? Don't you have access to modern technologies? Someone should feel pain for us too. Well! I was just giving one example. Maybe this was an easy thing but there are so many other issues. Actually, everyone wants mountains and lakes even if the ground becomes red. The people on the other side, too, want their sky ... the people on the other side.'

'Why don't you tell this to your leader?' Kishanlal said while contemplating something.

'If we had a leader than we would have not gone astray like this … the people we trusted broke our trust. They were merely concerned for a secure future for their generations. Otherwise, we never had soft corner for the people on the other side … desires for relations … we wanted to lead a normal lives … But …'

'Our leaders are also like that … generally they are all like that …' Kishanlal spoke in a meditative manner.

'Initially, if there was no oppositional behaviour then the situation would not have reached this impasse. If only the criminals were caught then the common people would have also helped. Every peace-loving human was himself troubled by all these. We have been caught in the middle … from both the directions … between devil and deep sea … Many people have chosen the wrong path only for their protection. Many have started believing that people, who have chosen the wrong path, were right and the people who were affected were … mother and father … caretaker … mother … leaving one's mother behind …' Again Hilal Ahmed's voice became inaudible. He held the bars tightly and rested his head on them.

'But even then these events will not come to an end,' Kishanlal said while looking from the side of window.

'This … because … you people catch their weapons and sell them back. One who is unable to purchase is killed. Otherwise the story goes on and on.'

'How do you know these things? Even I have heard such things … Somewhere perhaps …'

'Everyone, who does not have the capacity to buy weapons from you people, knows this,' Hilal Ahmed said while turning his face away.

'Your identity card shows that you are an educated man,' Kishanlal said while looking at him.

'You, too, appear educated,' Hilal Ahmed said slowly after maintaining silence for a while.

'Yes, BSc.'

'A science graduate and this job!' Hilal Ahmed said with shock.

'Even this position was gained by pawning all I had.'

'It means Life in exchange of wealth.'

'Yes … It can be put like that.'

'Aren't these issues taken to higher authorities?' Hilal Ahmed asked tenderly.

'No … even they come from authorities … gradually … step by step,' Kishanlal said haltingly.

Hilal Ahmed's lips had a peaceful smile. As he started moving towards the wall of the room he saw only darkness surrounding him.

There were no bodies, no blanket.

But, after taking few steps, he trained his eyes to see in the darkness. When he brought the blanket near the bars Kishanlal was taking out a cigarette from the packet.

'It is said that the conditions are improving … Do you smoke?'

'Yes … occasionally I do … perhaps it may improve. God alone knows.'

– *Translated from the Urdu by Haris Qadeer*

THE LAST LESSON

JOGINDER PAUL

On being kick-started, the motorcycle screamed as it left smoke, and those two had hardly seated themselves properly on it when, with a sudden leap, it began to run.

Seated at the rear Santa worriedly pointed out. 'Before starting at least allow one to sit properly.'

'If you sit down, Santaya, then how will you reach?'

Santa straightened his turban and said, 'When somebody's death comes, Bantaya, then Yam, the lord of death, transports one straightaway.'

Banta, laughing all the while, started telling him that the road was straight, and they would reach before daybreak.

Santa's eyes suddenly fixed themselves upon a stengun which hung from Banta's shoulder, its barrel raised towards his chest. Seething with anger, he deftly changed the position of his own gun inside his shirt instead, and still finding Banta's gun raised towards him called out in a troubled voice, 'Why is this mother pointed towards my heart?'

Raising his right hand from the motorcycle handle, Banta turned the direction of the barrel towards the front. 'Why be afraid, Santaya? Mothers, even if they be witches, do not eat their own children.'

Santa, relaxing, began to tell him that witches are childless. If they were mothers then how could they be witches? He had heard that during his birth either he could be saved or his mother and his mother had given up her life, repeatedly imploring with folded hands to quit worrying about her life and save her child's life at any cost. Thinking about his mother, six-footer Santa would, in his mind, turn into a small baby, thrashing about with his baby hands, bawling aloud or laughing, as he jumped up and down in his mother's hands. No, he was ignorant of his mother's face and appearance – how could he know? There was simply no photograph of her in the house. He had tried to understand from his father, but every time a different description by his father would raise a new picture in his mind.

'You are the limit, father! Hearing your description, mother seems a different person each time.'

'What can I say, son!' his widower father would reply, adding that his mother was a strange creature. Whichever woman one thought of, she'd look like her.

Listening to this often, Santa also began to feel that every woman was his mother; so much so that even when embracing his wife he would many times cry helplessly, as though he had laid his grief-stricken face on his lost mother's breasts.

The motorcycle was zipping down the straight road when suddenly Banta called out to his companion, and on receiving no reply impatiently called out even more loudly, 'Oye, Santaya!'

'Yes? – Ye-Yes-!'

'Have you fallen asleep? Who was crying here just now?'

'There's no one else here; so I must've been crying.'

'But you were sleeping Santaya!'

'So does one need your permission to cry in one's dreams?'

Banta was slightly irritated; he said, 'What is it to me? Cry in your dreams or while awake. I was only asking who was crying here just now.'

In the meantime the motorcycle let off a loud cracking sound and Santa felt as if the gun inside his shirt had gone off by mistake. He jumped …

'I felt as though my gun had gone off!' He tried to steady his quickened breathing.

'Guns don't take go off by themselves, stupid!'

'Say whatever you want, stupid, they do go off.' Santa paused, wondering how he could make his companion understand, and then began asking him, 'Tell me honestly, have we set out to fire the guns on our own?'

'You are a very deep man, Santaya,' Banta began to tell him. 'And therefore of no use. It's obvious, villain, if you disobey orders then you will only get yourself hanged.'

'Yes Bantaya, that is why I say, you – me who are we to disregard the will of Wahe Guru?'

Somewhat disturbed, he began to scratch his beard out of habit and as if to console himself he opened the conversation further, saying, 'On opening the mouth of my gun I feel as if I have no wish of my own, as if my gun's wish has become my wish.'

'May your children live long,' Banta said on a happy note, 'You have relieved me; otherwise I was thinking that whosoever has to be killed has to be killed by me alone.'

But on listening to him, Santa expressed his doubt, 'What if our guns turn their faces towards our own children then … then …'

'How can this happen?' Banta irritably increased the speed of the motorcycle. 'You are a very troublesome man.'

The troublesome man, in reply, gave off such a loud burst of laughter that on both sides of the road, the birds sleeping in the branches of the darkened trees started to flap their wings in alarm.

After the loud bursts of laughter Santa felt somewhat light of heart and with great reverence began to loudly repeat the 18th verse of the *Japji Sahib*:

'Countless the unwise, in black ignorance reel
Countless the usurpers and those that steal
Countless the rulers who force their way
Countless the cut-throats whom violence doth sway.'

'Santaya,' Banta opened his mouth to say God knows what, but afraid that it was a sin to interrupt the *Gurbani*, he just said '*Satnam Wahe Guru*' and kept quiet.

'Countless the sinners whom sin engages
Countless the liars who wander in mazes
Countless the wretches, have filth as fill
Countless the slanderers carrying load of Evil
Thus thinketh Nanak, the lowliest of the lowly
Sacrifice am I unto Thee a myriad times, O Holy
That what Pleaseth Thee is the only good done
O Thou, the Eternal, the Formless One.[1]

'The Blessed Guru's name is the only True Name!'

'Bantaya, the True King shall certainly forgive us.'

'But what have we done, Santaya?'

Santa began to pity Banta; the poor fellow was unable to understand his own misery. In his heart he began to pray that may the True King forgive them both; certainly, they did bad deeds but the True King knew that they were not bad men. If you don't know True King, even then forgive. Your forgiveness

1 Translated by Dr Gopal Singh, *Sri Guru Granth Sahib*, English version, Vol. I (New Delhi: World Book Centre, 1993, [1960]), p. 5.

is limitless … He was folding both his hands and bowing down his head when Banta increased the speed of the motorcycle, and he received such a jolt that he barely saved himself from falling down, 'You will kill me.'

'No Santaya, because of you I too shall be saved.'

Santa began to think that his friend Banta was like the water chestnut, thorny and black on the outside but on peeling a little a sweet and milky white kernel appeared, whose taste would not leave the mouth even after one had finished eating it. His maternal grandmother used to always place a heap of water chestnuts before him … Eat, son, eat to your heart's content! His grandmother had told him that his mother too could never have her fill of water chestnuts … Son, yesterday, you had opened your hair in the sun and you were eating water chestnuts, and I felt as if my Amar Kaur had appeared before my very eyes … His grandmother had suddenly hugged him and an innocent thought had passed through him that who knows … Yes, who knows, while giving birth to him his mother had died so that her spirit may descend into him … Standing before the mirror he would try to visualise himself in the form of a full-bodied woman … So this is my mother! Mother! At night, his grandmother would sleep holding him tightly in her arms as if she was afraid that he would disappear somewhere while playing in his dreams; whereas, while he slept his whole universe condensed itself on that bed and he, becoming his own mother, would in his own mother's hands be jumping uncontrollably, letting out peals of laughter.

'Santaya! Oye Santaya!'

'Yes … Aanh!'

'Slept off again?' Banta started laughing. 'Who was laughing here just now?'

Santa replied, 'If you weren't laughing then I must have been laughing, who else is there?'

'No Santaya,' he answered very grimly, 'Who knows, some ghost has started following us?'

'An apparition does not follow,' Santa began telling Banta. 'People themselves begin to follow an apparition.' He wondered why the metalled road had not ended till now! They had to keep going straight on this road where after about a mile, as if from within the charcoal road itself, began an unmetalled road. A few miles later, cutting through the middle of the fields, that unmetalled road naturally entered a village as if on bare feet. These two with a barrage of bullets from their stenguns had to kill the entire family of the headman of this village. Santa wanted to ask Banta if it was necessary to wipe off every trace of the poor village headman. They were going to completely destroy his entire family … Why? What harm had these poor helpless people done to them?

In the meantime, their motorcycle brutally ran over an old dog and sped on.

'Careful, Bantaya, you have unnecessarily taken the life of a mute.'

'If his life was precious to him then why was he blocking the road by standing there right in the middle?'

Santa began to understand why friends and well-wishers, on seeing him from afar, would move away here and there. They know that he comes rushing headlong. Just leave his path alone, let him go wherever he goes, what's it to us? What's more, now his bosom friend, Bachna, had also started running away from him. There was a time when even what they had eaten or drunk was discussed with heads joined together as if after revealing their deep secrets they felt greatly relieved.

'Oye Bachanaya!'

'Yes, Santaya!'

'Do you know what happened next?'

Bachana's ears would prick up, 'What happened?'

'I drank two big glasses of butter milk.'

'Really?'

'Yes, but even then I was not satisfied, so I stealthily gulped down even my aunt's share ...'

'Really!' Bachna asked, 'Then your aunt must've remained hungry?'

'No, my aunt smartly steals from my uncle!'

'Ha-ha-ha!'

Their loud bursts of laughter mingled as if, instead of two, only one of them was laughing.

'Alas! Why are the clouds beginning to thunder in the middle of such a sunny day?' His aunt would come running out into the courtyard, 'I hope my grain does not get wet.' And on finding these two laughing loudly she'd grow angry; 'If you laugh so loudly, you goddamned fellows, you will forget your way.'

Laughing even more loudly, they would retort, 'But we don't have to go anywhere; how can we forget the way?'

'Oye, son of a madman,' Banta jumped up from his seat and began to ask Santa, 'Why have you started laughing all of a sudden?' And then without waiting for a reply, he too began laughing loudly and began thinking that whatever one might say, really, enjoyment comes only from unnecessary Bang-Bang.

Their bursts of laughter showering bullets, Bang-Bang, ran ahead of the line of their motorcycle's light and with the breaking of dawn hid in the surrounding jungle out of fear.

'Bantaya, I feel, we have forgotten the way,' Santa again felt his gun pinching him, and putting his hand inside his clothes he settled it on his back, and said, 'We have still not reached the unmetalled road.'

Banta replied, 'It will come; the way is straight.'

But Santa was afraid that if a person were to go astray then he can go off track even on a straight road. He was thinking that he had joined the group of these good fellows because ten brothers were saying the same thing, they wouldn't be speaking lies. So when they raised the slogan, '*Jo Bole so Nihal*', his voice was the loudest amongst those that chorused, '*Sat Sri Akal!*' But the intention behind this slogan is to ask for everyone's well-being, view everyone's sorrow as one's own, among the believers of the true King there is no one who is a stranger, even those whom you don't know they too are your own. Santa folding both his hands, closed his eyes and swaying raised the slogan, '*Sat Sri Akal!*'

'Have patience Santaya,' Banta laughingly said, 'First let us find the whereabouts of the village headman.'

'No, Bantaya, just think ...'

'Oye, first let's do what has to be done, then we'll think.'

But Santa blurted out the words that came into his mouth, 'Before joining your group everyone felt like my own but now ...'

'Who is one's own in this transitory world? You think of your own well-being.'

'Damn my well-being; ask for my death, Bantaya ...' Santa's voice was filled with grief and anger, 'Those Sikh sons whose well-being I want to ask for, they have become strangers.' He was ruefully shaking his head, 'What kind of a life is this? One's own people have become strangers to such an extent that no one steps forward to even try and speak a little sense and make others understand.'

'Oye, why are you suddenly so morose, Santaya?'

'Something sad has happened, that's why. Even my close friend Bachna is scared that if he tries to make me understand then I, Santaya will put a bullet through him. Tell me, am I some demon ... I'm that same Santaya, that same friend of yours, Bachna, my friend. If I have gone a little astray then put me back on the right path with love ... But you speak right Bantaya, in this transitory world no one is one's own.' The motorcycle skidded on a pothole; he steadied himself and straightened his turban. 'You are no stranger to me, Bantaya; you find out some way, brother!'

'The way has been found, Braveheart!' In an extremely satisfied voice, Banta informed him, 'The unmetalled road is starting from just a few metres away.'

Santa, too, forgetting everything, fell silent, thinking that at least the way has been found. In his childhood his father used to often come home late. Once, when the next day he did not return even after dawn, Santa began to cry. His grandmother pulled him close to her heart and began to soothe him by saying, 'Why are you crying? Your father must've forgotten the way. Come, stand up in attendance of the True King and with folded hands pray that He puts your father on the road home.' His grandmother would often make him sit close to her and counsel him for hours to always take the straight path, the straight path that goes directly to *Baikunth*, God's abode.

'The straight path goes directly to *Baikunth*, Bantaya,' he said to his companion imitating his grandmother's style.

'Yes, get ready, Braveheart! We have to send the village headman's entire family there.'

But on imagining *Baikunth*, Santa had reached his mother who, in the True King's palace, was cleaning a huge heap of dirty utensils. Santa was angry with the True King that every day, unnecessarily he keeps a community kitchen open for gods and goddesses. 'No, son, to speak thus is a sin. It is my good fortune that I do the work of shining clean the dirty utensils of the great ancestors.'

'But mother ...'

'No, my son, if the utensils do not shine then the hunger of those who are hungry dies.'

Santa is sitting close beside his late mother and despite being this close he is still edging closer towards her, and edging closer and closer he has entered right into her heart and from here he has descended into his mother's womb and upon taking birth from her womb has started crying.

'Santaya! Oye, Santaya!'

'Yes … Aanh …!'

'Who was crying here just now?'

But Santa was still sobbing away, because immediately after he was born his mother had died.

The dawn hidden in the surrounding jungle, helpless in its eagerness to emerge, had now come out from behind the trees and guessing their intentions began running ahead of their motorcycle so that entering the village before them it could forewarn the village headman. The motorcycle was running at such speed that it seemed as if the riders did not need to reach anywhere; they were simply pursuing the dawn and so running on headlong.

'Bantaya!' The speeding vehicle on the unmetalled road had raised a lot of dust; therefore Santa stopped a little to pull the tail end of his turban towards his mouth, 'How has the village headman harmed us?'

'Oye, Santaya, what harm can that helpless man cause us?'

But Santa's confusion continued to increase: why, then, were they going to wipe off the village headman and his entire family? 'No Bantaya, just think …'

'You think too much; that is why you can't do anything.' Bantaya, heaven knows why, on seeing a few early morning white birds flying before him, held the motorcycle with his left hand and with his right held the gun … 'Dus-Da Dham-am- am!' In the blink of an eye many birds fell down together writhing in pain, and the motorcycle, continuously raising dust, sped on.

'Why did you shoot them down Bantaya!'

Banta, in the midst of triumphant chuckles, told him, 'It was just to set my aim; target practice, what else?'

'No, think about it and then reply.'

Banta wanted to warn him that it is the more sensible ones who are the first to come in the line of fire. He wanted to turn his head and speak his mind but because of the excessively fast speed of the motorcycle, he kept looking ahead.

'This village headman too, like you, was very sensible, that is why you are going to blow him off with bullets.'

But Santa was thinking that the village headman was a god-fearing Sikh, just like his maternal grandfather. In fact, he was such a decent man that one felt like standing before him with folded hands. His only fault was that, leaving all his work aside, he kept counselling all those who had gone astray. His maternal grandfather and grandmother also used to always keep counselling him and all others with great interest. Anyone who crossed their path felt as if he had been strained through a sieve, as if all the falsehood had been filtered. 'Listening time and again to their words all through my boyhood,' Santa thought, 'I had decided to don saffron clothes. Would I have roasted them too with my bullets had they been alive today?'

'No, Bantaya, let's turn back. I cannot lift my hand against the village headman.'

'Not to worry, stupid,' Banta said laughing, 'You stand guard and look around; I will do this work all by myself! There are only five people – the village headman, his wife, son, daughter-in-law, granddaughter; that's all!'

Santa reminded him that the village headman's daughter-in-law was carrying a life in her womb.

'Leave it; it will die crying in its mother's womb.'

'For heaven's sake, you are very cruel Bantaya!'

'Cruel? Why? I am merely carrying out the wish of God.'

'How's that?'

Banta said, 'It is like this: whatever is the wish of the entire gang, that is God's wish too.'

At this Santa protested, 'God is everyone's protector. How can He wish someone's killing?'

Banta was exasperated, 'Stop sermonising and quietly follow the order, otherwise you know what will happen.'

Santa really felt frightened but in such a way that he didn't realise that he was afraid, otherwise he would have scolded and chided himself and fallen in line. For a while, both kept sitting silently. In the meantime, their motorcycle went past a Gurudwara that was at a little distance from the headman's village. From the Gurudwara, words from the following devotional hymn could be heard:

'*At day break the light came, at day break the light came.*'

In the dim light around him, heaven knows what Santa suddenly saw but once again he sat up straight and addressed Banta telling him clearly that he would not let even a single hair of the village headman be harmed.

Banta's ears pricked to such an extent as if touching Santa's beard and this time he replied in a very angry voice, 'Listen you spineless effeminate, stop your nonsense, otherwise, before the village headman, I will have to wipe *you* off.'

Banta's harsh words raised Santa's temper to such a level all of a sudden that he lost his mind and throwing caution to the winds, just took out his gun and from behind fired at Banta; and on that flying vehicle both of them entangled with each other and fell on the ground; and on finding them unable to move from their place, at that very moment a monkey sitting on a tree, thinking God knows what, got down from the tree and picking up their guns from the unmetalled road, tip-toed away ghost-like into the thick jungle nearby and disappeared.

'No, Bantaya, no!'

Santa was trying to drag his broken bones towards his companion, still wanting to counsel him that they had not been following the straight path, 'God is one only Bantaya, the only one God, higher than all, the God of the whole world, Bantaya … No, don't speak, just think …'

And when after having thought long, the thread of Banta's breaths began to break then Santa with a great effort, gathering his broken breaths, spoke into his ear thus, 'Bantaya, many gods have put the human race on the wrong path!'

– Translated from the Hindi by Anita Samkaria

THE CULPRIT

JEELANI BANO

I wonder whether it was my eyesight that had weakened or was it the world that had changed so drastically?

Nisar would rub his eyes again and again. Everything was in disarray. Even familiar faces could not be recognised.

It was as dark as night. On waking up at night it would appear as though people were yelling or crying.

What kind of noise is this? Is some mob coming to attack us? Nisar woke up with a jolt.

'I can't hear anything. I can't understand why you are feeling so scared?' Amina said.

'Yes, I am feeling scared. I hope the door is closed. Have you shut the windows?' he sat up with a start. Once, when he had opened the window to see what was happening on the streets, the police had come into his house. 'Who started this?'

'You know perfectly well who the attacker is,' he wanted to tell the inspector, but didn't. These days one was scared to speak thus. It was possible that someone may perchance recognise him. If someone came and stood close beside him, his heart would begin to beat faster. Why did he stare at me? What is that young man hiding in his sling bag? Why did that car go ahead and then stop?

When there was rioting in my colony, Venkatesh called me. 'How are you Nisar? Is everything all right in your area? I just called to find out if you are at home or not.'

Why did Venkatesh call me so late in the night? Why did he want to know whether I was home or not? From what was being shown on television about the riots, it seemed as if he had instigated it. People were looking at him with hatred and wanted to seek revenge. No matter where the riots or who the people, Nisar always saw himself in the role of a culprit.

Each time he would leave the house, it was with the belief that something dreadful would happen that day. Maybe a bomb would explode in the office or he would be murdered. Maybe some terrorist would kidnap Maryam.

'Baba, if terrorists enter our house I will jump from the roof and die.' One day when he heard Maryam say this, he was much relieved.

'Listen Amina, the insurance papers are in the bottom shelf of the almirah. Sadiq has not yet returned the twenty thousand rupees. In my opinion Ahsan is the most suitable match for Maryam.'

But instead of sharing his anxiety, Amina worried about other things. 'There is no flour and curfew will be re-imposed in the evening.' She seemed more concerned about the lack of flour than about Nisar.

In the lab, Ashwini went on repeating just one thing. 'Everywhere everything is ruined.'

'I don't think so,' Nisar was emphatic. 'Until you and I don't change it, how can the entire environment be corrupted? Till now I have not heard of any person killing his friend.'

'Now look at me very carefully.'

Ashwini started laughing.

He mixed poisonous medicines in the lab and was now infusing poison in the entire lab. Anyway, the mood in the office was spoilt. Now when tea would be served in the staff room the camaraderie was missing. Everybody sat in silence. Someone spread the newspaper out in front of him. Another pretended he was searching for something in his briefcase. Time and again people looked up hopefully and then would be disappointed. It seemed as if everybody had lost something which they felt was impossible to regain.

Uff, it is so hot! I am sweating. It is so suffocating. Ashwini's words are tormenting everyone like drops of poison. And then silence also seems like a crime. Nisar cleared his throat and said to Venkatesh. 'Where had you gone yesterday during lunch hour? I waited for you till three o'clock.'

On hearing this, Venkatesh was scared. With trembling hands he placed the cup of tea on the table.

He lit a cigarette and in a subdued voice said, 'The doctor has advised me to stay off meat so I can't share your lunch anymore.'

'Really?' Nisar hung his head as if there was an addition to his list of crimes. When Venkatesh was talking to him, Ashwini was scrutinising him closely. This was the staff room of gazetted officers of the lab. They were all brilliant scientists who spread toxins and their antidote in the world. They travelled to all corners of the globe to attend high-level seminars. They were aware of the changing scenario of the world, but paid no heed to incidents like the one that occurred that night where twenty people had died and where the entire settlement had been burned down.

Dr Reddy pretends he is a Marxist. The President of the Qaumi Ekta Committee and Secretary of the Relief Fund he says that today the biggest criminal is religion. He makes fun of religious festivals. He says that religious slogans are poisonous weapons. But now even he is silent. He related how one day some miscreants in his locality threatened everyone that if they refused to participate in the Rath Yatra, they would be punished.

'Yes, I am suffering because of this. My wife is too scared to even step out of the house. My children don't go for tuition. I now have to drop Pinky to college.'

'I guess that is why you forgot to invite me for dinner this Diwali. However you remembered to send me sweets the next day,' said Nisar sarcastically.

'No, that's not correct.' Reddy held Nisar's hands in a warm clasp. 'It so happened that ... Okay, now get up. It's time to get back to work.' Everybody got up except Nisar. He continued sitting. It was only a half past ten but no one wanted to listen to Reddy. They immediately buried their faces in their files. They did not even lift their heads when Nigar sailed into the hall enveloped in a cloud of perfume.

Nigar was a piece of magnet to which everyone was drawn. The whole atmosphere in the lab seemed to take on the colours of her sari. The colour even permeated outside the window, all over the road and across the sky till it went and settled on the faces of the screaming and screeching housewives who lived enclosed in flats with shuttered windows. There it would fade. Today she laughed at something and listened intently to another. She laughed at someone's joke. She took a bite from someone's lunch box.

They would feel thrilled just by taking Nigar's name. Like young giddy college lads they would simply giggle loudly.

Nigar entered and looked around. Sensing the solemnity in the air, she stopped. Then she opened the door of her cabin and went inside.

Nisar noticed that instead of looking at Nigar, Ashwini had been staring at him. Frightened, he wiped his sweat and bent over the files.

It was curfew time and everyone was rushing out, briefcases in hand. Venkatesh emerged from the washroom, a huge red vermillion mark shining on his forehead. Venkatesh was Nisar's childhood friend. One day Nisar asked him why he had started applying a tilak on his forehead. Venkatesh replied that he had started going to the temple every morning. During the day he washed his face so often that the tilak would eventually be gone but today, just before leaving the office, he had re-applied it. Everyday Nisar would drop him to his house in Basheer Bagh.

'Okay, I'm off,' said Venkatesh.

Nisar looked at him and quickly gathered his files.

'No, you sit.' Venkatesh's abruptness left him stunned.

'I am not feeling well. I will visit the doctor.'

The hands that had been tying the files stopped midway. Nisar bent his head and started wiping imaginary dust off the table. Something has definitely happened, he thought. People are suspecting him and a very good friend like Venkatesh has left him alone and walked off. When we heard the news of the death of my uncle in the Aligarh riots, the entire neighbourhood was shocked. Everyone in the office was frightened as if he had been involved in the plot to kill his own uncle.

One evening when Raman and Raveena were playing in his lawn, he noticed that their maid forcefully took them away. When he went for a morning walk, Dr Narayan's daughter-in-law saw him and froze in her footsteps as if she was waiting for someone.

Nisar lifted his head and looked around. After Venkatesh's departure he seemed to have lost the strength to get up. The whole office had emptied out. As always, the door opened slowly and Anand, the peon entered. He looked intently at Nisar and then walked out. Nisar was alarmed. Why had Anand come into the office? What did he expect to see? Nisar all alone in the entire office … a lonely Nisar Ahmed … all alone!

Should I close the door from inside? How can I go out? How will I prove my identity? Curfew must have been imposed.

He started the car but there was no petrol. The petrol pumps had been closed for the past two days.

'Taxi, Taxi! Please stop, brother, drop me home. Take as much fare as you want.'

'No, sir,' said the taxi driver, starting his cab, 'At this time I cannot take the responsibility of dropping anyone home. In any case, I doubt whether you still have a home. You will unnecessarily make me drive around looking for it.'

'I do not have a home!' Wiping his tears, he joined the queue for the bus. Ahead of him were two burkha-clad girls. They were frightened on seeing Nisar. One old man, sensing their discomfort, asked them to move away.

Here also I am listed among criminals.

He was worried as no bus appeared. Riots must have erupted somewhere nearby. Firing could be heard. People started running away but there were a few who, like Nisar, were at a loss and who could not find solace anywhere. They just awaited death.

'This firing is taking place in Brahmwadi,' said a thirteen year old boy.

'Really?' Nisar was surprised. For many years he had been on the lookout for bullets. But he had not yet learnt to distinguish between Hindu bullets and Muslim bullets. But these poor kids of today, bitter experience had taught them a lot.

'Run along, if anyone is seen on the streets they will be shot at.' The police was warning everyone.

Nisar wanted to ask a policeman if they would really be safe within their homes. But then he too started running. After some time he realised that he was with those people who did not consider him one of their own. He had come to a place which was not meant for him.

'Go, go away from here.'

But where could he go? He was asking everyone, those who were seeking shelter, those who were watching the scene from tall buildings, and the lathi-wielding policemen.

The next day when he regained consciousness, he heard Amina speaking with someone over the phone, 'Yesterday he fell down unconscious. He has been suffering from depression and anxiety for the past several days. Oh, Venkatesh is also unwell? Please convey my regards to him.'

'What happened to Venkatesh?' Nisar sat up.

'His wife was saying that he is suffering from hypertension and has become very weak,' replied Amina as she handed him a glass of water and his medicines.

One week later Venkatesh came to visit him. He had indeed become very weak.

'Are you ill? You haven't even been coming to office. Everyone is worried about you.' His breathing was uneven as he sat on the sofa.

'First tell me about your health. You are looking very weak indeed.' Nisar looked closely at Venaktesh.

Venkatesh sat with his head bent. His hand trembled as he attempted to light a cigarette. He averted his eyes and in a troubled voice he said, 'I don't know what has happened to me. I feel scared all the time. You will laugh when I tell you that I am even scared of you.'

'Even of me!' It was Nisar now who hung his head.

'It seems as if everyone suspects me – as if I am a culprit.' Nisar's head remained bent.

Venkatesh's cigarette slowly turned to ash.

After a long time, Nisar picked up the packet of medicines lying on the table and held it out towards Venkatesh.

'Has Dr Singh prescribed these medicines for you?'

'Yes, exactly the same. Has he prescribed these for you too?'

Both hung their heads in unison.

– Translated from the Urdu by Bushra Alvi

ANOTHER GREAT WAR

RATAN SINGH

The war was like a war.

It was bigger than the First and Second World Wars.

No! This wasn't a war between two nations or two superpowers where borders get stained with human blood because of mutual enmity and Death begins to dance – in sheer happiness over its victory.

In those wars the earth gets drenched with the tears of life and the sky begins to shower rain as though it were weeping tears of blood.

This war was not a war between two emperors, but ...

This was a war between two beggars.

The problem was the same, as it was between the emperors.

The issue was of one's survival, to keep one's existence intact, to preserve the pride in one's ego.

In the same way that two countries sometimes come to loggerheads over some trivial issue, the root of their differences was also a petty issue.

As always, they had sat side by side to beg on the footpath. A man passing by had tossed a rupee coin into the bowl held in one beggar's hand.

The coin didn't fall into the bowl; instead it ricocheted off the rim of the bowl and bounced off and, as the beggar looked on, lurched its way along to the sheet spread in front of the other beggar.

The first beggar quickly stretched his hand to pick it up but by then the second beggar had picked it up and clasped it tightly in his fist.

And now they were looking at each other with hate-filled eyes.

The first one said that since the coin had been tossed in his bowl, therefore he had a rightful claim.

The second maintained that the coin had fallen not in the other's bowl but on his sheet, therefore it was his.

'But he dropped it in my bowl.'

'But it fell on my sheet.'

And in the way that war breaks out between the armies of two countries, a bitter battle ensued between the two.

But this war was not between two strong forces; it was a fight between two people who had been enfeebled by poverty.

You could call their scuffle a bid to overpower the other.

The filthiest of curses that they were heaping upon each other could be likened to the roar and thunder of guns and canons.

In these twin attacks there was such fire and so much smoke that their little world was being scorched.

They were breaking and scattering into little pieces but both were unwilling to withdraw from the battle lines. They were facing each other with the greatest determination.

'Let there be as much bloodshed as there has to be,' both were thinking. 'But that one rupee coin is mine. I will not give it up at any cost.'

When there is a war between two nations, the newspapers of both countries carry nothing except news of the war. So much so, that their news is broadcast by radio, television and newspapers all across the world.

As a result, a strange sort of ardour seeps into the people of the two countries. They begin to consider themselves oppressed and call the other oppressor.

But no one was turning to see the battle between these two beggars, whose worth was less than a zero when compared to the rest of the world; and zero by itself has no value.

And the person who had given the rupee in the first place, had long since moved on.

And those who were walking on the footpath were so engrossed in their own lives that the fighting beggars held no significance whatsoever in their eyes.

It is only the attacks of the 'big' people that have any significance.

And that is why they could see and yet turn a blind eye.

In any case, people try and avoid catching the eye of a beggar. They try not to even look in their direction for if, by mistake, the feeling of mercy rises within them they might have to lighten their pockets.

What is more, the other beggars who were sitting in a row on either side, too, were pretending not to notice anything.

It has been seen that among those engaged in the same business, if the shop of one is closed, the other benefits.

And indeed some good came of it. The pious who were coming out of the house of worship across the road gave alms and money to the other beggars, skirting the two who were fighting.

A rich man gave *halwa-puri* and savoury vegetables to all the beggars; he did not give any to the two who were fighting.

It so happened that, after some time, a long, sleek, gleaming car came and stopped beside the row of beggars. A rich man stepped out; he was fat and looked prosperous.

And he had a wife with him, as portly and wealthy-looking as he was.

The rich man held a wad of crisp new notes in his hand. He stopped before each beggar and placed five hundred-rupee notes in front of each one of them. No sooner had he placed the money, his wife would pick up a dhoti from the bundle of dhotis the servant accompanying them was carrying and keep it in front of each beggar.

Just as nations who are engaged in prolonged battles get poorer and poorer still and the rows of beggars become longer and longer in their cities, the same happened to these two beggars.

They, too, remained bereft of the largesse of the charitable rich man.

For the two who had become mortal enemies of each other – over one rupee – the immense tragedy of being bereft of the princely sum of five hundred rupees was akin to being bombed by an atom bomb such as the one that had fallen over Hiroshima and Nagasaki.

Longingly, they watched the rich man's car retreat into the distance and then, unable to bear the tragedy, fell back to fighting and grappling with each other till they fell so hard that they could not get up again.

No! The news of this tragedy did not appear in any local rag, forget any newspaper anywhere in the world.

And so I have written this story: so that the world knows the fate that befalls those who keep fighting amongst themselves.

Life turns its face away and moves on, leaving them behind.

And if you happen to belong to the lowest rung of the Ladder of Life then it makes very little difference whether you exist, or you don't.

– Translated from the Urdu by Rakhshanda Jalil

PIGEONS OF THE DOMES

SHAUKAT HAYAT

A flock of homeless pigeons was soaring high in the skies, swooping and constantly flying away. They would occasionally descend, anxiously and restlessly look for their home and, finding the old domes missing from their place, fly back in a state of despair. Their wings were exhausted with the continuous flying, and their eyes were bloodshot as if blood from the whole body had accumulated in the eyes, just about ready to boil over.

The neighbour's children were quite mischievous. When humans are forced to live in hen-coops and hens have the privilege of sauntering around in wide and expansive spaces, many serious issues need to be considered afresh. But then, children are what they are – whether they belong to apartments or to common suburban slums. They are so unruly. They make such noise, and create such a ruckus around the whole flat. But to create a ruckus, could they only think of his flat – the smallest one-bedroom unit in the largest apartment complex of the city, least suited for playing and fooling around? His carpet area was barely enough for a few people to just about breathe and simply twist and turn, only to keep breathing. The only silver lining in this otherwise closed hen-coop, which provided some comfort, was a small balcony, a large portion of which was decorated with a number of flower-pots containing a variety of plants of different species – rose, jasmine, zinnia, croton – all symbolising man's desire to live.

Deadbeat from the day's work, he would breathlessly climb up the stairs to the fourth floor of the elevator-less apartment and ring the doorbell to his flat, exhaustion writ large on his very being. His children would clasp and cling to him and try to climb on to his shoulders. 'You have not become "cultured" yet. Look at the other children, learn from them. See how they conduct themselves quietly – almost as if they don't exist. That, in fact, is their very identity!'

But when he would go and sit in the small balcony and get himself a cup of hot tea while his children were busy and silent, it would seem to him that he did not need anything else in life. Even paradise would not be more delightful, he would think. All his exhaustion would instantly disappear.

The builder had left the large peepal tree in the apartment complex intact. One of its branches stretched out towards his balcony. This collage formed by the peepal tree alongside a large mass of cement looked like a masterpiece of modern art. A flock of chirping sparrows would hover around the balcony and keep singing songs of the beauty of life. A naughty squirrel would run into the balcony, stare at the sparrows with a glint of mischief and make a hurried retreat to the peepal tree through one of its branches. There would be a distinct chill in the air. In this chill, the gentle warmth of golden rays would give the pleasure of a delightful harmony – far more pleasurable than the warmth of a cherished lover or a desirable beauty.

He would softly hum a song, 'Life, don't be so cruel. I've managed to acquire you putting everything I had at stake. I am in the quest for you.'

If you mix whiskey and beer, the bitterness of the concoction produces a jingling sensation in the mind which is very pleasurable. Your body and mind loosen and begin soaring in the skies. If you look from above, people walking on the ground appear dwarfed.

Strong winds started blowing. The leaves of the peepal began fluttering and young unripe fruit began falling from the tree … The chirping of the sparrows was making for an unusual treat to the ears.

The next-door neighbour was saying, 'This time the heat is not as scorching as last year. The days shall pass smoothly. The weather is fine. The desire to live continues. You live happily too. No problem.'

'All these children from the apartment! Could they find only my flat to crowd? Are they having a conference? Leaving all two-bedroom and three-bedroom flats, why did they have to gather only in a single-bedroom one? Everywhere the big fish is swallowing the smaller one. But what if all the small fish get together and transform themselves into one big fish?'

The television was on. Private channel programmes were running. On a milky screen, long centuries of history were, on their own, breathing their last on the brink of moments.

'Someone should explain to these children; do they intend to raise a storm in these hushed times? I just hope my buds, flowers, tulsi leaves and flowerpots are not damaged. I have put in a lot of effort in growing them. Listen – just look; never mind, forget it. A gentleman has to eventually suffer … Don't say anything … children are but children. Neighbour's children … even if they hop and jump, how far will they go?' he mumbled to his wife before going out on a long walk with his next-door neighbour, Sen Dada, the young man of sixty-two.

Dada was saying in Urdu, 'Yes sir, there is no cause for worry. Everything is normal. Uncontrolled actions do not sustain for long. Only by accepting the path of peace and stability can all of us lead a peaceful and happy life. I am finding a major difference from last year. The chronicler is writing about peace and solace.'

When with him, Sen Dada, an old-timer, would deliberately use difficult Urdu words.

Cars were moving on the street as usual. The familiar hustle-bustle on the street which is usually missing on holidays was missing that day too. The neighbour drew a long drag of his cigarette.

'Oho, why are you in such a mournful mood? I can understand you are anxious about the safety of your balcony and your plants and pots. Nothing will happen. All your pots will be safe. Now that we are going to meet friends, stop looking so sad. Enjoy yourself. Look at the shape and sharp protrusions of these round domes. Just look at them …'

'Dada, even at this age, you ...' he left the sentence incomplete.

While his heart was going through a dreadful state, engrossed in some other domes, Sen Dada was smacking his lips at the thought of groping soft and tender domes of flesh.

'Why discuss age. Always consider yourself young. This is life. To look at them and immerse into these colourful pictures … repeatedly immerse and emerge,' Sen Dada repeated. 'Young man, you have grown old in youth itself. Just look up and see …'

Sen Dada's grip on his shoulder tightened. In front of them were three stunning women, busy strolling like doves, chit-chatting among themselves.

'Sen Dada, you are engrossed in these birds. Just look up. A flock of homeless pigeons is continuously hovering around the sky. Look at the feelings of homelessness and turbulence evident in their restlessness, their home having disappeared after being so barbarically and brutally wrecked and ruined. Can you see the eyes of those pigeons? Can you feel the blood gushing down their eyes, their helplessness and the burning desire to somehow do something drastic?'

Sen Dada was absorbed in his own thoughts. Why would he need to look at the sky? He had the whole earth to himself; an earth on which there was no dearth of celestial splendour. He was one of those old men whose eyes sparkle with lust after their wives' deaths.

This reminds me – once when the guard informed us that a snake was spotted in the apartment complex, everyone went into a state of bewilderment. A red alert was declared in the entire complex. People couldn't sleep that night. Sticks and rods were borrowed from all over and collected. Doors and windows were locked. All eyes were keeping a vigil. With every moment there was fear that the snake might bite someone if the lights went out or if someone fell asleep.

He was only anxious that the squirrel and the flock of sparrows that visited his balcony might get scared away, and worried that the snake might bite them. God forbid, dark clouds began hovering around the beautiful collage created by his colourful flowerpots, squirrel and sparrows.

He picked up an iron rod and quietly went and sat in his balcony where the sparrows had made a small nest. Their chirping seemed like the sound of colourful bright fountains. He heaved a deep sigh of relief. In one of his hands was a three-cell torch.

His wife kept muttering, calling him names and ordering him to leave the balcony. She tried to scare him in different ways with the fear of snake poison but he did not pay heed.

Finally, he had to tell her that if she was so scared, she could lock the balcony door from inside. He would keep guarding the sparrows' nest.

For a long time his wife and children kept begging and pleading, declaring him crazy and stupid. But at no cost did he agree to be careless about the lives of those tiny sparrows.

They couldn't find the snake in any of the flats. All nooks and corners were combed and screened. Boxes and cupboards were thoroughly searched. Children are children, after all. For some time, they found the snake business an entertaining show. They were helping their elders with complete dedication. After a while, tired and exhausted, they went to sleep here and there. The elders kept awake throughout the night and, finally, by morning they had unanimously arrived at the conclusion that it was a rumour floated only to keep them harassed all night. Who had initiated this rumour? They began investigating. Finally, the apartment guard came to be suspected. It was his mischief. He was trying to evade his responsibilities.

With the gentle morning breeze were seen butterflies fluttering away towards flowers. Bumblebees also began hovering over the flowers. The flock of sparrows came out of its nest and flew off to collect food. When gentle and fresh sunrays touched his balcony, he felt that reasons to live were not yet dead.

'Dada, I am not enjoying this. Let's go back. I don't know what fate my flowers will meet. Those rowdy children don't seem to have the right intentions.'

'You are unnecessarily getting worried. They regularly get together in some flat or the other; this time it was your flat. After all, your own children are also amongst them. What's there to worry?'

'Dada, I don't know why but I am feeling uneasy. This flock of restless pigeons is creating a strange disconcert in my mind. Their peaceful home has been snatched away. Those tall domes have been reduced to dust. Where can these pigeons now go, Dada? Where will they seek refuge?'

'Young man, if you think positive, you will find that there's a home just about everywhere: in domes, on hill tops, in rocky caves, on branches of trees in dense forests – just be ready to endure the change in season. Toughen your skin, my friend,' replied Sen Dada.

He felt some strange sensations inside. On the one hand, he could hear celebrations galore with firecrackers and, on the other, a mournful elegy being played on a flute. After ages, that bizarre moment had simply frozen over a single point, from where streams of happiness and sorrow flow simultaneously, though ostensibly there was a perplexing silence all around which seemed to be the sign of an impending storm.

Sen Dada was oblivious to both sensations. His carnal senses had got the better of him. He was greedily eyeing the women in the households he was visiting. After having visited several, they reached Mr Thomson's. Mr Thomson was a hospitable man. He instantly took out a new bottle and kept some glasses on the table. His young housemaid, Miss Reza, was continuously helping with everything. She quickly took out some meat from the refrigerator, chopped it into pieces, fried it and offered the fried pieces to the guests. A spurt of sensation gushed through Sen Dada's body as he smelled the steam emanating from the hot meat. Mr Thomson had been drinking for a while and was already way too drunk. By now, Sen Dada was also quite tipsy. He couldn't stop himself.

As Miss Reza brought a plate of cashews, he touched her bare warm legs with his trembling fingers. Very lovingly, she took Sen Dada's hands in her own and kissed them with a certain sense of devotion. She then poured a peg for him and held the glass to his lips. For a moment, his old thirst was quenched and his heart found solace. The very next moment his craving and desperation were back. His blood pressure rose. Once again, his fingers began touching Ms. Reza's bare legs and creeping towards her thighs. For some time, Miss Reza kept still. There was simply no facial reaction. She did not raise any objection. As his fingers kept moving ahead, Miss Reza's eyes welled up.

Actually, Sen Dada reminded Miss Reza of her past. She got lost in her memories, reminiscing her childhood.

'My dear Reza, life is an endless sky … You have to go a long way … Very long,' her affectionate father had such dreams for her. She hugged her father and, with her tiny feet, climbed up his shoulders.

It was Mr Sen's resemblance to her father that had cast a spell on her and brought her close to him. Her father had already found his peace in his coffin.

Like a leaf drifting tossed about by the wind, having been to many places, she had finally found refuge at Thomson's who was known as a highly respectable gentleman of his area. She was forced to look happy and surrender herself to Thomson with a fake smile. She didn't have an option. She had changed many an avenue. On each one of them she had only found voracious red-eyed beasts, tongues hanging out. Then what was wrong with Mr Thomson? A neat and clean man who smelled good, at least his touch didn't physically repulse her.

Unmindful of what was going on in Miss Reza's mind, Sen Dada continued to be immersed in his own world of intoxication and pleasure. His eyes had begun lowering with passion. Miss Reza, even though she didn't want to, was standing close to him. Though drunk, Mr Thomson had assessed Sen Dada's intentions.

He was a generous man. He loved sharing his food and drink but didn't allow anyone to share his personal belongings. He looked angrily at Miss Reza. Miss Reza, who by now had developed sympathy for Sen Dada, was baffled. She picked up the empty plate and, wiping her tears, went off towards the kitchen, becoming invisible; so much so, that when her services were required, Mr Thomson had to shout out loud for her.

Whose grief was worse, he wondered, Miss Reza's or his own? A flock of cooing pigeons began hovering around his head. He admitted that worse than his grief was the grief of these homeless pigeons, who will now have to just keep suffering the painful ordeal of travelling all their lives. For generations they had been living in these domes. But now …

He was getting annoyed at Sen Dada and Mr Thomson's continuous drinking. 'Sen Dada says, "Young man, forget your sorrows. Enjoy." Can someone enjoy in this situation?'

From inside the house came the noise of falling utensils. A somewhat terrified Reza came out running, 'Uncle, a pigeon has entered the house. The neighbour's cat was trying to pounce on it. The pigeon has now hidden itself somewhere in the stack of utensils. With great difficulty I managed to shoo away the cat and shut the kitchen door.'

His heart skipped a beat. He first looked into Sen Dada's eyes and then at Thomson. Despite being drunk, they seemed to be disturbed about the pigeon. Their heads bowed, as if some disaster had struck. Just then someone knocked on the outer door.

'Mr Thomson, Mr Thomson!'

Sad and disturbed, Reza opened the door. It was their neighbour, Mr John.

'Miss Reza, call Mr Thomson.'

'What's the matter,' a drunk Mr Thomson came out taking heavy steps.

'My pigeon has entered your house. You know my mother-in-law has been ill for a long time. Nowadays her hands tremble. Doctor has prescribed pigeon meat soup. I was just about to slaughter the pigeon when it flew away to your house.'

'Yes, yes, it's hiding in my house. Miss Reza just reported to me … There's a cat as well who is after its life. Miss Reza, go, return his pigeon to him … Come, sit in the drawing room, Mr John. In the meanwhile, would you care for a drink?'

'No thanks. I only drink on weekends. The next day is off, you see. There's no hurry to get up early. This bloody thing makes me sleep a lot.'

After facing a thousand internal conflicts and defeats, the helpless Miss Reza had caught hold of the pigeon. He saw that her whole body was trembling. Mr Thomson heard her inner voice. For many days he had been hearing her talk similar things to herself. With silent eyes, she was muttering to herself, 'Loser, if you can't fight, run … fly away … run away from this habitation towards the boundless skies and jungles.'

But the petrified pigeon was busy hiding in her palms, shrinking and shrivelling. And when Mr John, profusely thanking them, extended his hand to catch the pigeon, it seemed that something literally jumped out of Miss Reza's inner-self. It was difficult to decide who was shivering more – the pigeon or Miss Reza. Or was it he who was trembling the most.

'Could this pigeon be …?' it suddenly struck him. Those homeless pigeons … Perhaps one of them, to provide warmth to the old lady's hands, had been captivated in an abattoir.

Miss Reza loosened her grip. She felt as if someone had jumped from inside and shrugged her hands. 'If you can't fight, at least run. Oh loser! Even this ability you have lost.'

The pigeon flew away and sat on the ventilating window. Mr Thomson gave her a tight slap. He was infuriated. Miss Reza was shell-shocked. He commanded her to place a stool on the table and catch the pigeon.

In an attempt to do so, she climbed the stool but it wobbled and Miss Reza fell down. Sen Dada moved forward to pick her up but, by then, Mr Thomson had already picked her up. Clinging to his chest, Miss Reza was trembling. Both of them got up.

'We'll take our leave, Mr Thomson. Your company was most enjoyable.'

'But this gentleman seems so depressed, he didn't enjoy at all.'

Sen Dada affectionately placed a hand on his shoulder, though he was constantly looking sideways at the endlessly trembling Miss Reza.

'His sadness is understandable. But what's the point of being sad all the time; it would have been fine had it provided a solution. I brought him over in the hope that indulging in alcohol will cheer him up. But watching the cat and pigeon drama here, he has become even more depressed. Never mind ... You were far too generous. Thank you very much for your warm affection.'

Before leaving, Sen Dada gave Miss Reza one last complete look. Even in her terrified state, she looked stunning. 'Bye bye, Reza. Bye, Mr Thomson. Good night.'

That day they had visited a number of friends. Everyone had avoided talking about the most fateful event of the day. In their heart of hearts, people were either crying or laughing.

People were either in a state of helplessness or a state of happiness – handling it in their own way. But despite these states of mind and oblivion, there was one question bothering everyone, 'What will happen now? What is going to happen in the future?'

He was fed up. He had also indulged at Thomson's. But, far from getting drunk, he didn't even feel high. Every now and then he would just think about the plants in his pots, his balcony and the crowd of children. He found himself caught in a strange uneasiness all the time.

After enjoying to his heart's content with all his friends in that neighbourhood, Sen Dada finally decided to go back. He was staggering. A rosy intoxication had riveted his very being. Reza's momentary intimacy had filled him with a strange sense of pleasure and ecstasy.

But he was still conscious enough to know that he had to take care of his companion, to reassure him of the safety of his flowers, plants and pots. Throughout their return journey, he kept cajoling and coaxing him, 'Don't worry, my child. Everything will be all right.'

At the gate, the apartment guard let them in. There was silence all over. Had he not held Sen Dada on the stairs, he would have stumbled and fallen. On the third floor, with immense difficulty, he took out the keys from Dada's pocket, opened the lock and made him enter his flat.

After having ensured that Dada had fastened the latch from inside, he left towards his own flat. His legs were trembling while climbing the stairs, his heart quivering with an unknown fear.

On the doorbell being rung, when his wife opened the door, her eyes seemed swollen; as if she had been crying for a long time.

'How are my flowers doing?'

'Go and see for yourself …'

The children were fast asleep on their beds. Their faces seemed tormented; as if they had been watching a very scary and painful dream. After all, his fears had come true. All the blood in his veins seemed to have dried up.

As soon as he opened the balcony, its wrecked and ruined state gripped him. Nipped flowers, crushed petals lay scattered over the mosaic floor … Broken pots and mounds of mud all over … Broken straws of sparrow-nests … And the sparrows not to be seen anywhere … The squirrel, the butterflies and the bumblebees were unlikely to be seen for a long time now … The entire beauty of his balcony had been ruined.

'Finally, everything I had, in their game these children have …'

His suspicion came true. The other day, some children had caught hold of the snake that had entered the apartment complex and, by now, had become used to the dangerous game of playing with it. That is why they had become so venomous and barbaric.

Up above, the flock of those warm-blooded pigeons from the domes was continuously hovering around in search of a home, desperate to say something, to just speak out.

When he finally managed to look at his wife, he suddenly realised that there was a corpse lying in the house and, to bury it in this state of curfew was going to pose a serious problem.

– Translated from the Urdu by Saif Mahmood

HYSTERIA

KHALID JAWED

Outside a dog was barking loudly. Probably that is what woke him up. It seemed as if he had just fallen asleep. It was a cold December night. He could hear the terrifying sounds of conflicts raging outside. He pulled away the quilt from over his head. There was complete darkness in the room, but he could grope his wife's bedside. He was familiar with her light snoring sounds which meant that a major part of the night was still left and that there was still time till daybreak. Even in her old age, his wife would wake up quite early, and it is common knowledge that the aged cannot sleep till late in the morning. He himself would wake up early. For the past few years, he had been regularly going for morning walks, but after he suffered a mild attack, he had difficulty in walking as his body would lose balance. Even though he could walk with some effort, his gait appeared awkward and rickety. Even his handwriting and speech were severely affected and had become shaky and incoherent. Actually it was a small accident. Four years ago, he was a prominent journalist, and had a reputation of uncompromising fidelity for the highest ethical standards. However, the changing ethical standards of journalism deeply pained him for this had robbed the profession of its gentle connect with humanism. Subsequently, he spoke passionately in the seminar. He already had high blood-pressure and due to his age and condition, it was not advisable to speak so vehemently and with such anger.

He became intensely emotional in the seminar, and spoke vigorously about the degrading values in journalism as evident in the mindless publication of five newspapers in a small town. He then raised a strange question. Why does man need to know? According to him, man should aspire to be well-educated rather than be well-informed. Some people found his words comic or maybe his facial expressions appeared comic. Certainly, with age, his frail body shook while he spoke animatedly, which amused some people. Anyway, whatever it was, as soon as the sentence ended, everyone attending the seminar laughed loudly. Soon, the contagious laughter spread to the entire hall, so much so that a young journalist passed a snide remark. Then his face turned red, his body began shaking violently, and he fell down.

After three months of hospitalisation, his life was saved, but a blood clot had formed in his brain. An operation could remove it, but at his age it was risky and moreover, there was no guarantee of a complete recovery after the operation. Nevertheless his life was saved. The only effect was that his speech was incoherent. Often he would forget things and names of people or would call them by wrong names. While walking he could not maintain balance, and would walk inside the house using the walls as support.

But, despite all this, he had not forgotten either his name or his profession. Even now he would write articles on current affairs. He would often lose direction while writing and become incoherent. His articles were politely put in the dustbin by the editors. He had also not forgotten his wife, who had remained by his side, even though she could have left for America along with their two sons. Both his sons were in America along with their wives since long. They had almost lost touch with their parents. In response to their mother's letters, sometimes one of the sons would make a telephone call of two and a half or three minutes. Recently, this also had not happened.

On peering out of the quilt, he could feel the chill.

'I had fallen asleep just now,' he thought. Then he felt something cold under him near his thighs. He could feel the clammy inside of the wet and cold quilt mingled with its warmth.

It is urine, he thought irritably.

'Listen, it has again come out … urine has come out.' He called out loudly to his sleeping wife. He would stutter while speaking and often the slippery phlegm in his throat would make his voice unrecognisable even to his wife. But that tone of fear and helplessness in his voice would immediately alert her and she would attend to him. Cautiously, she would try to understand his words. At that time she was asleep but hearing him, she woke up with a start.

'What happened?' she said as she got up.

'Urine … urine has come out,' he spoke slowly.

She switched on the light.

'It's extremely cold,' she muttered. Then, coming near, she pulled out a dirty bit of sheet from under him, which was completely wet. Throwing it aside on the floor, she pulled out another dry and clean piece of cloth and wiped his lower body with it.

'Do it quickly … I am feeling cold,' he said shivering.

'Be patient … I will keep another cloth underneath. How many sheets and mattresses can I change? During these days you should get that pipe fitted. In winters it becomes quite problematic,' she grumbled.

Since last year, he had been suffering from weak bladder control, and often urinated involuntarily while getting up or sitting. To avoid further hassle, the doctor had suggested catheterisation.

During those days, when he had the catheter, he had found a new engagement. A plastic bag used to hang from the foot of his bed, which carried markings of a measuring scale. Usually the capacity of the plastic bag is two litres, while the urine collects in it drop by drop. He would keep watching this process while lying on his side. It had almost become his quirky habit.

'Let me check the amount now,' he would keep watching it intently. He would often ask his wife,. 'Check it. I can't see it clearly. How many millilitres is it?' His wife would get irritated.

'No … I was thinking … compared to yesterday, is it less or not.' Concerned, he would bend over to check the reading on the urine bag. On days when there would be less urine in the bag, he would be depressed and ask his wife for more water.

The biggest advantage of the catheter was that the bed and the clothes would not get wet. Holding his urine bag he would walk slowly towards the bathroom or reach the chair in the veranda. But all the time his interest and focus would remain on the urine output. But this catheter could not be put beyond twenty to twenty-two days. His blood sugar was also a bit above normal. That is why any injury was best avoided. The doctor had to remove it after the fixed period.

When his wife was wiping his weak and thin legs with a towel, he was reminded of his elder son. Just like this, this new born baby would lie next to him on the bed, while she would clean him with a towel rubbing his legs and thighs. The shape of the lower part of his body and legs resembled that of his father. For a moment his wife paused to take a long look at his face, and he felt at that moment his face contort as if he was about to weep, just like his son who, on such occasions, would frown and cry with his mouth wide open.

'Sometimes you should turn on the other side as well. You keep lying on one side. This can cause bedsores … wounds on your body.' She told him while turning him on his side. While doing so she felt a slight stench emanating from his body. She spotted a whitish pink patch on his hip. This was a bedsore and she knew how dangerous it could be. She had seen patients with bedsores, who had been bedridden for long or had not been cleaned properly, to an extent that they had become septic and infested. More often than not these bedsores had proved fatal.

'Have a bath tomorrow,' she spoke softly covering him with the quilt.

Outside, the wind was blowing, banging the door of the room loudly.

'Now keep lying on this side,' she instructed him and switched off the light on her side of the bed. She had also become quite weak and winters were harsh on her lungs. At that time also her breathing was heavy, as she worried over her aged husband lying on one side, and the bedsore not healing.

But the problem was somewhere else. His bed was set along the wall of the room and next to the bed was a small round table, on which were piled up papers, mostly old newspapers, books and pens. The light bulb was placed at such an angle that its light fell on the table, enabling him to read and write only towards the table. His own shadow would block the light preventing him from reading or writing anything. He could only stare at the wall which, with its dirty paint and broken plaster, formed a canvas of shapeless forms, and scared him. Hence, he would again turn his side. Furthermore, lying on this side was more comfortable for him and he could sleep.

He had not slept. When his wife retired to her bed he opened his eyes wide in the dark room. He could see nothing. There was complete silence outside. But then the siren of a police van from afar passed by, highlighting the dreadful night. Presently the country was passing through a bad phase. The city was under curfew. All night the CRP patrolled the city and police sirens blared.

A sound came from the terrace. Since past few days a wild black cat had been frequenting their house and would often lie all day in his room. At night she would roam atop the terraces and awnings. Sometimes, due to extreme cold or fatigue, she would return and scratch the door with her paws or mew meekly to gain entry, and wake them up. His wife would get up and open the door. Now also it was the cat. He heard the sound of her paws scratching the door.

'Listen … she has come,' he almost shouted. Often he could not keep the link between his words, tone and voice. Sometimes when he wanted to say something softly, his tone would get high pitched.

'Open the door … she has come.' He said it again loudly. He was getting irritated with himself because he had suddenly forgotten who was coming.

'She is a nuisance … this cat has forced herself on to us,' his wife grumbled. But not getting up was also not an option for she had a soft corner for animals.

'Open … open the door,' he shouted.

'For God's sake … speak softly.'

On opening the door, two bright glassy eyes fixed themselves on the dark walls of the room.

'Switch on the light,' he said it in a manner that only his wife could understand.

'Why … it is only 1.30 a.m.'

'I want to read,' he said in an emotional tone and then turned towards the table. For a moment, the wife paused, and then switched on the light. Then she turned to look at him. He was staring at her. But she knew when he gazed like that he was actually not looking at anything. The cat squatted under the bed, while his wife returned to her bed.

Now he was lying on his side and his eyes were on the newspapers piled on the table. There were pictures of three domes amidst thick trees, where they stood quietly, thinly covered by moss and grass. At a distance, a river gushed along her deserted banks. There were some dried red marks on the picture, but the newspaper was folded at places and the only legible word was 'skeleton.'

'Skeleton … what do these idiots know about skeletons,' he said this in a weak and shaky voice even though his uneven breath and facial expression revealed the intensity with which he wanted to utter these words.

'Are you not feeling sleepy today?' Bored, the wife enquired.

'Listen … I had written this article to open the eyes of those idiots,' he said picking up a bundle of papers from the table.

'Why are you tiring yourself unnecessarily … show some concern for your ailment! You bother yourself needlessly. This article of yours was returned a month ago with regrets and marked non-publishable.' The wife said in a counselling tone, which carried an element of sympathy, but probably this is what he hated the most.

'They are donkeys … non-publishable … because I am writing only the truth … do these illiterates even know what a "skeleton" is … Listen, you listen to … what have I written.'

His face was flushed and his breathing was heavy. He paused to control his breath. Then he shifted closer to the edge of the bed, propped himself on his elbow and cupping his face in his palm, began reading from that bundle. His face was cupped in his palm in such a way that his cheek and half of his lips were pushed towards the ear, because of which his voice sounded different. His wife found his voice extremely pitiful.

'Regarding the skeleton, a human skeleton has 206 bones. Other animals can have a different count of bones. It is the skeleton that provides motion to a body. Not only this, actually the skeleton gives form to the body and more importantly, it is inside the bone-marrow that red blood corpuscles are produced. Regarding the bone count, the skull has a total of fourteen bones and the face has eight types of different bones. However, some experts are of the opinion that this count is like this … that from the arms till the shoulders and the fingers, there are thirty-two bones …' Now he was explaining the minutest details of a human skeleton. His wife was watching him with pity. She had read this article once and had found it incoherent. Further, the article mentioned the different kinds of skeletons ranging from crawling creatures to birds of flight, followed by a detailed listing of the different types of bones in each. Then the article suddenly moved on to a study of history and architectural styles of different periods. Midway, he began discussing linguistic theories and concepts regarding words and language. She started feeling drowsy.

'The fossilised remains of skeletons are aiding the study of life forms on earth.' He stopped reading, he was getting breathless and his hand, which was bent at the elbow, had lost sensation due to the cold. He slowly removed his hand from his face. With this his head dropped heavily onto the pillow. Then he began moving his hand slowly in the air. His blood circulation returned, causing discomfort, and made him clench his teeth. The bundle of papers had slipped from his other hand and fallen on his chest. His wife was lying on her side with folded legs and was probably sleepy.

'There were times when snails, sea grass and jelly fish swam in the waters with no bones, but then the time came when vertebrates arrived and engulfed all life.' While reading he suddenly shouted, as if annoyed while conversing with someone. His wife was startled and sat up in her bed.

'Why are you shouting? Neither will you sleep peacefully nor will you let me do so.' She was extremely annoyed, and began rubbing her eyes with her hands. But he did not even look at her. Now he began reading the article as if he was whispering it in someone's ear. His wife was quietly watching him. While reading, his voice again became loud.

'Simple life forms and complex bony animals evolved over a long period, but the evolutionary journey was accomplished after all.' Now he was reading in a much lowered voice as if what was being read was not of much importance. He continued reading in this tone for a while and then suddenly his tone became excited. His weak chest again felt breathless.

'There is not much of a difference between men and monkeys, except that the monkey is dancing to the tune of its keeper and his ridiculous depressive face makes some people laugh. Possibly, it could be a sign of dejection of having lagged behind man in the evolutionary process or the sadness of having a crooked thigh bone, preventing him from walking erect like man.'

'Oh for God's sake keep quiet now! Calm down,' the wife said troubled.

He looked at his wife with blank eyes and cleared his throat loudly. His throat felt very dry. He tried to wet it by collecting saliva in his mouth. While turning over the next page, he once again glanced at his wife in the same manner and continued reading loudly.

'What is the connection between the humans atop the dome, the snails swimming in the ocean and the monkeys on the trees? Actually, this issue needs to be resolved on a priority basis.'

His wife took a long breath and changed her side. Now that she was not looking at him, his voice seemed to have become laden with an intense pain and hurt; it resonated among the moving shadows on the walls of the room. She felt restless.

The wife again turned towards him.

'Listen … read the rest of it tomorrow. You should also sleep, please,' she pleaded.

'After dispelling misconceptions and doubts about the skeleton, it is imperative to clear the issue concerning the construction of architectural styles. In this regard, I am of the opinion that … that …' He paused for a moment. Outside, a police van zipped past blaring its siren. He kept aside the bundle of papers and began opening and closing his fist. Holding the papers aloft for so long had strained his hand. He flipped the page and glanced at his wife, before returning to his article again.

The wife closed her eyes feeling helpless. She realised that now he would not sleep before finishing the article. The sound of the cat licking her fur could be heard from under the bed. Both these sounds, of the cat's licking and his reading the article, merged for a while. Later, only his voice gradually sounded like a lullaby to his wife and her eyes became heavy with sleep. It seemed as if the light in the room had been switched off.

'In India, the Muslims introduced the dome, minarets and the arches. They knew the art of constructing arches, and hence did not require pillars. Architecture is a reflection of innate qualities. All constructions are basically brick, mortar, lime and mud. Construction is, in fact, embedded in every particle of mud. Sometimes it reveals itself and sometimes it vanishes within the folds of mud and its particles. Construction is defined by its styles and forms. The point is to change from "formlessness" to "form."' He turned the page. His wife was drowsy and her heavy breathing indicated that she was about to start snoring. He ignored her and began reading as if he was before an audience.

'We should see things in their actual form. Words have relative connotation. Hence truth cannot be expressed through words and dialogue. I advise the government, lawmakers, sociologists and historians to keep this aspect always in mind that all conflicts and discords in this world are merely an outcome of mistakes of language, its expression and loosely understood meaning of descriptive words. A connection has always existed between clarity and confusion, which has often clouded our perception.'

Suddenly he felt a strange bitter taste in his throat. He was drooling, and wiped the saliva with the sleeve of his shirt carelessly. His wife was snoring.

This time, he began reading almost smiling to himself.

'As far as our poets and scholars are concerned, after this catastrophe, there is only one aspect that can become the topic of their interest. For instance, if they can visualise it … when a four hundred and fifty years old mud had descended forcefully on the earth, then what a terrifying sound must have resonated. And the life forms hidden in that mud would have been displaced and scattered and would be desperately searching for alternatives, which has now become their fate. The river banks must have become even more terrifying and bewildering. It is also worth pondering that now the sun would have altered its presence there. The sunlight would fall in different patterns now and the wind would blow differently, so much so that the surrounding trees would sway or maybe stay still. Nothing can be said regarding this with certainty.'

He paused and suddenly began feeling extremely cold. It was then that he realised that his writings lacked coherence and connectivity. His thoughts were not being penned at all. They appeared illogical. What he wished to write was the 'truth.' He had lost direction while penning it down. What he had written in the article was also the truth but was bereft of words and language, and was relative in nature. He also realised that it was useless to look for any coherence or substance in these disjointed writings.

He felt lost but the very thought of finding the missing link and coherence caused him extreme mental stress and agony. An intense depression engulfed him. He felt feverish. He quietly lay down and pushed aside the bundle of papers sadly. Sleep overtook him. The yellow light of the bulb began hurting his eyes. He covered his face with the quilt but the frayed quilt could not stop the light. He tightly closed his sleepy eyes.

Sleep that is induced under the glare of a light differs from that induced in darkness. The former has a restlessness about it and is filled with depressive images.

He dreamt that he was standing with his school bag in a corner of his ancestral home.

'Go change your shirt as evening is approaching and the call for *maghrib* is about to be sounded. You must pray for passing your exams,' his mother said while caressing his head with her hand.

He stepped out from the corner and stood in the deserted but large courtyard of that dilapidated house. There was a guava tree in the courtyard, on which the evening was fast descending. It was then that the call for *maghrib* came from the nearby mosque. His mother covered her head with her white dupatta. She began feeling a strange purity in her heart.

He was running fast on the road. There was a red rubber ball before him but then that ball disappeared. He saw himself standing before his mother like a culprit.

'Now prayer is compulsory for you and you don't even know how to perform the ablutions. Go and do the ablutions. Begin by pledging your intention of undertaking the ablutions for seeking God's benevolence and blessings.'

His face and hands began getting wet with cold water.

'Yes now wet one-fourth of your head and after washing your feet till the ankles, get up.'

He got up. He felt fairer than before.

'Now start the prayer. Do you remember it?' In a large veranda of three arches, a prayer mat was lying in a relatively clean corner. Large cobwebs were hanging on the walls of the veranda.

'No, first you pick me up in your lap,' he insisted.

'No, grown up children do not sit in the lap.'

'No … first you take me in the lap,' he yelled again.

Those soft arms reached out towards him and picked him up on her lap. All around there was light. His mother's soggy clothes smelt of the aromas emanating from the kitchen.

'I am seeing your heart is not in the prayer. Good children don't do this. God gets annoyed. What is your problem in praying?'

Mother's voice was angry but her face was not visible.

'My knees get bruised,' he said fearfully.

'Idiot … Ask Allah's forgiveness otherwise you will face His wrath,' Mother shouted loudly and began beating him with both her hands.

Suddenly, the sky is filled with colourful kites and he steps outside the house gazing upwards. But moving on, he finds himself inside the local mosque and starts praying along with everyone else. While praying, his attention is caught by his feet repeatedly, those black feet with large veins and a shapeless big toe … uneven, overgrown nails with dirt under them. He forgot the prostration. Everyone else was in prostration, only he was staring at his ugly feet in shame. A stormy blast blew across and threw him out of the mosque.

Now he was lying on top of a heap of garbage and dirt and was without any clothes. He was extremely embarrassed and despite his utmost efforts could not get up. Before him were three high domes of the mosque, graceful and pure. He began staring at those domes but soon felt the flesh from his face melt away and fall off.

Now he was no more, only a skeleton was left. Only teeth, bones and the eye sockets in place of eyes were left. Who had emerged from inside him? Probably, he screamed loudly but the sound got stuck in his throat. He was very thirsty.

Suddenly, this scene also changed. He found himself lying on a worn-out cot covered with a white sheet. Both his toes had been tied together tightly, due to which he seemed the same from head to toe, absolutely straight. His cot was lying in front of a mosque. This was a small brick mosque, the domes of which had holes in many places, covered with weeds, which some wild birds were pulling out with their beaks. A huge bare field surrounded it. He was sitting on the broken stairs of this mosque, dejected and depressed. His dead body was kept in front. Then, from somewhere, men dressed in white wearing caps, arrived and stood there.

Then, one of them, probably the Imam, came and stood near the head of the dead body. The rest of them stood in rows and began praying for the departed soul and its redemption.

Now it was evening. Again the day and night were meeting. The sun was setting and darkness was descending. At that moment, far away the sound of dumping of garbage could be heard. Again, the earth shook. Now, he was all alone and at his wits' end in that vast field. Now, there was no mosque nor his dead body or those people. Then, he heard the call for prayer from afar, a strange sad voice. Along with the call for prayer, he saw the clear shining face of his mother. Crying loudly he began grasping her.

'What is it? … You are ranting … get up,' his wife woke up on hearing his dreadful sounds. She was awake and he was trying desperately to sit up. His quilt had fallen off and he was shivering.

'What is the matter? Why are you getting up?' His wife came to him almost running.

'Nothing … I will pray,' he said and looked at his wife as if at a stranger. In fifty years of marriage she had not seen such a look in her husband's eyes. Completely alien, absent and detached. The look in his eyes terrified her.

'Have you ever offered prayer in your entire life?' she enquired while covering him with the quilt. Then she realised he was feverish.

'Oh! You have such a high fever and you have not covered your head. Keep your head inside the quilt,' she said while covering him.

'I will offer prayer. The call for prayer has been given,' he pleaded.

'Call for prayer … it is night now. If you are restless, I will get some warm milk,' his wife said, sounding worried.

'I will offer prayer,' he said this as if he had not heard his wife at all. For a moment his wife was terrified and apprehensive. Due to his fever he is talking nonsense, she thought and prayed for the morning to come soon. The night seemed unbearable. She was feeling cold. She switched off the light and lay in her bed.

He was lying quietly with eyes closed. It was true that except in his childhood, he had not offered any prayer in his lifetime. He had never been attached to religion ever. As far as he could remember, during his childhood whenever he offered prayers he would pay more attention to comparing the feet of others, than to the prayer itself.

When it was dark in the room again, he removed the quilt from over his head and began staring into the darkness. He was remembering his mother passionately. Momentarily, he imagined himself as a small boy and turning on the other side spread out his arms wide to embrace his mother. Both his arms hit the dark wall and fell on the bed. His eyes welled up with tears. His body was burning with fever but his feet were ice cold. He closed his eyes tightly and his tears rolled down into his unkempt beard.

A dog was barking outside. This time, instead of a police siren, he heard the whistle of a distant train carried across by the wind.

Winds have their own sixth sense, which allow them to understand the fleeting time and change accordingly. The wind blowing outside had lost its vigour and was now blowing intermittently, as if tired and dejected. This meant that the night was almost over and daybreak was near.

Suddenly, he sat up feeling restless. Far away the call for the *fajr* could be heard.

'I will offer prayer,' probably he wanted to say it aloud but his voice failed him. Then he realised that he had been unclean for so long. He should bathe first, he thought.

Pushing aside his quilt with his feet he tried to raise himself up by holding the sides of his bed.

At last he sat up. Then, he lowered his shaking legs on to the floor and supporting himself with the wall, stood up.

Being in one place for so long has its advantages. He could find his way to open the door in that darkness. On opening the door, a blast of cold air entered the room. His body shivered and set his teeth chattering, which bruised his tongue. A trickle of blood flowed out on to his lips and chin.

Now he could not move without support. His body was shaking and it was impossible to control it while standing. Compelled, he sat down on the floor and began crawling on all fours. The cold floor was hurting his hands, knees and heels. After ages, his knees were moving today.

The bathroom was not far from the door. The cat had come out from under the bed. His wife had had a disturbed night and was fast asleep.

He crawled into the bathroom. He silently repeated the three steps of bathing in his heart. Splash water all over the body, cleanse your mouth with water and clean the nose.

First of all he had to splash water all over his body. He reached the tap by guessing the right spot and opened it. Icy water began flowing from his head towards his feet. Vapour formed over his feverish body. His sickly aged and weak body drenched with icy water became listless. He felt a sudden pain in his chest. Lifeless, he fell headlong on the bathroom floor as if in prostration.

– Translated from the Urdu by Sameena Hasan Siddiqui

A LIFE IN TRANSIT

NOOR ZAHEER

She had never felt so angry with herself. Not that she hadn't taken many wrong decisions in her life and paid many a times for her stupidities and her inability to smarten up. But never before had she felt so desperate as to want to bang her head against the wall. She knew she had made a huge mistake this time. Why did she answer that man; what did he say his name was? She recalled it now, yes, his name was Shyam Bihari Garg. How could she have swallowed his bait? Why couldn't she have kept her mouth shut when he goaded her? What had she gained in the end by tangling with him? Why had she even bothered to go to the party? After all, she is as lonely today as she was before Soumya came, perhaps even more so.

Perhaps none of this would have happened if Soumya hadn't been here.

Shabnam was almost forty when she had finally managed to save enough money to buy a small flat and leave behind her nomadic life of having to move every two or three years from one rented place to another. Twice she had failed in her quest for a life partner and so was single. She had never listened to her relatives, even as a child, and when they advised her to buy her flat near Jamia Millia Islamia or in Nizamuddin, she had laughed it off. Most of her neighbours here were Hindus. Two families were Sikh and one was Buddhist from the north-east. The colony had a temple where *aarti* was performed morning and evening. But that did not seem to be enough and idols had been placed under the old, majestic peepal tree in the park, which everybody called Joggers' Park, and you could see a clay lamp burning there on Saturday mornings. After some time, a Hanuman temple also got built, and a large and noisy procession was carried out to celebrate the installation of the idol. One evening, on her walk, Shabnam noticed clay lamps burning under every big and small peepal and banyan tree. A couple of them even had a red *chunri* tied around them and flowers lay around their roots. Not being a religious person herself, this over the top religiosity of her neighbours had made her laugh.

It was a very hot day when she came with all her possessions in a tempo to move into her flat. Her next door neighbours had given her a drink of water twice. Their young son had come out to help with the heavy pieces of furniture. And when she came back with her groceries, they put her milk in their fridge so it wouldn't spoil while her own fridge kicked in. The people living on the floor below came up on their own to give her ice cubes and kept insisting that she join them for dinner.

Alas, such solicitousness lasted only until she put her nameplate on the door. All the seven flat owners in the building became so quiet then, as though they had seen a ghost. She was the same Shabnam. Then what had changed because of her religion? Anyway, Shabnam was used to such sudden bouts of indifference. And she believed that if she continued to behave normally with her neighbours, then at least half of them would warm up to her. In any case, where did she have the time for friendship? She came back from school around four, did her household chores and then sat down to prepare her lessons for the next day.

Shabnam had bought the flat on the top floor for two reasons. For one, the flat on the third floor was the cheapest; second, the roof above was included. Shabnam had put up flowerpots on the roof soon after moving in. Gradually, the roof had turned a pleasant green. After the summer, the flowering plants were laden with flowers. But soon, the flowers started to disappear. Early in the morning, she would often hear footsteps on the roof. She thought it was a kid trashing her roof garden. One day, she quietly followed the footsteps on the roof and found two women plucking all the freshly opened buds. They laughed embarrassedly when they saw her. Shabnam had also smiled and said, 'One should always ask before taking something that belongs to someone else.'

One of them had replied with a confident demeanour: 'It is for the puja, ji, for God.'

'Oh, I see, one doesn't need to ask permission if one is taking them for God?'

The woman's voice was edged with anger when she said: 'Everything is God's. That is what our religion teaches us.'

'Then why come so early, like a thief hiding in the dark?'

She had got really incensed then: 'How dare you call it theft when it is for God? You say it because you are a *vidharmi*.'

Shabnam had raised her voice too. 'You don't have a problem with taking a *vidharmi's* flowers to offer to your God.' She had wanted to ask them not to pluck all the flowers. That God didn't want them to plunder the whole garden. But before she could say all this, the two had thrown their polythene bags full of flowers on the ground and muttering to themselves, had climbed the parapet to their side of the roof.

Gradually, some of the neighbours began to say 'Hello.' After all, she was a Class 12 teacher in a prestigious public school and this raised her status in some eyes. One day, Mrs Gupta from the flat below hesitatingly spoke to her about her daughter's 10th class board exam. 'She is weak in maths and her whole career depends on this board exam.'

The news about Shabnam coaching the girl had spread like wildfire within the colony. Other children started to come. Shabnam made some money taking tuitions and now her time did not sit so heavy on her. The neighbours now were nicer but none of them visited her or invited her to their homes.

Then Soumya got a great job in Delhi. Soumya, Shabnam's childhood friend, great socialite, chartered accountant. Laughter sat on her lips. Shabnam's best friend Soumya. Where else could she live except with Shabnam until she got her own flat from her company? Meeting after four years, Shabnam and Soumya's first evenings were spent catching up: memories of hostel life, whereabouts of old friends and so on and so forth.

The fifth evening Soumya asked her bluntly, '*Yaar*, what is the matter? Your neighbours don't drop in at your place or invite you to theirs?' Shabnam had tried to pass it off: 'What can one do? That's how they are.' She had quietly gathered the teacups and walked away towards the kitchen, but Soumya being Soumya, followed her there. 'They give me weird looks.'

'Well, you are so pretty. Why won't men ogle?' Shabnam had tried to make a joke of it.

'I am not talking about that kind of looking. They open their doors just a chink to examine me as I pass by, as though to figure out what sort of a creature I am. This morning Mrs Gupta couldn't help herself and asked me.'

Shabnam's teacup slipped from her hand and fell into the sink. 'What did Mrs Gupta say?' Shabnam knew that Soumya got very upset with anything smelling of communalism. She feared that Soumya might have fought with Mrs Gupta.

'She wanted to know my name. And after she learnt that I am Soumya Adhikari, she grabbed my hand and took me inside her door.'

Shabnam felt a ton of bricks fall on her heart but she kept quiet.

'She said that my bindi had indicated to her that I was a Hindu. I replied that Shabnam too wears a bindi quite often. She appeared slightly embarrassed and then started probing me about our friendship. I figured out why she was asking me all that. So I told her in great detail about your Hindu friends and my Muslim ones. And in between I took a swipe at her by speculating about the kind of people who discriminate on the basis of religion, who let stereotypes about religion blind them to the common humanity of their neighbour.'

'Oh, God, Soumya! There was no need to talk like that!' Shabnam chided her friend.

'What do you mean there was no need? This attitude has to be nipped in the bud.'

'Time would have straightened them out. You can't rush such things.'

'Since when have you become a defeatist who leaves everything to time? And my rebuke did have an effect. We are invited for tea at Mrs Srivastava's tomorrow evening!'

'What?' Shabnam couldn't believe her ears.

'Yes! People get to know each other only if they spend time together. Your neighbours need to learn that there is no difference between the yearnings and aspirations of well educated, progressive Hindus and Muslims.'

All the residents of 'F' Block were gathered at Mrs Srivastava's flat. Her son had had his *mundan* ceremony three days ago in Jaipur at her in-laws' place. Hence the party. Both the husband and wife and their other guests were being very nice to Shabnam, so much so that she began to curse herself for not having arranged an ice-breaking party herself. Had she only done that, she wouldn't have spent a whole year of loneliness, waiting and hoping for things to change. Why hadn't she thought of taking the first step, she cursed herself.

Mrs Srivastava looked very flustered, frying pakoras and holding on to the little kid somehow. When Shabnam hesitatingly asked if she could help her with the pakoras, Mrs Srivastava was delighted, 'Please do call me Archana,' she said.

'I will, if you also call me Shabnam. And "*tum*," not "*aap*".' A fountain of laughter erupted among the gathered women.

'Oh yes. Exchange must always be equal,' Mrs Gupta said.

Mrs Bhatia joked, 'Yes, you are a *bania*. Who knows more about weighing and measuring than *banias*?' The women laughed again.

After snacks, the coffee tray was passed around. A man sitting across from Shabnam kept staring at her. The way his gaze kept returning to her as he spoke to people nearby, made Shabnam feel that they were talking about her. Just when she was planning to leave quietly, the man spoke out to her, rather loudly: 'Oh, Miss Shabnam Bilgrami, I wanted to ask you something.' The aggression in his voice put Shabnam on her guard as she looked at him. 'Although it is I who ask, everyone here would like you to answer this question. You can say that it is a *collective* question.' He looked around the room and smiled, as though saying, 'Don't be afraid. I will convert your thoughts into words.' Shabnam didn't say anything, her eyes focused on the man.

'So, we would like to know your thoughts on Ram Janma Bhumi.'

Everyone in the room was quiet now. Shabnam swallowed her saliva. 'I don't know what you mean,' she threw the question back at him. 'I mean,' he said, 'what do you want? Should the Babri Mosque be rebuilt or should a temple to Ram be built there?'

By now Shabnam had gained her composure. In a sombre tone, she answered, 'It is possible that I want neither of the two.'

'You are trying to avoid my question,' the man argued.

'Why? Why is this avoidance?' Now Soumya had jumped into the fray. 'Why is it necessary to choose between a mosque and a temple?'

'You will have to take sides. In my opinion, every Muslim should side with the Hindus and contribute to building a grand Ram temple.'

'What is your name?' Soumya asked him a bit rudely.

'My name wouldn't change the truth. Anyway, I am Shyam Bihari Garg.'

'What truth are you talking about?' asked Shabnam.

'The Muslims came to India from outside, as plunderers. Their intent was to destroy the ancient Hindu religion and establish Muslim raj. That is why they demolished the temples and built mosques on those sites. Justice should be done. All old mosques should be demolished and temples built there. This is the demand of Hindu *rashtra*.'

'Since when did India become Hindu *rashtra*?' Soumya asked.

'Since these people demanded and got their Pakistan,' he fired back.

Seeing that Shabnam was in a state of shock, Soumya took up the cudgels. 'But no one in Shabnam's family left for Pakistan. Nor did they ever ask for Pakistan.'

'Then she should have no objection to accepting Indian culture. Why is she still an outsider?' Shabnam could figure out that he was bent on provoking her, but why did no one else in the room except Soumya speak up? Swallowing her saliva, she said, 'Does Indian culture mean Hindutva? Do you think religion and culture are the same thing?'

'Of course, they are one,' he said confidently.

Soumya boiled over. 'People like you promoted Hindutva in the name of Ram Janma Bhumi. A collective madness took hold of the country and some protectors of Hinduism got hold of goons to demolish the Babri mosque. Now that the mosque is done away with, how do you plan to provoke the populace next? You haven't got another issue.' Soumya's words brought an oily smile on his lips. His eyes kept goading Shabnam. Although it was Soumya who had spoken, he directed his reply towards Shabnam.

'Why do you say we don't have an agenda? There is Kashi, there is Mathura. Who knows how many temples were demolished and mosques built on top of them. We have to snatch them all back.'

All this while Shabnam had been trying to control her rage, control her blood from boiling, to somehow keep her mental balance. She felt something crack and break into pieces with a huge bang, right near her heart. She heard someone screaming. Had something precious broken apart? After a second, she realised that the voice screaming was hers. 'You people are right. Do take Ram Janma Bhumi. Do take Kashi and Mathura. And we will take Kashmir. We have taken half of it already.' She rushed out sobbing loudly and climbed up the stairs to go to her flat, disregarding Soumya's voice calling after her.

She calmed down after crying hysterically for a few minutes. She washed her face with cold water, combed her hair. Rather than go on cursing herself, she thought of doing something more sensible. She ought to go down and apologise. And tell them that what she had said was uttered in a fit of anger. But will people forgive her after what she had said? And Soumya? How will she face her? Soumya who had always stood against communalism. She had completely humiliated that Soumya. Pain, sadness, fear and anxiety flooded her mind. How can terrorism be the answer to communalism?

She pulled out a thick file from the bottom rack of the bookshelf. Dusting off the file with the end of her sari, she put the file on the table carefully, as though it was a precious and fragile thing and not a discoloured old file. She opened it and black headlines, large and small, began to dance before her eyes …

'Kashmiri Hindus should get their homes back.'

'Kashmiri Pandits have become refugees in their own country!'

'We still remember the fields of saffron!'

There was lots of stuff in the file. Clippings of articles she had written over several years. Articles that had caused her Muslim friends to shun her. She had gone into the Kashmiri refugee camps collecting statistics, buoyed by the belief that no circumstances justify taking away another human being's home. She turned the next page: 'Who needs the temple or the mosque? Ayodhya should get a university instead.' 'Let Hindus and Muslims join and build a hospital in Ayodhya.' The file had pieces about her travels on foot in Ayodhya, Fatehpur and Allahabad, her interviews with ordinary people whose opinions go every which way, like a heap of dry leaves that fly off in all directions with the wind, when riots break out. People who explode in communal frenzy. She had tried to understand and write about what these people really wanted. The people whose flights of ambition do not dream of majestic temples or palatial mosques, the people who get bloodied and maimed in the riots and who then drag their mutilated bodies to courts and offices, pleading for justice.

She wiped her mouth with the same dusty end of her sari and moved towards the door, the file in her hand as proof. She pulled the door handle towards her. The door did not open. 'It has been a month since the rains stopped. How come the wood is still swollen,' she thought. She pulled it harder but it still didn't budge. Now she pulled with all her might. This time she heard the latch clink. So the door had not got stuck because of the swollen wood, but someone had locked her in.

A strange premonition encircled her heart. She came out on the balcony. The balcony door of the flat next door was open.

She took a deep breath to control her racing heartbeat and then called out: 'Mrs Negi! Mrs Negi!'

Silence echoed in the next door flat, a silence of someone who had heard her and yet was ignoring her. She pushed back her panic and called out again. After about twenty calls, Mrs Negi's young son came out on the balcony. His face had the look of someone who had been forced to come out. She had started to tell him that her door was locked from outside when she saw the smirk on his face and stopped. The young man looked at her for a second and then went back in, without saying a word. Shabnam stood in shock for a few seconds then ran in and started to look for her mobile. But she knew that the mobile was not in the flat. It was in the purse she had forgotten in the downstairs flat.

She came back on the balcony again. A wave of fear enveloped her body and pierced her heart. Her nerves, carrying her blood to her lungs, were filling it up with her fear and circulating it around her body. Pure fear! What will happen now? Will these people just leave her locked up here? So she dies a slow and painful death? She ran and opened the fridge. There was a loaf of bread, three or four tomatoes, a cauliflower. Yes, the freezer had four packets of meat, but how long could this food last? And what about water? What if they cut off her water connection? She quickly filled up all the water bottles. Then she ran into the bathroom and filled up all the buckets. Oh, the electric meter is also downstairs. What if they disconnect that too? Maybe one evening a petrol bomb will fall inside her house and burn everything down. They will find an anonymous dead body after the flames have died down.

She put her hand on a chair to steady her shaking legs, and sat down. Although she had sympathy for the Jews who had suffered terrible atrocities in Europe during the Second World War, today, for the first time, she was beginning to grasp what they must have gone through in their hearts and minds. Were they also tormented by the thought that while the German Gestapo were their enemies for sure, what had happened to the ordinary Germans? Why did they allow themselves to float away on this sea of hatred? Why did they collaborate in the hunt for Jews? Why did they spy on the Jews in hiding, and sent them to concentration camps laughing and clapping? Is our country walking on the same road? When being born in a particular religion will be such a huge crime that its followers will have to go around with their heads bowed?

No, no, nothing like this will happen here. The thought made her feel a bit better. She took a deep breath to lighten the burden on her heart. The city, after all, has law and order. There are other people near about besides the Negis. And most important, there is Soumya after all. Right this second, she must be arguing with those people, trying to crack their communalist mould of thinking. She will not leave the battlefield without winning. And even if she loses, she will return to the flat, and free her.

Shabnam's wait had now changed its tenor. Was she now waiting in the same way as a Jewish family might have waited in some basement in a European home, waiting for a kind Christian who might bring them some food, some medicines, some day to day necessities? Who might help them cross the border so that they might once again set up a new home on some other piece of land, leaving their homeland? Will the minorities have to lead a life in transit in every century?

– Translated from the Urdu by the Author

BLANK CALL

KHURSHID AKRAM

Fakhruddin Ahmed, manufacturer of iron bolts and nuts, hence better known as Fakhru Nutraj, rose for the *Zuhr* namaz but something else was running in his mind. Even as he became aware of the call to the prayer, he was thinking of Gupta Lala, whom he had to meet after the prayer. When the congregation voiced praise of God, he shook the notion from his mind … he was in the presence of Allah, the Bountiful and Merciful. But even as he stood behind the Imam, praying silently while trying to discipline his thoughts, his attention wandered again. He was unable to work out how to deal with Lala, who seemed to have no intention of repaying the amount due. If only Lala was candid about his unwillingness to pay, then he might be able to figure out a plan, even if it meant open conflict … Standing in the posture of prayer, he strove to dismiss the thought … The Imam was reciting, albeit silently, the verses from the Quran which is in Arabic and which he did not understand. Being a tradesman, he was often distracted by such worldly matters, like the affairs of business, which he would inadvertently think about for a while and then summarily dismiss. It occurred to him that he was so deeply immersed in worldly affairs that he was simply unable to expunge such thoughts from his heart. What could he do; this was what business was all about. All his life he had veered between truthfulness and prevarication in order to meet his family's needs. It was not just one occasion, as if you could shunt the matter aside and stand in the court of the Almighty, dismissing the whole affair. Even at this moment he was hearing one thing, and thinking about something else. Business matters, not always clear, the matter of plates, about the press, about Lala, ebbed and flowed. With the call of '*Allah-hu-Akbar*' he bent down – impulsively, willingly, without any thought. Even if his mind was otherwise preoccupied, the power of routine was such that he prostrated himself, bowing down, then standing up ... until the end of the prayer, with the utterance of the *Salaam*. Although he was attuned to the ritual observances of namaz, it was as if his limbs truly remembered when to bow, and when to rise.

As he came out of the mosque, he was free from the dilemma. He had already decided that after namaz he would not return home to have his meal. He would first visit Lala, since he had asked to meet him at 2:00 pm. Even if a little late and who knows Lala would come up with myriad excuses for not paying his dues ... Ah! Maulvi Sahib, you have come late, I've already made payment to another party. Fakhruddin Ahmed, alias Fakhru Nutraj, maker of nuts, was not a Maulvi, definitely not. He had studied up to primary classes in a madarasa, hence remembered some chapters and verses of the Quran, without really understanding their meaning. However, for the last two-three years, after being diagnosed with a liver problem and told by the doctor to stop drinking at once, it was the craving for alcohol that troubled him more than the malady. One day he thought of *namaz* as a way to calm his restless mind, as *namaz*, they say, is a cure for many evils. Once he took to *namaz*, he stopped shaving. As his beard grew, *Tablighis*, the orthodox preachers, began pestering him to sit for lessons and accompany them for their proselytising rounds, but being a hard-boiled tradesman, he would give them the slip. However, the faithful were determined to bring him in line. Somehow, he was taken by them on a three-day religious trip. Yet when he returned, neither had his interest in religion grown, nor had he benefited from the lessons given. Neither did the intensity of feeling for *namaz* grow any deeper, nor did he adopt the custom of eating with legs folded beneath in the prescribed posture. Even so, he did start wearing a cap along with the beard. The combination of cap and beard led to people addressing him as Maulvi. As for Lala, he did not even know Fakhru Mian's real name. His business was being run in the name of F. A. and Sons, and at the time of receiving payment he would sign his name in Urdu, which Lala did not understand. But Lala was least bothered about his name – he was a lala, first and foremost and after all, business is business. Initially, his dealings went well, indeed, very well. When he started his small enterprise he had two small presses. He was readily able to make ends meet. When life looked like settling down, he thought of expanding the business. It was at this time that his transactions with Gupta Lala, a major supplier of small parts, began. At the outset, Lala was first-rate in his dealings. He would place large orders for materials and also make timely payments. Fakhru Mian thought that his business had indeed begun to flourish as a result of the good fortune bestowed by *namaz*. He took a loan and installed two big presses, and the pace of supplies picked up momentum.

Once business ties were well established, Lala gradually began to withhold payments. Lala would make you believe that this was the way the business should be run. He began to hedge and delay matters. His tone became somewhat dismissive. However, Fakhru Mian put up with this. Why blame the milch cow even if it kicks? He had to maintain business relations with Lala, since there was so much competition in the marketplace. There were countless numbers of smaller manufacturing units all around. If he stopped supply, someone else would take his place in no time. With this in mind, he took it all on the chin. The problem, however, was that the supplier of iron sheets had a large business, and did not extend credit to smaller enterprises like Fakhru Mian's. Yet he somehow managed and kept sending supplies to Lala. For supply worth a thousand, Lala would pay just five hundred rupees, saying he would settle accounts later. In this fashion the outstanding amount from Lala rose to a whopping sum of Rs. 70,000. And so, that day as Fakhru walked to meet Lala he was seething with anger. He felt like wringing Lala's neck; but he knew his hands were tied.

When he reached the shop, Lala was not there. And Fakhru Mian was feeling hungry. He drank some water, steeled his heart and kept sitting. During this hour, transactions at the shop continued while he sat and fumed. With a kind of smouldering resentment, he realised for the first time that the amount Lala owed, on account of which his business was floundering, was only a small part of his daily dealings.

One and a half hours later, when Lala arrived, he took his place without paying any attention to 'Maulvi Sahib.' He began by abusing his servant. 'You are putting on too much flab, it seems. I had told you to send Kanodia's consignment yesterday, but it has still not gone.' The servant remained silent, and left the shop. After this, Lala began making phone calls. 'Yes, Bhatti Sahib, your order has been dispatched. Send the payment … Oh, if you do not pay, then how will my business run? I too have to pay my clients. There is someone sitting just in front of me right here,' with this Lala cast a glance towards Fakhru Mian. He felt a certain relief that the scoundrel hasn't forgotten. However, after so much pleading, Fakhru Mian's patience had worn thin. He looked at Lala and wondered if he was being taken for a ride. Perhaps he was making excuses to delay. Can any business grow big otherwise? Such businesses grow by trampling smaller enterprises underfoot.

Who knows, perhaps the cursed fellow is making imaginary phone-calls. He's putting up a charade to befool me.

'So, when are you sending the payment,' Lala spoke. 'Fifteen days? That's too long. Send it next week … Yes, you will receive the materials meanwhile.' After this he made another call. By now, Fakhru Mian had understood his true intention. He was sure that he was up to no good. Lala would not pay up. As his anger mounted, he also felt helpless. By the time Lala had finished his calls and turned towards him, Fakhru's rage and sense of helplessness were overlaid by a slight weakness induced by hunger. Still he wanted to hear what Lala had to say. 'Maulvi Sahib, keep the supply coming.'

'But Lalaji, you should also keep making payments.'

'Payments will be made sooner or later; that is the way business runs.'

'Lalaji, you had promised to clear the amount due today. Please make some payment.'

'Oh, how am I to make the payment? You heard what I just said. Parties take delivery of material without payment, but business has to go on.'

Lala's rationalisation was more than what Fakhru Mian could endure.

'Lalaji, I am not concerned with your transactions. Please make my payment.'

'How can I make payment?' Lala became incensed. 'When I get my payments, only then can I do so. If this arrangement does not suit you, by all means stop supplies.'

'I will stop supplies, but you clear my dues,' he said without mincing any words.

Lala shot back in an even sharper tone. 'Yes, stop delivery immediately. I have no interest in dealing with a party who keeps pestering me. Our thirteen lakhs are stuck in the market; we don't lose our temper before anybody. Go now; you'll be paid in small sums by and by. Stop supplies.'

He had gone to collect his dues, but found himself in an even tighter fix. He knew very well that all dealings are done without a valid record. All receipts, and all dealings were on non-cognisable plain papers, largely on word of mouth. He would lose this money, and he along with his trade would sink. Seething with anger, helpless, weary, trapped in an impasse, and afflicted with a sense of apprehension of it all slipping away, Fakhru Mian walked back home. It was the time of the call for the *Asr* prayer. He was passing the Hindu neighbourhood. After the cross-roads one enters the Muslim area where he lived in an inner locality. In the centre of Chowk Sita Ram, surrounded by congested tenements and houses tumbling pell-mell one over the other, narrow streets and stinking drains, tangles of electric wires just above head-height and different kinds of odours and commotion, was a somewhat open space. In the middle of the road there was a peepal tree enclosed with bricks, where a small temple had been built, which had a red floor and in which the idols of Ram and Sita had been installed. On both sides of the street there were shops and houses. In some buildings the Hindus resided, in some others the Muslims. From the construction of these houses with mostly wooden balconies, it was difficult to tell who was living there. However, there was one feature that was easily identifiable. In the buildings where Muslims lived, salwars and kameezes could be seen hanging on the railings, whereas in the Hindu homes, dhotis and saris used to hang. However, Fakhru Mian had perhaps not reflected on these subtleties, nor was he mindful of which area he was coming from or where he was going. He was simply conscious of being cheated, of going home to meet the children he was responsible for with less than what he had hoped for. It was in this distraught state that a rapidly moving rickshaw tried to overtake him. The rickshaw's rusted mud-guard caught in his kurta. He was pulled along for a bit, and then fell with a jolt at a distance. His kurta was torn, and he was injured as well. Rage overwhelmed him. He got up, charged at the rickshaw puller and started beating him. He was a frail fellow. He ran on to the temple platform. Fakhru Mian, blinded by fury, lost all awareness of his surroundings. He began belabouring the man on the temple platform. The rickshaw puller started wailing, 'Hai Ram, save me, he's killing me.' This cry of a defenceless man became a challenge for the onlookers. A man caught his hand and said. 'Hey Maulvi, have you gone mad – why are you hitting the poor fellow?' At any other time, being addressed in this fashion, 'Hey Maulvi,' which came as a summons from a dark chapter of history, he would have reacted differently. On another occasion, he would not even have beaten the rickshaw puller so harshly, since his offence was not so grave. Such bothers and brawls were the order of the day in these densely populated settlements. If instead of a man with a beard and cap, someone else was hitting the rickshaw puller, the onlookers too would have watched the goings-on with inscrutable attention. If rather than the temple's doorstep it had been another place, then the rickshaw puller, whose name could have been 'Raju', 'Raghu', 'Bholu' or something like that, might not have called out Hai Ram, save me However, it was that strange moment … the time when sharp claws come out like that of a crab's and spread all around. At such a time when a bearded man wearing a cap was found beating a Hindu rickshaw puller at the entrance of a temple, some Hindus in the vicinity became enraged. Even as some of them attempted to intercede, others began raining blows on Fakhru Mian. Collective pride, collective obstinacy and collective rage can become dangerous. Although only a few blows reached their target, for Fakhru Mian it was as if thousands of cruel blows were landing on him. There were just a few stares, but for Fakhru Mian, it was as if innumerable terrifying and hate-filled glares were directed at him. In his injured state he began wielding his rather weak limbs in retaliation and it seemed as if many extra limbs had sprouted and joined the struggle. Actually, after seeing Fakhru Mian being beaten near the temple wall, some Muslims rushed to his aid. Then there was as if the rights and wrongs of the case would be decided later, those attacking the brethren must be killed … Soon, just as Fakhru Mian was losing consciousness, the news reached the neighbourhood where his house was located and where his two young sons and other relatives and many of their friends were to be found. 'Kill the scoundrels, they have made life unbearable,' someone screamed in a fit of rage after which everyone picked up whatever came to hand and headed towards Chowk Sita Ram. In the meantime the news reached the other side. There too were many people. There too the cry of fury spread far and wide.

At the time when the riots broke out and spread in the old city, employees working in government offices were returning home. Only a few officers and subordinate staff remain in office till the last minute. It was an office under the Home Ministry and in one of its corridors, there was a well-appointed room, where Deputy Director S. S. Sharma was sitting, looking through some files. He had to take a decision about an important file. Before him was the personal file of Suhail Abbas, who had been charged with misuse of government facilities. He was a clerk who had been appointed not through competition but on compassionate grounds. His father Aqil Abbas had been the A. O. in this very office. Some two years ago he had died while still in service. At the time Suhail was working as a computer operator in the Gulf, where up to date computers were in use. He was smart and industrious. He quickly learned programming and the various operations of computers. There he had access to many amenities. The money was good and the chances of promotions bright. There was no need for him to return and take up his father's clerical post. However, he was the Abbas family's only son. And now his mother did not wish her son to remain far away. Out of this compulsion, Suhail took up this job. In those days the government offices were being equipped with computers. However, most of those working in these offices did not have either the interest or ability to understand these computers. It was as if Suhail had won a lottery. Instead of having to deal with boring files, he became a computer operator. Although this made little difference to his grade or pay-scale, he had the satisfaction that he was in the computer section. His task was to transmit confidential information and messages on behalf of the Ministry to departments concerned with internal security. It was assumed that he was discharging his duties with a sense of responsibility. Once, he was sent to Bangalore to assist in the purchase of specialised software. In the meantime the director received a note from a confidential source regarding some e-mails that Suhail had sent containing business correspondence that had nothing to do with office work. Suhail was issued a memorandum and an inquiry committee was set up to investigate the matter. Mr Sharma, though, wanted to hush up the matter, and have him transferred to another section after reprimanding him. Although he was aware that Suhail had misused government facilities, he did not want any harsh action to be taken against him, since he knew that there was no one as skilled in using computers as Suhail. Furthermore, he did his work diligently. But the matter went to higher levels; therefore an inquiry committee had to be instituted … At this moment Mr Sharma was reading this very report. He was unable to decide whether to let him off or take harsher steps, since Suhail's reply was couched in such technical language that only a computer expert would be able to assess the rights and wrongs of the matter. A further argument Suhail made was that the note had been deliberately prepared in his absence as part of a conspiracy against him. Mr Sharma was convinced with his arguments, and after satisfying himself, was mulling over the grounds for letting him off, just then the phone bell rang … on the other side there was one of his friends who lived in the old city where riots had broken out, indeed were spreading. He told Sharmaji that some people had even tried to attack a temple there. They were receiving reports from here and there about people being stabbed. The sound of firing was audible. He could spot a house burning from the roof of his building. Fear and anxiety, even hatred underlay the voice that emanated from the other side of the wire. On hearing this news, Sharmaji was deeply disturbed. He had read the tracts of Guru Golwalkar and Hedgewar and the likes in which certain observations about Muslims appeared that would indeed agitate any Hindu who came around to their cause and believed what they said. He had read these books in his youth, when he had been considerably influenced by their views. After hearing about the riots, he instantly began thinking along these lines, without actually wishing to do so. For it so happened that despite his faith in the views of thinkers like Golwalkar and Hedgewar, he had not come across any Muslims who were really so bad. Many were even remarkable individuals as, for instance, Suhail Abbas. However, at this time a wave of hatred rose from his spine to his brain, clouding his thought processes, which were now dictated by its effects. At this time, he started looking through Suhail Abbas' file again, but was unable to concentrate, since the pages of five hundred years of history began flapping in his mind, while cruel rulers from Mohammad Ghori to Aurangzeb with unsheathed swords began splashing blood in the recesses of his consciousness. Even as he read the file, it was as if his mind was engorged with a cloud of dust, and he came to the conclusion that there was enough evidence against Suhail Abbas for action to be initiated. As a result, after careful deliberation he jotted down his comments on the file concluding that since Suhail Abbas had misused government facilities as verified by the inquiry committee, he should be suspended from service. It was a Thursday. The next day was a holiday on account of Good Friday, followed by off-days on Saturday and Sunday. He did not wish to face this dilemma for three days, so he immediately sent for his personal assistant and instructed him to type the suspension order for Suhail Abbas.

Although this work took quite some time, he was satisfied that the matter has been dealt with justly. Nevertheless, he was sweating profusely and was even running a temperature. By this time his chartered bus would have long since left. He contemplated the thought of being jostled on an ordinary bus. Sharmaji lived in a government colony where he had been allotted a three bedroom house. However, the place was at quite a distance from this office. Sharmaji did not possess a vehicle, while most of his fellow officers owned cars. He was an honest officer, and had never taken a bribe or asked for a commission. He belonged to a pundit family from Agra, having high moral values. After the abolition of zamindari, they did not enjoy the same level of prosperity. Even so, the disciplines and social graces of yore had remained intact in him. Once upon a time there had been quite a bit of social interaction between his family and that of zamindar Sayyid Ali. However, this became a casualty of the movement spearheaded by Mohammad Ali Jinnah. Once the nation attained Independence Sharmaji had begun to grasp the ways of the world. After that, whatever he saw, read or understood in his early years, there was no place left for Sayyid Ali's family. Around this time they lost their landholdings with the end of zamindari. For generations there had been a tradition of education and learning, which came in handy. To begin with, he had some doubts at the thought of taking up a job, since no one in the family had gone into service before this. But he did, and now was quite content that he held a government position and wielded so much power. He was even more satisfied that in such a society in which bribery and dishonesty were rampant, he had retained his sense of integrity. This was the reason he did not possess a car. Yes, he did own a Bullet motorcycle, but that too had become rather old and often caused trouble. That's why for some time he had begun coming to the office by bus. He thought that after saving some money he would sell the old motorcycle and buy a new one. He had never really thought about purchasing a car.

As he was coming out, a car's horn sounded close to him. He turned and saw Qureishi Sahib, the executive engineer, who was in charge of the civil construction wing in the same office. Although younger than him, he was an officer in the same grade. He lived in the same colony as Sharmaji. The car's window rolled down. 'Come Sharmaji, I assume you're going home.' Sharmaji did not like Qureishi because he was known to be corrupt to the bone. Qureishi was the son of a poor Ghosi from Muzaffarnagar; he had completed his diploma and obtained a government job through bribery. After that, he had ensured his own promotion in various places through assiduous wheeling and dealing. The worst part was that he was a rather shallow person. He took bribes, made plenty of money and talked only about making money. And at this time there was another reason for Sharmaji's loathing. Qureishi himself opened the door of the car. Sharmaji sat down reluctantly, but remained silent. He liked to talk about social and political issues. However, it would not be proper to speak about such subjects with this fellow, he thought. As was his wont, Qureishi brought up an office matter relating to bribery. 'So what? He knows nothing. Even though he has a mobile phone …', he went on talking, even as Sharmaji kept thinking about something else.

At 8:30 pm the national bulletin carried the news about the spreading of the riots through the old city. Many had been killed. A place of worship had been damaged as well. After that curfew had been imposed everywhere. The person who had told him about the riots could not be contacted now because the telephone lines to the riot-afflicted areas had been cut. That night Sharmaji was extremely restless. This was despite the fact that his colony was fifteen kilometres away from the old city, where even the smoke from the riot could not reach if it were not for the newspapers and television. During the night pages of books he had once read in a state of hopelessness kept fluttering in his dreams. In these dreams it was as if he was transported to a land where the Golden Bird lived. It was the map of that land which he had put together from stories, legends and myths. Then a dark shadow would fall over the map, over which the ghosts of figures like Mohammad Bin Qasim, Babar and Aurangzeb strutted, and then he would suddenly wake up.

Two newspapers were delivered daily at his place. He would read the English paper for news about politics and the Hindi paper for social and religious news. But most of the time he would simply browse through the papers. That morning he opened the Hindi paper first. 'Three Hindu youths killed, temple set on fire, even as the police remained mute observers. A Maulvi beat up a devotee after entering the temple. Despite the curfew the rioters kept shouting slogans like *Nara-e-Takbir*.'

After such a sleepless night, these headlines added fuel to the fire. The anger that he had tried to hold back began to flow uncontrollably, like a filthy sewer gushing into a river.

He at once shot off a letter to the newspaper with the heading 'Muslims start riots.' He wrote, 'Once again this riot has proved that all riots till now have been started by Muslims. These are the heirs of those cruel rulers who thirsted for Hindu blood.

They divided this country. They massacred Hindus and Sikhs in West Punjab. Politicians and social and religious thinkers should ponder how to deal with the aggressive attitude of Muslims. It is a matter of concern that police and administration remain silent witnesses to the slaughter of Hindus and burning of temples. The time has come for the Hindu community to think seriously whether a hard-line stance needs to be taken to enable them to lead a life of peace and self-respect in their own country.'

As a government servant he could not publish such a letter under his own name. So he wrote Shyama Prasad Mukherji as his pseudonym below. Then he realised that Shyama Prasad Mukherji may be his ideal, but if the letter was published with this name, readers would become suspicious. So he deleted this and wrote: Shyam Prasad. Beneath, he wrote a fictitious address.

The same morning the Urdu paper *Sada-i-Millat*'s headlines read: 'After Bhagalpur, Meerut and Moradabad another massacre of Muslims has begun: bomb thrown at mosque's minaret. Seven young men martyred by police bullets while offering the holy namaz. Reign of terror unleashed against Muslims. Policemen dishonour Muslim women in their homes.'

It was Friday. Despite the curfew some people roamed the streets with mikes announcing that Muslims should congregate for the Friday prayers. They should compel the administration to lift the curfew for the Friday prayers. This news spread in all directions like wildfire. On one side there were those ready to die in order to perform the Friday prayers and on the other those getting ready to kill them. The police were alert and the administration remained strict. Permission for collective worship was not granted. In spite of the curfew, riots restarted soon after sundown.

Next morning the headline of *Sada-i-Millat* ran: 'Muslims deprived of the right to carry out religious duties in *Dar-ul-Harb*, the war zone. Communal decision of the police and administration in not permitting Muslims to perform *Namaz-e-Juma*. Muslim leaders across the country condemn the administration and threaten nation-wide protest demonstrations.'

Hindi newspaper carried the headlines: 'Four more Hindu young men killed in the riots, Muslims offer Friday prayers in violation of the curfew. Muslims goons roam around freely with bombs and pistols while the administration is helpless and incapable.'

This news prompted Sharmaji to once more write a letter. Today he was even more belligerent. Muslims – quit India! 'Muslims, instead of making life intolerable for peace loving and non-violent Hindus, should leave the country. They have already claimed one country in 1947. What right do they have to remain in this country, make trouble, start riots and cock a snook at the system while stubbornly getting their own way? Today I believe the entire Hindu community is with those organisations who have said in plain words that if Muslims wish to live in this country they should say Vande Mataram. Either they should remain here as Hindus, or leave for their beloved Pakistan. The need of the hour is for the entire Hindu society to give their full support to such organisations so that Muslims can be thrown out of this country, and this land be purified by sprinkling Ganga water.' And this time, he signed the letter in the name of Nirmal Pande.

In the old city, after day-long peace and quiet, communal violence would begin at sundown. Even as curfew remained in force, the riots continued. In the Hindi newspapers such poison-pen letters kept appearing under the names of Shyam Prasad, Nirmal Pande, Ram Nath Chaturvedi, Deen Bandhu Rathore, etcetera. Meanwhile, *Sada-i-Millat*'s sales shot up because of its gory headlines. The well-wishers of the community started making plans for a gherao of parliament. They threatened to take the matter to the United Nations. Appeals were made to Arab countries to put pressure on the Indian government to halt the massacre of Muslims. In a lithographed news sheet with a print run of two to three hundred brought out primarily to carry advertisements of the D.A.V.P., a letter by 'a servant of the community' appeared urging that this was the moment for Pakistan to attack India. All believers will rise to help their brothers in faith and the flag of Pakistan will be raised over Hindustan from Kashmir to Kanyakumari, Inshallah!

All this while, Fakhru Nutraj was hovering between life and death in hospital. On the fifth day he gained enough consciousness to understand where he was and the reasons for being there. He had a vague feeling that he made some mistake: what and how he could not remember.

For several days Suhail Abbas wandered around in a state of worry about his suspension order. He was not so much concerned about retaining the job. For him it was more a question of self-respect. The humiliation of the reprimand, after being found guilty, had driven him mad with rage. For two days he had been trying to meet Sharmaji to ask him if this was the only reward for his capability and hard work; it was not so much about the job. The option of taking the matter to court still remained, and Suhail was sure that he would emerge victorious. However, Sharmaji had issued strict instructions to his P. A. to the contrary, since he did not wish to meet Suhail Abbas, or face the dilemma of reviewing the decision. In the past few days letters by him had been appearing in the papers under false names. The letter today appeared under the title – 'Muslims are Traitors.'

After a week Fakhru Mian had regained complete consciousness. It was his good fortune that he remembered everything. He also found out about what had transpired in the interim and he felt a pang of regret for what he had done. He realised that if he had not beaten up the rickshaw puller so badly, matters would not have gone so far and the riots would not have happened. Despondently, he thought to himself, how can I be blamed? Whatever I did was on account of that crooked Lala …

Rioting began to abate. For how long could one exchange blows, after all, without a square meal! When people become desperate for food and water, who could worry about reports about numbers of people being killed by those on one side or the other? And then the children's education was being interrupted. Somebody had to take his father to the hospital for an eye-operation; another person's pregnancy had come to term. Somebody had to arrange his daughter's marriage; a girl wanted to make a call to a boy in the neighbourhood. There were so many tasks to be attended to, for sure!

After the office opened, Sharmaji's workload increased. After all, he had major responsibilities. He had piles of files to dispose of, so the mania for writing letters diminished. A few days later he received a call from his son, who was studying for his MBA in Ahmedabad. He told his father that the fees for the final semester had to be deposited the next month. Sharmaji became busy with the matter of paying the fees. The money he had saved for the motorcycle would come in handy. Preoccupied with how to raise the remaining amount, he often forgot to open the newspaper.

However, there were many others reading the newspaper. In the colony, and beyond – in the city, in the villages and townships, in small neighbourhoods, at the barber shops, in the tea-stalls. Those young men who did not have to deposit a son's fees, or worry about a cataract operation tended to read with excitement and fervour such news and letters announcing that Muslims should quit India, that Muslims who wished to live in India would have to say Vande Mataram, and that Hindustan was for Hindus.

Sharmaji became so immersed in this worry about his son's fees that he had become unaware of the extent to which the atmosphere had been vitiated in the colony, and the kind of hot wind that had begun to blow in countless *bastis* and settlements. He was consumed by his own concerns. Truly, how difficult life had become! His ancestors could not have possibly experienced such hard times, he thought piteously. A few months ago another problem had unsettled him. This difficulty, though unmistakable to the ear, remained out of plain sight. Just as in villages and small communities young unmarried girls sometimes get possessed by spirits, who, swaying wildly, declare themselves to be their lovers and threaten to take the girl away with them to the spectral world, his daughter Nisha, so well-proportioned and fair, had become the recipient of blank calls. Life had been going on well up to this time. His son was pursuing an MBA, his daughter was attending college, he had had an air-conditioner installed in his room in the office, and there was time to discuss social and political issues. Unexpectedly, Nisha began getting such blank calls, where the speaker sometimes made declarations of love, at other times threats of kidnapping. Nisha became pale with anxiety in just a few days. After all, which shaman could exorcise this city ghost! Sharmaji, who had had a traditional upbringing, became terrified by this unseen calamity. He became so tense that at times he would think of getting the phone disconnected, leaving the colony or even leaving the city altogether. He became suspicious of every passerby. When someone spoke to him, instead of listening he would strain to ascertain if this was indeed that voice. But luckily this misfortune too passed. In his view, the police was not of much help; in other words, they did not beat up any likely suspect. At his request, the telephone exchange began monitoring his calls. After this, as often happens, the anonymous calls stopped. Now Sharmaji heaved a sigh of relief. However, since the culprit had not actually been caught, his anxiety remained. At present, he had to worry about his son's fees, and his wife added another concern. She felt it was time for Nisha to be married.

If life had its difficulties, by God's grace there were also some consolations. For instance, in the village, he owned forty bighas of land, which he had left in the care of his older brother-in-law. As per the custom he should have received a good amount of grain. However, every year Jijaji would make some excuse and fob him off with just enough rice and dal for basic needs. Sharmaji began to wonder whether he could rely on these landholdings. Who cares for anyone anyway; even Jijaji's intentions may change and he might grab the land. He had already taken over his own brother's land, after all, and Sharmaji was only his younger brother-in-law and lived in the city … So, he thought, half the land should be sold off. Quite a good sum could be raised. This would take care of Vikas's fees, Nisha's marriage expenditure and a new motorcycle for sure. Yes, this was the right thing to do. Accordingly, the family started planning their visit to Agra, and Sharmaji took two weeks leave from the office. Mrs Sharma and Nisha purchased small gifts for close relatives and began packing these. However, just before their departure, news came that riots had broken out in Agra.

Sharmaji heard about the rioting on the national bulletin with annoyance and unease. However, he was unable to immediately fathom the reason for the riots on the basis of this news.

– Translated from the Devnagari version
by Tarun K. Saint, with crucial inputs
from Chand Kishore Saint and Naghma Zafir

BARS

KEKI N. DARUWALLA

We dropped the subject we were discussing when the subject walked in. Five minutes earlier she had said, 'The expression on this Jailor's face is always satirical.'

'How many Jailors have you seen?'

'Just this one.'

'And how often have you seen him?'

'Twice.'

'And that makes you so certain, geometry class … end of theorem. He's just like any other Jailor – that's his job, keeping people within bars.'

'Behind you mean.'

'I prefer within. Incidentally I have never heard of satire being parked on a face, even if it belongs to an unfortunate Jailor. Anger yes, cruelty too; such attributes get etched on a face perhaps, eye and the turn of the lip giving a man away. But satire?'

I could see the anger in her eyes. 'Correction, it is not jailors who are unfortunate, it is the ones they jail!' Feisty girl. Pointless telling her, I thought, that jailors don't jail, it's the courts. She would know that but what do you do about passion, anger.

'Let's face it, you had made up your mind before you saw him, isn't it? You thought of a jailor as someone louche, sinister, possibly with an eye patch, no?'

'No!' she barked.

And here he was, the Jailor I mean. 'O here you are again.' he said looking at his wrist as the watch came out sliding through his cuffs. He pretended not to notice me, just looked at Gabriela and nodded. 'Still a half hour you know. I could let you see him, but visiting hours are sacrosanct, as you know.'

'I don't.' Stubborn angry look, eyes squarely meeting the Jailor's. These young girls, so ready to pick up fights! Gabriela was not one to be cowed down, what if her uncle was in the tub and Authority Incarnate stood there, a baton tucked under his armpit.

'Well rules are sacred and so are Visiting Hours.'

'Why should rules stand between niece and uncle or daughter and father?'

'Because rules are rules Lady, stern and immovable, like bricks, fired in a kiln.' He nodded rather kindly at her and walked off; didn't want to be interrogated by this aggressive girl. Interrogation was not a nice word in Jail, reeked of illegality, cops barging in at odd hours and 'interrogating' prisoners.

The Jailor's look is nondescript, the colour of his face colourless. A job requirement I thought when I first called on him on my transfer as the new Jail doctor. His office was a few yards away from the main building. An old Jail it is, weather-beaten and mouldy, with thick walls and sharp battlements, a once-imposing edifice in a princely state in what was then known as Central Provinces. His office looked modern though, with chessboard tiles and steel tables.

'Look after them,' he told me pointing to the inmates inside, 'they need you. We can't do much for them but at least we can look after their physical health.' For the next few months those were the only sympathetic words I heard from him. Whether he had a soft chord somewhere, I had no idea. 'One thing more, I would like you to wander around the meeting place during visiting hours. Don't misunderstand, not to ferret out what transpires between inmates and visitors, but to keep a finger on the pulse generally. You don't have to tell me, I am not asking you to snoop. As for hardened criminals, murderers and kidnappers, I have my ways of knowing what is going on.'

I was about to get up, but he kept silent, grimly lost in thought. Then he added, 'The Deputy Jailor is no good. I will have to lean on you at times.'

Two people landed an hour earlier always, Gabriela, the niece of Father Baptista and Aadila, wife of the 'terrorist' Abrar Hasan. The terrorist bit had started being downplayed when another investigating agency had taken over the case. The press was saying that the whole group was innocent and the new investigators thought so. He had been four years with us. We in the jail know that between what the police and the courts say and the jailbird's version there's not just a gulf but an ocean. Aadila hardly said anything interesting. She just repeated each time that Abrar was a head mechanic at a big service station and one day the cops came and took him away. He was innocent.

Gabriela, who after a meeting or two had asked me to call her Gaby, as everyone else did, was just too angry to talk about her uncle's case. I also never probed. One never knew about her temper. The Deputy Jailor had got a mouthful from her once. When I asked her she said, 'The fool tells me, why do you come to see your uncle? Why not his wife or daughter? Because, I told the fool, my uncle is a Catholic priest. He can't have a wife and so he can't have a daughter! Have you understood that? He stared at me vilely but didn't say anything!'

I decided to ask Father Baptista one day. He was given a cell and a decent cot, allowed food from home every now and then. The Jailor even allowed him his own clothes in the cell, but when he came out for his constitutional he had to be in 'stripes', our prescribed jail attire. And he had the use of a mobile phone – all this went unappreciated by Gaby. Ungrateful people! He was even allowed paper to write on, though there's a story to it. For when the new Deputy Minister came to have a look at the Jail (he called it 'inspection' – though we never got an inspection report) he went into the 'paper business' as he described it.

'No diary, *shiary*, you understand! I don't want inmates writing gory story – bad food, *maar peet* in jail, drug, *charas*. MLAs ask questions. They have nothing else to do. Only allow to write *shlokas*.'

The jailor intervened. 'Sir, what about Christians and others? Can they quote from their books?'

'Not understanding! Only *shlokas*!'

Talking with Father Baptista was rewarding. He was tall, shaggy haired, spoke excellent Hindustani, had no trouble sitting cross-legged, Indian style on his cot; didn't look the proselytising type. I asked for a chair which was brought in.

He was a good talker. 'Do you get bored?' I asked him.

'Now and then. I try to keep myself busy in prayer to our Lord, but even prayer has to end sometime. And then how much can the mind wander and forage for memory, sponge on it? But these ten months have not been very hard, if that's what you want to know.'

I tried to convince him that this was simple conversation, I wasn't keen to know anything. Have no idea how much he believed me. His looks betrayed nothing. I presume it is a quality which only those few possess, who serve God. I was unhappy to see some of the lower staff keep an eye on uncle and niece as they talked through the grill during meeting hours. What were they looking for, sign talk, inflection of brow, a blank look, a Morse code of expressions? Or perhaps they were watching for the transmission of a dark thought from one to another.

Slowly over weeks I zeroed in. What brought him here, in the tub? Surely you know all that, he said. The whole town knows. There was nothing to it. This man by name Sunil Manohar came to the church and said his father had died. He wanted him to be buried in our Christian cemetery. The man looked under the weather with two day's stubble. He looked distressed. I asked him if he was a Christian? No he said. What about your father? He smiled. 'If I am not a Christian obviously my father will not be a Christian?' Not necessary I thought but I nodded. No point arguing. 'Why do you want him buried? Why can't you take him to the burning ghat?'

Straight question. He, meaning his father, wanted his body to be interred here. The man was always in mortal dread of fire – he carried a few burns from his childhood. You can't really argue with that. And our cemetery looked good, a small island of stone crosses, with bougainvillea draped on the enclosing wall. I had been entrusted with two novitiates who were on their way to becoming priests. The Bishop wanted me to assess their beliefs and desire to take the plunge. As you know it involves celibacy, tough decision for modern men. These youngsters had enough sense to advise me against the burial, but they couldn't give a convincing rationale. I saw no harm. In most things we have very little say. Fate decides them for us. But surely a man could decide what happens to his outer shell after he is dead.

Next morning I conducted the skimpiest of ceremonies. You can't let a man go into the earth without a prayer surely! I read a short prayer from the 3:1-9 *Book of Wisdom, He accepted them as a holocaust.*

The souls of the virtuous are in the hands of God,
No torment shall ever touch them.
In the eyes of the unwise, they did appear to die,
Their going looked like a disaster,
their leaving us like an annihilation;
But they are in peace ....

I was especially keen on one line in this prayer which read '*their hope was rich with immortality.*'

'Was that all you read?' I asked.

'One other passage. I couldn't refrain from reading out from the *Acts of the Apostles:*

"Peter addressed Cornelius and his household:
The truth I have now come to realise" he said,
"is that God does not have favourites, but that anybody of any nationality who fears God and does what is right is acceptable to him."

That was all. It was a short service if that's what you can call it. I hope you know Doctor that in a church service we consider Jesus sacramentally present. By the evening someone complained. The constabulary came with a sub-Inspector in tow, or vice versa, talked of this and that and after two hours of futile questions arrested me. It was the anti-conversion law of the state. I told them we were not converting anyone. Someone wanted to be buried in our cemetery; we buried him. That was all. But would they listen. It's ten months now since ... he shrugged his shoulders.

I felt like assuaging him and asked, 'Hope things are okay here?'

He nodded. 'Yes, thank you, but they wouldn't allow other inmates here to come to me. They thought I'd convert them!'

It was rumination time on occasions. He would close his eyes and start reminiscing. Once he said I am not sure if I am a good believer. I am not sure at all if St. Thomas the Apostle ever came to India but I dare not say that to a Catholic from Kerala. I have been to a seminary for a course with members of the Syro-Malabar Church. There were also St. Thomas Christians there, they call themselves Nasranis, a Syrian term meaning followers of the Nazarene. I couldn't last in a church in South India for more than a month, I am sure. Belief has to be absolute, blind – no place for the rational in it. That's the terrible danger in reasoning. How could a first century rickety boat set out say from Jaffa or Tyre or wherever and make it to Malabar? And hardly a reference in any chronicle! Doubt is the Devil. You believe in the divine just as you believe the earth is round. Lack of belief gets mapped on the face, however much you may dissemble. It is something people of my calling need to be wary of.

Sometime back I had asked him what he would do once he got back; was there anything particular he yearned for? Let's face it, inane questions. One could ask that of anyone in Jail. 'All I want is quiet around me,' he said, 'silence thick as fog, silence that you could cut with a knife. Too much hustle bustle here in this place. (He never called our jail by its name.) Too much of coming and going, unlocking of cells, food passed through little openings, guards talking loudly when they are not shouting at the prisoners, aimless rounds by your officials. I just want some greenery around me and quiet, the silence even more important than the greenery.'

Father Baptista was worried about one inmate – Abrar who was just two cells away. They allow him to talk to me now and then as they bring him back from his constitutional. 'He was alright the first few months I was here, by which I mean resigned. Resignation is the best state to be in when in jail. Those newspaper reports have disturbed his equilibrium. He is tense, almost frenetic; he would blow up the doors if he could, blow up the walls and get out. If the investigators say he is innocent, why can't his release be hurried through, that's what he seems to be saying and thinking about all the time. Sad case, needs sympathy.'

The Jail grapevine is a pretty sure thing, and has the habit of turning out right. Abrar's orders from the court were on their way. But what can you say of people who jump the gun, or are impelled to jump the gun? Abrar felt almost forced into it. As it is his innocence was weighing heavy on him and one evening another inmate accosted him, picked up a fight and beat him up. If you are known as a 'terrorist', someone accused of planting a bomb that spat out shards, you are marked. Guys are itching to get at your throat. I was not there and the different versions are bit of a blur. This much is certain that Abrar ran out through that forbidding stone corridor, and once out he made a beeline for the heavily bolted gate on the outer wall. Here the different versions fork away tangentially. According to one, the guard grappled with him and brought him to the Jailor. According to another the guard at the gate scurried into the sentry post and brought out his gun. Abrar pounced on the gun and held it against the man's chest. Later he tried to blow the lock, but the gun was not loaded!

He threw the gun and tried to climb the wall, but obviously failed. Old walls, high battlements, what can one do? The guards were loading their guns when the Jailor arrived on the scene, took command, got the searchlights switched on though it was still dusk, ordered the staff to see that the other inmates were securely locked in, and asked the guards to unload their guns. Then he began a dialogue with the man. 'Your release orders are here, Son, in my office, right here. Don't spoil things.' The two, I believe, could be heard hollering at each other.

'You don't believe me?'

'I don't.'

'Whom will you believe then?'

There was no answer. The Jailor sent for Father Baptista. Before the priest could come, he went into the office, and came out holding the paper. Then he started his long walk towards Abrar and showed him the paper. They talked for a few minutes and then walked back. In less than an hour Abrar was released from Jail. I have no idea why the staff sat on his release order for more than a day.

Next day I had a chat with the priest. 'The papers say the case against you is being withdrawn.'

'It should never have been lodged in the first place,' he answered.

'Looking forward to anything particular?'

'I told you … silence and greenery. I am not sure of the first now, because silence for me doesn't just mean lack of sound, there are other things to it. I am wary of clamour.'

'What do you mean? What sort of clamour ?'

'Doctor, I was also thinking of a different kind of noise – denigrating Gandhi, extolling Godse, the majority being asked to produce more children, the division of people into legitimate and illegitimate people. All this for me is clamour.'

Two days later the orders for his release arrived. Some of the lower staff had gathered around to pay their regards to him. I was surprised. Gaby was there and for once she was not hot under the collar, and even gave me a smile, a bit of a rarity. Father Baptista was wearing a shawl and had a walking stick on which he leaned a little. He looked like a swami as he walked out and I almost felt like bowing to him and touching his feet.

– *(This story was written in English especially for this volume.)*

THE VULTURES OF DOONGERWADI

ALI IMAM NAQVI

The two of them were flabbergasted by the strange happening. Without quite meaning to, they put the stretcher down on the ground. They looked at the corpse in amazement and then their glances met and their eyes asked many questions of each other. For a long time, the orbs of their eyes kept moving in their sockets, and when they paused, the two shrugged their shoulders to show their ignorance. In unison, the two stretched the muscles in their neck and turned their face first to the left and then to the right. Then their eyes turned upwards to circle the dense trees at the edge of the doongerwadi.

Not even a single vulture could be seen till the far distance. It was the first time such a thing had happened. The warning bell had rung two hours ago. Fifteen minutes later the helpers in *bungli* number two had given the corpse in their safekeeping. They had brought the corpse inside the safe walls of the tower and shut the gates. Then, opening the small window in the door, Feroz Bhatena had looked out at the mourners and asked who the deceased was.

'What about some tip …?'

The attendant smiled and pushed two ten rupee notes towards Feroz. He immediately put one in his own pocket and, extending the other note towards Hormuz, he shut the window.

'O Lord …' Hormuz raised his head and looked towards the sky peeping through the dense foliage of tall and mighty trees. Then, he signalled to Feroz with his eyes; both bent and picked up the stretcher and began to move towards the tower.

'Feroz …' Hormuz addressed his companion as they walked.

'Hunn … '

'How long … how long are we going to do this work?'

'Come on, come on, don't chew my brain.'

'Is this the only work we are fit to do?'

'What do you think?'

'I don't know … I am just asking.'

'Yes.'

'I swear by Zarathustra,' and he raised his eyes heavenwards as he swore. For a couple of minutes, both were quiet; then, Feroz said, 'Look here, Hormuz, the Parsi Panchayat raised us. What can we do if our destiny is flawed? Do you understand, or not? Tell me.'

'That's your story, brother. But to tell you the truth, I am quite fed up … fed up of this life.'

But the chain of their conversation broke. They had reached the tower. With one nudge from Hormuz's foot, the door to the tower had flung open and in the next moment they were inside it, with one standing at the head of the corpse and the other at its feet. The dead person's face, smeared with curd, looked white. Hormuz raised the head a little while Bhatena whipped the shroud off the body. Then they took turns to touch the dead person's feet and brought the hands to their eyes and chest. Then, both stood aside. By way of covering, the corpse had only a handkerchief tied around its waist. Hormuz and Feroz left the handkerchief where it was and turned and left the tower. They returned to their room and sat down on two chairs beside a table. Hormuz took out a bottle of alcohol and kept it on the table. Both took turns filling their glasses. Feroz Bhatena put a piece of *patrail* in his mouth and said, 'Hormuz!'

'Yes?'

'What a life!'

'What happened?'

'Tower … One … Two … Four … And …'

'Yes, and?'

'What else.'

'And corpse, corpse.'

'I don't understand.'

'Look at the life of a Parsi?'

'Life?'

'Yes.'

'Why? What happened?'

'Our youth is fast-paced but our old age is slow. You are absolutely right, brother.'

'Yes, absolutely true.'

For a long time the two sat talking idly, and drinking. After some time, they began to sob and cry. Suddenly the bell rang; this time the corpse was coming from *bungli* number four.'

'Good! The Lord Zarathustra has arranged for our drinks today!'

'Hurry up! Come on!'

They hurried towards the outer gate of the *bungli*. Once again, the door had been opened and an empty stretcher had been laid outside. In a short while, the corpse from *bungli* number four was given to their charge. Once again, the attendant had handed them two ten-rupee notes; this time Hormuz had stepped forward and taken them. The door of the *bungli* was shut. The two of them picked up the stretcher and began to move outside.

'Hormuz!'

'Yes?'

'One day, we too shall go like this, won't we?'

Hormuz stopped in his tracks. He turned his neck and looked at Feroz. Then he asked Feroz in a terrified tone, 'Why did you ask this question?'

'Everyone has to die.'

'True, but I have no intention of dying just yet.'

'Intention? Well said, brother!'

'Shut up, you scum! What have we seen in our life so far? Corpses, corpses, and more corpses, and vultures and, at the most, cheap liquor from the roadside stall with a dash of pungent rock salt! Ten rupee notes … I ask you: isn't there more to life than this?'

Feroz kept silent. He kept looking at Hormuz.

'Tell me, brother, is this all there is to life?'

'What can I say? All I know is that if we have come, we must go too one day. And when I go, someone else will come in my place.'

'Shut up, you sister … bastard …' Hormuz screamed.

'Don't shout, brother. And don't talk about life; we are carrying a corpse in our hands.'

In silence, they walked till the tower and when the gate of the tower opened …

The two of them were flabbergasted by the strange happening. Without quite meaning to, they put the stretcher down on the ground. They looked at the corpse in amazement and then their glances met and their eyes asked many questions of each other. For a long time, the orbs of their eyes kept moving in their sockets, and when they paused, the two shrugged their shoulders to show their ignorance … Then their eyes turned upwards to circle the dense trees at the edge of the doongerwadi.

And it was the first time such a thing had happened. The vultures were missing and the corpse was lying there intact. For, what had been happening all this while was that the corpse would be laid out, Firoz and Hormuz would leave the tower and in twenty or twenty-five minutes the corpse would be transferred into the bellies of the vultures. They would see the vultures flying away, then go into the tower, soak the skeletal remains with acid, whereupon it would turn into ash and run down the channels into the deep pits under the tower – deep, down God knows how far into the innards of the earth. Sometimes, it so happened that no corpse would come. At such times, the Panchayat would buy a goat for the vultures and give it to Hormuz and Feroz, to stop the vultures from flying away for want of sustenance. But today was the strangest sight ever! The corpse was lying there intact and the vultures were missing!

Hormuz and Feroz kept looking at each other with wide open eyes. After standing still for some time, they deposited the second corpse too on the grill of the tower. Then they looked at each other with many questions in their eyes.

'What do you think? Should we tell Kaikubad?'

'Yes, we should.'

They reached their room and pressed the switch of the emergency bell. A red bulb fitted on the wall of the doongerwadi began to switch on and off. Surprised, the clerks came out of their office. And the bulbs for the different *bungli*s too began to flicker on and off. The priests stopped their chanting. The dogs roaming around here and there in the *bungli*s stopped and cowered. The mourners who had come with the new corpses were bewildered; they too came out of the *bungli*s. Everywhere, there was the same question on everyone's lips: 'What happened? What happened?'

Kaikubad ran out and looked at the sky; then he turned back. Everyone surrounded him. 'What happened? What happened?' These words echoed all around. In answer, Kaikubad announced, 'The vultures have gone.'

'The vultures have gone?'

'The vultures have gone?'

'But why?'

'Something must have happened!'

'But what could have happened?'

The secretary of the Parsi Panchayat received Kaikubad's phone and his forehead creased with a network of frowns. He heard the entire story, put the receiver back in its cradle and informed the director through the intercom. Immediately, an urgent meeting was called. The matter was placed before the board of directors. But the question still remained.

'Where had the vultures gone?'

'What did you say … the vultures have gone?' there was the slightest trace of disbelief in the police commissioner's voice.

'Yes, our vultures have gone,' the president of the Parsi Panchayat stressed each syllable and repeated his statement. Then he listened to what the police commissioner had to say with rapt attention. The colour came and went from his face. He kept listening to the police commissioner for a very long time. When the story ended from the other side, he put the receiver back in its cradle. All the other directors were looking towards him. He gave them the gist of his conversation with the police commissioner. Everyone came out of the meeting carrying some satisfaction but a lot more worries back with them. The secretary called the doongerwadi. Kaikubad conveyed the gist of the conversation between the president of the Parsi Panchayat and the police commissioner to the honourable priests and the assembled mourners. The news reached Hormuz and Feroz from the priests, via the attendants of the *bungli*. Feroz heard the entire matter with the closest attention. Then he began to look up at the sky. From the windows between the dense foliage on the trees, the sky could be seen clearly. There were no crows or kites or vultures.

And then they were startled. The warning bell was ringing. A corpse was coming from *bungli* number three. Once again, they found themselves standing at the door of the *bungli*. The corpse came. This time, the attendant extended two fifty-rupee notes towards Feroz. Taking the corpse inside the tower, Feroz made a face and said, 'Hormuz!'

'Speak, brother.'

'Why are all the Parsis dying today?'

Hormuz remained silent. He was looking upwards at the sky. 'There is not a bird in sight and the corpses are piling up one after the other.'

'But where have the birds gone?'

'The police commissioner said that all the vultures have gone to the Sunday and Monday markets.'

'But why?'

'*Arre*, those Hindus and Muslims have fought with each other. There have been riots. They have burnt the hearse van, and also the ambulance. The road is littered with corpses and our vultures are having a feast. And that police commissioner, he said that once the roads have been cleared, our vultures are going to return on their own.'

'So what if the roads clear … will the vultures return … After all, this is India … there is a riot here every day. Everyday there is burning and arson, everyday people die … What then … what the hell … will the vultures ever return?'

– Translated from the Urdu by Rakhshanda Jalil

GLOSSARY

Aarti: part of the puja, when the ceremonial lamp is lit and offerings are made to the deity

Ababeel: species of bird

Allah Miyan: colloquial reference to Allah or Prophet Mohammed

Arre: exclamation of surprise

Atta: flour

Baikunth: abode of Vishnu of the Hindu trinity; in text means abode of God

Bakerkhani: type of baked bread, popular in Kashmir as a snack and eaten along with salted tea

Bania: Hindu who belongs to the trading community

Basti: settlement, smaller than a city or town but larger than a village

Bathwa: greens cooked and served as a side dish with chappatis

Behen: sister

Bhadon: the month of the rains corresponding to July-August

Bibi: form of address for a woman younger than one's self or for a young lady

Bigha: unit of measurement of area of land

Biradari: community

Bulbul: Indian bird with a sweet song

Chakki: flour mill or rice mill

Chaupal: assembly-place or assembly-room in a village; a common meeting place for villagers

Chinar: deciduous tree known for its longevity; popular in Kashmir

Chunri: scarf or dupatta

Churails: witches

Darji: shortened version of 'sardarji'

Dham: Hindu place of pilgrimage. As per the Hindu scriptures, there are four *dhams* which a devotee should visit in his lifetime

Doongerwadi: Doongerwadi, literally meaning 'garden on the hill' was the name of a piece of land on which a Tower of Silence was built by the Parsi community in Malabar Hill, Mumbai; it has since become a generic word and come to be used almost synonymously with the Tower of Silence. The doongerwadi compound includes the *bungli* where the corpse is kept and the last rituals are observed and from where it is taken to the actual tower. A *bungli* is an ante chamber where the corpse is kept and funerary rites performed before it is taken to the tower where vultures will pick it clean

Fajr: the pre-dawn prayer, first of the five daily namaz

Gamcha: long rectangular piece of cloth worn by men as a scarf

Gamla: gardening pot

Gharara: elaborate two-legged garment with an excessively flared hem, worn with a short top and dupatta

Gully: extremely narrow alley

Haay/Hai: exclamation of surprise, regret, alarm even lament

Hai re daiya: exclamation of surprise or anger

Halaal: kosher meat or the meat of an animal over which a prayer has been recited in accordance with the Muslim practice

Insha Allah: if Allah wills

Janeu: sacred thread worn by Brahmins

Kirpan: short dagger-like knife kept by Sikhs on their persons; one of the five 'Ks' prescribed by their religion to be kept by a Sikh on his person

Kirtan: devotional songs often accompanied with drums and cymbals

Krishna Ashtami also *JanamAshtami*: eighth day of the month of *Bhadon* in the Hindu calendar when Lord Krishna is said to have been born to Devaki and Vasudev. However, due to a prophecy that the child would destroy his evil uncle, the King Kansa, Vasudev hid the new-born infant in a basket, swam across the swollen Jamuna River on that dark rainy night and gave him to Yashoda to be raised and reared in safety

Laahoulvillaquwwat: verse used variously to express disgust or dissatisfaction, loosely translated it means, 'I turn my face from Evil'

Langar: community kitchen, such as the one run in Sikh gurudwaras

Maghrib: the fourth of the five daily *namaz*, it is offered at sunset

Mahua: plant from the flowers of which an intoxicating drink is brewed

Maidan-e-hashr: Plain of Resurrection

Milaad: abbreviation of Milaadun-Nabi, when congregational hymns are sung in praise of the Prophet Muhammad, interspersed with prose passages on his life and teachings

Mohulla: old-fashioned neighbourhood with closely built houses; usually very congested and crowded

Mundan: ritual head shaving ceremony among Hindus followed by naming a new-born child

Nauhas: graceful poetry

Ojha: country doctor or sorcerer; a sub-community of Brahmins

Paathshala: village school

Papiha: bird whose plaintive notes are interpreted as '*pi kahan*' meaning where has my beloved gone or simply where is my beloved?

Patrail: dumpling of colocasia leaves in a spicy chickpea flour batter that is first steamed, then fried; eaten as a side dish or a snack

Purbi: dialect spoken in the eastern regions of Uttar Pradesh

Ram Naumi: festival celebrating birth of Shri Ram

Rashtra: nation

Sakhu: teak tree

Salaam: referring to the ritual of offering salutation on either side, first right and then left, at the culmination of the *namaz*

Sarkanda: reed; reed-stalk

Shisham: deciduous evergreen tree commonly known as Indian Rosewood; its wood is glossy and used in furniture and fixtures

Subhanallah: Praise be to Allah!

Tablighis: orthodox preachers

Tehzeeb: etiquette, manners

Thakurain: thakur's wife

Tola: measure of gold

Vidharmi: one from another religion

Wahe Guru: the Sikh chant meaning 'Praise the Guru'

Yaar: friend

Zubaan: literal meaning 'tongue'. Generally used to mean a person's language or literary utterance

Relationship Terms

Bhau: brother

Ammajaan: mother

Bade Chacha: elder uncle

Bapuji/Babuji/Bauji: father in Hindi and its dialects

Abbajaan: father in Urdu

Kaka: young boy

Chachi: aunt; father's younger brother's wife

Bibiji: respectful way of addressing an elderly lady

Jijaji: elder sister's husband

Slogans

Jai Bajrang Bali: Praise be to Lord Hanuman

Allah-hu-Akbar

Khoon ka badla khoon: blood for blood

Jo Bole so Nihal

Sat Sri Akal

NOTES ON CONTRIBUTORS

AUTHORS

Gulzar Filmmaker, poet, translator and one of the most popular lyricists of Hindustani cinema, writing film songs for the last five decades. Standing comfortably on the crossroads of high and popular culture, he successfully blends and juxtaposes the two with his sharp poetic craft. Although, his fame, by and large, rests on his contribution to cinema, it being a more popular medium, he has a body of significant work in the literary arena as well. Known for his choice of imagery and characteristic use of language, Gulzar has bagged innumerable awards, ranging from the National Award, Sahitya Akademi, Filmfare, Grammy, Oscar and so on.

Abdus Samad Professor of Political Science, he began his writing career in 1961 with the children's Magazine *Ghuncha* from Bijnour. His first collection of short stories, *Bara Rangon Wala Kamra*, appeared in 1980 and his first novel, *Do Gaz Zameen*, in 1988. This has been followed by six collections of short stories, eight novels (including one in English), one collection of literary sketches, two books related to Political Science, and two works of translation. He has received the Sahitya Akademi Award in 1990 for *Do Gaz Zameen* and the Bhartiya Bhasha Parishad in 1998 for the same novel. He has received the Ghalib Award for prose in 2014.

Tariq Chhatari Starting his career as a programme executive in All India Radio in 1984, he is at present a Professor in the Department of Urdu at Aligarh Muslim University. His notable contributions include a collection of short stories entitled *Bagh Ka Darwaza* published in 2001 (2nd ed. 2011) and *Jadeed Afsana: Hindi-Urdu* (Comparative study of Hindi-Urdu short stories after 1960) which was published in 1993. Many of his short stories have been translated and published in English, Telugu, Marathi, Punjabi, Odishi and Hindi. The central theme that pervades many of his short stories is changing human relationships, mental conflicts and loss of identity.

Zakia Mashhadi Coming from an urban educated middle class family with roots in western UP, she did her BA and MA in Psychology from Lucknow University in 1966. An avid reader, she started her writing career in 1974 and has since published five collections of short stories in Urdu and translated more than a dozen books for prestigious literary organisations like Sahitya Akademi, National Book Trust, and Khuda Bakhsh Oriental Public Library, Patna from English and Hindi into Urdu, and vice versa. She has also written more than a dozen booklets for rural neo-literates in simple Hindi and Urdu.

Syed Muhammad Ashraf Born on 8 July 1957 at Sitapur, a town in the Awadh region in UP, he belongs to a family of devout scholars and Sufi saints of Marehra Shareef, district Etah, UP. Presently posted as Chief Commissioner of Income Tax in Kolkata, he has steadfastly pursued his career as a senior officer in the Indian Revenue Service along with his literary and academic interests. His major work includes two collections of short stories: *1994 Daar Se Bichchre* (1994) and *Baad-e Saba Ka Intizar* (2000) for which he received the Sahitya Akademi Award; and a novel *Number Dar ka Neela* (1997).

Ajeet Cour Well-known Punjabi fiction writer, author of nineteen collections of short stories and novels, nine creative translations of fiction and poetry, over twenty edited works, and numerous articles. Her works have been widely translated into several Indian and foreign languages. Her forte lies in the passion and commitment she brings to bear from creative writing to cultural activism, from preservation of environment and heritage to empowerment of marginalised women. The spirit behind the Foundation of SAARC Writers and Literature, and Academy of Fine Arts and Literature, a Cultural Centre in Siri Fort, founded by her in 1975, she also initiated the idea of cultural connectivity among the SAARC countries for peace since 1986.

Asghar Wajahat Hindi scholar, fiction writer, novelist, playwright, an independent documentary filmmaker and a television scriptwriter. His best-known works include *Saat Aasmaan, Jis Lahore Nai Dekhya O Jamyai Nai, Kaisee Lagi Lagaee,* among others.

Deepak Budki Born on 15 February 1950 in Srinagar, Kashmir, he obtained his Master's degree in Botany and Bachelor of Education degree from Kashmir University. Later, he also graduated from National Defence College, New Delhi and became Associate of Insurance Institute of India, Mumbai. He joined Indian Postal Service in 1976 and retired as Member, Postal Services Board in 2010. Budki has four collections of short stories and three collections of critical essays and numerous book reviews to his credit. He was awarded Bharat Gaurav Award by International Friendship Society, presented to him by Shri B.N. Singh, Ex-Governor of Tamil Nadu and Assam States.

M.K. Mahtab: Born in 1926 in Lyallpur, Pakistan, his full name was Mahindar Kapur Mahtab. But he was better known to Urdu readers as Meem Kaaf (M. K.) Mahtab. He was a prominent short story writer of his time who wrote extensively for popular literary magazines and digests such as Beesween Sadi. He died in Delhi on 5 November 2005.

Tarannum Riyaz Recipient of SAARC Literary Award 2014, she is a senior fellow with the Ministry of Culture. Born and brought up in Kashmir, she writes in the Urdu language. She is a poet, critic, columnist, short story writer and essayist. Her works include *Barf Aashna Parindey* (novel, 2009); *Mera Rakhte Safar* (short stories, 2008); *Fareb-e-Khitta-e-Gul* (four novellas, 2008); *Purani Kitaabon ki Khusbhu* (poetry, 2005); *Chashme Naqshe Kadam* (critical essays, 2005); *Beeswi Sadi Mein Khawateen Ka Urdu Adab* (anthology, 2005); *Moorti* (novel, 2002); *Yimberzal* (short stories, 2002); *Ababeelain Laut Aaengi* (short stories, 2000); and *Yeh Tang Zameen* (short stories,1998).

Joginder Paul Born in 1925 in Sialkot, in Pakistan, he had his first story published in the well-known Urdu journal *Saqi* in 1945. The Partition of the country led to his migration to Ambala as a refugee. His marriage led to another migration, to Kenya where he taught English, throughout expressing his angst of being in exile in his stories. Back in India in 1965, he was principal of a college in Aurangabad, Maharashtra for another fourteen years before coming to settle in Delhi for full-time writing. He has published over thirteen collections of short stories, including *Khula, Khodu Baba ka Maqbara* and *Bastian.* Amongst his novels are, *Ek Boond Lahoo Ki, Nadeed, Paar Pare* and *Khwabro.* He has three collections of short short stories (*Laghukathayein*). Paul is a recipient of many important literary honours including the SAARC Lifetime Award for his contribution to literature, Iqbal Samman, Urdu Academy Award, All India Bahadur Shah Zafar Award and the Ghalib Award.

Jeelani Bano One of the foremost Urdu writers today, she has written short stories, novels, plays, essays and children's stories. She has published two novels, seven collections of short stories, two collections of novelettes and a translation of Malayalam stories from Hindi. Her themes deal with social and cultural oppression, bonded labour, poverty, powerlessness, stress of urban life, and suffering of women. Her short stories have been translated into many Indian and foreign languages. Awarded the Padma Shri in 2001, she lives in Hyderabad, lectures and travels extensively. She is Principal Advisor, Child & Women Human Rights, International Human Rights Association (India).

Ratan Singh Born in 1927 in Daud in District Narowal, Pakistan, he did a BA from Lucknow University. While he retired as Station Director, Radio Kashmir, Srinagar, he was also editor of *Aaftab-e Jadid*, Urdu daily from Jabalpur and has written several collections of short stories, many of which are included in the textbooks of various state boards. His Urdu collections include: *Pehli Awaaz, Pinjare Ka Aadmi, Kath Ka Ghoda, Gah, Pani Pe Likha Naam,* etc. His autobiography is *Beete Hue Din*. He also writes in Punjabi.

Shaukat Hayat Lives in Patna and writes stories about namelessness and alienation. His collection of short stories are titled *Bang* and *Gumbad ke Kabootar*, and a novel *Sarpat Ghora*. He was awarded the National Katha Award in 1997 and Lifetime Achievement Award in 2009 by the Government of Bihar.

Khalid Jawed Born in 1963 in Bareilly, Uttar Pradesh, he is a well-known fiction writer in Urdu. His collection of short stories was titled *Akhri Dawat*. He has received the Katha Award in 1997 for his story '*Bure Mausam Mein*'. His writings have been translated into English, Hindi, French and Spanish. His debut novel *Maut Ki*

Kitab is considered a landmark in contemporary Urdu fiction. He is an Assistant Professor in the Department of Urdu, Jamia Millia Islamia, New Delhi.

Noor Zaheer Writer and social activist, for the last fifteen years she has been involved in researching the culture and oral traditions of the North-western Himalayan tribes. She has written more than fifty short stories, four full-length plays, twenty-four plays for children. *My God is a Woman, Barh Urraiye* both novels, *Mere Hisse ki Roshnai* (My Share of the Ink) – a memoir of the Progressive Writers Movement and *Surkh Karavan ke Hamsafar* (Fellow-travellers of the Red Caravan) a travelogue based in Pakistan are her major published works. She is at present working on another novel based in Kinnaur.

Khurshid Akram Born in Calcutta (now Kolkata) in 1963, he has worked in the All India Radio and NHRC and was, earlier, the editor of *Aaj Kal* (Urdu). His books include: *Ek Ghair Mashroot Muafinama* (short stories); *Pichhli Peet ke Kaaraney* (poems); *Andaz-e Nazar Mera* (criticism); *Jadeed Hindi Shairi* (compilation). He has translated four books from English, Hindi and Bengali into Urdu. His short stories, poems, critical articles, and reviews have been published in mainstream magazines and journals. A couple of his short stories have also appeared in various anthologies.

Keki N. Daruwalla Lives in Delhi and writes poetry and fiction. His last two books (published in 2014) are *Fire Altar* (Poetry) and *Islands* (short stories) about life on islands and on people as islands.

Ali Imam Naqvi Novelist and short story writer, he has the following collections to his credit: *Naye Makaan ki Deemak, Mubahala, Ghat-te Badh-te Saaye* and *Mausam Azabon Ka.* His novella, *Teen Batti ke Rama* and a novel, *Bisaat* are also remarkable works in contemporary Urdu fiction. He has been honoured by the Urdu Akademies of Uttar Pradesh and Maharashtra.

TRANSLATORS

Saba Mahmood Bashir Poet, author and translator, her first book was a collection of poems, *Memory Past* (2006) brought out by Writers' Workshop and her latest book is the analysis of the poetry of Gulzar, a culmination of her PhD thesis, *I Swallowed the Moon: The Poetry of Gulzar* (2013), where she places Gulzar as a progressive poet in popular culture. Her forthcoming book is an analysis of the 1975 film, *Aandhi*. She lives in Delhi with her husband and daughter.

Javaid Qazi Fiction writer since four decades, his collection, *Unlikely Stories*, was published by Oxford University Press, Karachi in 1998. His stories have appeared in *Massachusetts Review, Chelsea, Toronto South Asian Review, Kansas Quarterly* and *Sequoia*. He has also translated and published the stories of well-known Urdu authors such as Intezar Hussain, Nayyar Masood and Ahmed Hamesh. He was born in Lahore in 1947 and in 1968 went to the United States to study English literature. Over the last forty years, he has taught English literature in various universities in the US, at Manas University in Bishkek, Kyrghyz Republic and at Girne American University in the Turkish Republic of North Cyprus. He has also worked as a technical writer in the computer industry. He lives in San Jose, California with his wife, and has published a novel *Well Met in Cyprus* with Niyogi Books, New Delhi.

Fatima Rizvi Teacher of literature in the Department of English and Modern European Languages at the University of Lucknow.

Her areas of interest include postcolonial literature and literature in translation. Her academic papers have been published in journals of national and international repute and anthologies of criticism. She is on the board of the 'Centre for Cultural Texts, Records and Translation of Indian Literatures' set up in the Department, under the State Government's 'Centre of Excellence Scheme.'

Sohail Akbar Practitioner and teacher of still photography, Sohail Akbar's association with photography goes back more than two decades. He has taught photography at AJK Mass Communication Research Centre Jamia Millia Islamia, New Delhi. He has also been a filmmaker, curator and photography researcher. His interest in the visual arts has been nurtured by the very idea of storytelling in any medium. Contemporary Urdu and Hindi literature are areas of special interest to him. He has translated stories from Urdu to English.

Haris Qadeer Teacher at the Department of English, University of Delhi. He has previously taught at Aligarh Muslim University and Gautam Buddha University. He was awarded University gold medal for his MA (English) and later earned his PhD from Aligarh Muslim University, Aligarh. His areas of interest include writings by Indian Muslim women, postcolonial literature and translations.

Anita Samkaria Associate Professor of English at Satyawati College, University of Delhi. She is also the coordinator of the Family Counselling Centre in her college. The centre focuses on sensitising students on gender issues and addresses a gamut of social issues. She is interested in Translation and Gender Studies.

Bushra Alvi Freelance writer and editor and contributes regularly to various magazines, newspapers and websites. She is a permanent blogger at *The Huffington Post* and is currently co-authoring the biography of a senior Indian politician. An avid poet, her work has been published in various anthologies. She looks forward to publishing her collection of poems soon, illustrated with photographs taken by her.

Saif Mahmood New Delhi-based litigating and corporate lawyer, with a doctorate in Comparative Constitutional Law in South Asia. He speaks and writes on diverse issues ranging from law to literature. Founder of the South Asian Alliance for Literature, Art & Culture (SAALARC), he blogs on besabab.wordpress.com

Tarun K. Saint Associate Professor in the English Department at Hindu College, Delhi University. His area of research interest is the literature of the Partition. He has edited *Bruised Memories: Communal Violence and the Writer* and co-edited *Translating Partition* (with Ravikant). His study *Witnessing Partition: Memory, History, Fiction* appeared in 2010.

Sameena Hasan Siddiqui Associate Professor, Centre for the study of Comparative Religions and Civilisations, Jamia Millia Islamia, New Delhi. Her area of research is socio-cultural history of Medieval India with special interest in Sufism. She received her doctorate from the University of Delhi, and was teaching in Delhi University from 1985 till she joined Jamia Millia Islamia in 2005. Her published work includes: Islam and the Frontier Zone; The Dargah of Shaikh Nizamuddin Auliya: References in the Revenue and Judicial records (1859-1973). Her forthcoming work is on Tasawwuf defining intertextuality: The Indian experience.